Murder Must Wait

If you have difficulty obtaining these
titles from your local bookshop, write
direct to Angus & Robertson Publishers at:

Unit 4, Eden Park, 31 Waterloo Road,
North Ryde, NSW, Australia 2113
or
16 Golden Square, London W1R 4BN, United Kingdom

ARTHUR W. UPFIELD

Murder Must Wait

ANGUS & ROBERTSON PUBLISHERS

ANGUS & ROBERTSON PUBLISHERS
London • Sydney • Melbourne

First published by William Heinemann Ltd in 1953
This Arkon paperback edition first published
in Australia by Angus & Robertson Publishers and
in the United Kingdom by Angus & Robertson (UK) Ltd in 1984

Copyright © 1953 by Arthur W. Upfield

ISBN 0 207 14905 4

Printed in Australia by The Dominion Press – Hedges & Bell

CHAPTER 1

THE MURDER OF MRS ROCKCLIFF

IT HAPPENED at Mitford some time during Monday night. Sprawled on the northern bank of the River Murray, and in the State of New South Wales, Mitford is wide open to the cold southerlies of winter and the hot northerlies of summer. A broad tree-shaded boulevard skirts the river, and Main Street is flanked by squat emporiums crammed with goods likely, and unlikely, to be needed by people who own the surrounding vineyards and who operate the canning works for ten weeks every year.

It wasn't Sergeant Yoti's first homicide case, but it was destined to give him a new and not altogether unpleasant experience. He wasn't much to look at . . . in civilian clothes. He was square and grey, and the foolish ones thought him soft. You think of a kind, understanding uncle when at the point of inebriation you own the town, and you may wake up and faintly recall that what Sergeant Yoti failed to do with his fists, he accomplished with his boots.

This Wednesday opened as every other day in February: hot and windy and dusty outside the Police Station, still and hot and boring within. The morning was governed by dull routine, and the afternoon was given by the Sergeant to polishing his cases for presenting to the magistrates the following day. Shortly after three o'clock the mail was delivered, and Yoti read a letter penned by the Chief of the State CID, in Sydney.

> Dear Yoti [wrote Superintendent Canno], I've seized the opportunity of snaffling Napoleon Bonaparte to look into those baby cases out your way. Don't know if you have ever met this bloke, but you must have heard of him. Anyway, give him all the rope and he'll pay dividends. You'll find him the most aggravating feller you could think of, but there's nothing lousy in his makeup. How's things up your street? Drop me a line sometime. Remember me to Joan. Your George is shaping well in the Traffic Branch, I'm told. . . .

Yoti permitted himself to smile. Canno had gone high; he himself had remained almost stationary, and the day was long back on life's road when they had joined the Department together.

Napoleon Bonaparte! What a name! And, by all accounts, what a man! Sergeant Yoti pondered, his friend's letter gripped by a sizeable fist. The tales he had heard about this Napoleon Bonaparte, this detective-inspector of the Queensland CID, this cross between Sir Galahad and Ned Kelly.

Well, the stolen babies would deflate this Bonaparte. They'd stir his grey matter and dry up his sinuses. He boasted that he'd never failed to finish an investigation. Well, well! Old Canno must be putting the yoke on this Mister Bonaparte, doing a snigger up his sleeve while urging him on to tackle the disappearances of four babies, babies who had just vanished, vanished from a pram or a cot, out of a house, off a veranda, even off Main Street one busy afternoon.

Yoti wasn't amused when thinking about it, even though the only gleam of comfort in a dark night was the failure of Canno's city experts to do better than he had done . . . which was just nothing in clear results. The first baby had been a routine job; the second baby, an upheaval. The third child had brought Canno's boys; photographers and fingerprinters and dust collectors. And the last baby had loosened all hell in Mitford so that even his wife had looked at him with eyes of disillusionment.

Napoleon Bonaparte! Coming to try his luck weeks after Baby Number Four had vanished like a penny in the river. No wonder the cat laughed.

Sergeant Yoti loved cats, and was stroking the enormous black specimen on his desk when the telephone in the outer office blasted the peace. Yoti smiled at the cat, almost unconscious of the voice acknowledging the telephone call. He heard the receiver being replaced, then the quick, heavy footfalls of the uniformed constable who entered his office and stood stiffly beyond the desk.

"Essen rang through, Sergeant," reported the constable, not yet old enough to keep his face masked or his voice controlled. "His brother-in-law rang him to say he was worried about a Mrs Rockliff who lives next door. Essen went round. The woman hadn't been seen for a couple of days and the milk and mail not taken in. He tried the front door and found it unlocked, and went in. The woman's lying dead in a bedroom. Essen says he thinks it's homicide."

No eruption rocked the Police Station at Mitford. No sirens screamed through Main Street. The police car driven by a constable negotiated the cross-street with normal care, and Yoti smoked his pipe and returned the greeting of a man who waved to him.

Elgin Street consisted of detached villas, guarded by small front gardens. At the gate of No 5 two men waited: one obviously a policeman in mufti, the other elderly and obviously nervous. First Constable Essen came forward.

"Woman appears to have been murdered," he said. "Body's in the front bedroom. This is my brother-in-law, who last saw the woman alive on Monday. Rang me about it because there mightn't have been anything to it."

Yoti nodded.

"I live next door, Sergeant," admitted the elderly man. "The name's Thring. We haven't seen Mrs Rockcliff since Monday, and there's two lots of milk and letters at the gate. I thought. . ."

"You did right, Mr Thring. Stay here with the constable. We'll go in, Essen."

Essen opened the door by the handle of the ordinary catch, and Yoti noted the Yale-type lock was snibbed. The hall was small and had the imprint of the house-proud slave. A hat and umbrella stand stood against one wall, a small table flanked by a chair fronted another. On the table was a bowl of dying roses; above it hung an oval mirror reflecting the open front door. Dark green linoleum covered the floor of the hall and passage leading to the rear.

"Room to the right, Sergeant," Essen said tightly. "The door was shut, but I managed to open it without mucking up possible prints. She's lying on the floor at the foot of the bed. And the baby's cot is empty."

Yoti closed the door, and the light from the open fanlight emphasised the lines which suddenly appeared about his wide mouth. Abruptly he strode to the bedroom, paused just within the door frame. The scene was registered as a succession of pictures: beginning with the meticulously made bed, then the blind-protected windows, the body of the woman on the floor, and finally the empty cot beyond the foot of the bed.

"Thring says he and his wife are sure that Mrs Rockcliff left the child alone in the house," Essen said. "None of the neighbours have seen it since last Monday. Looks like the woman returned to find the baby-thief on the job, and was done in because she recognised him."

It was a pleasant room, the drawn linen blinds creating a pseudo-coolness, and the sunlight penetrating at one side to fashion a finger of gold to caress a dead hand upon a blue rug. There was light enough to see the lacy draperies of the baby's cot, the feeding bottle on the small table, the miniatures on the walls.

Only now was he conscious of the flies blundering about, of the staleness of the air, of the silence about him and of the noises without. On tiptoe he left the doorway to step over the body and reach the cot. He could see the valley on the tiny pillow where the baby's head had rested, and his mind was so crowded with the consequences of that empty cot that the murder of the mother was then of small moment.

He went back the road he had come . . . over the body . . . again paused in the doorway, to look at the cot before permitting his eyes to concentrate on the dead woman, lying partially on her back, one arm above the head, the other outflung.

"You been through the house, of course?" he said to Essen.

"Yes. Back door locked. All the windows fastened. Nothing out of place."

"We'll begin at the beginning . . . your brother-in-law."

Passing to the porch and so into the brilliant sunlight, Yoti addressed himself to Thring.

"You live next door, Mr Thring. When did you see Mrs Rockcliff last?"

"Matter of fact, several days ago," replied the neighbour. "My wife last saw her about eight on Monday evening. Mrs Rockcliff was then going out."

"Without the baby?"

"She never took the baby out with her at night."

"Just left it in the house . . . alone?"

"Yes. That's what made us worry. Yesterday morning Mrs Rockcliff didn't take in her milk and paper, and didn't collect her mail from the box. When more milk was left this morning, and more papers, and another letter, we got concerned about the baby in case Mrs Rockcliff hadn't come home on Monday night. I knocked at the front door several times this morning.

8

I went round the back and knocked again. I didn't think to try if the front door was unlocked."

"Mrs Rockcliff never left the baby with anyone when she went out?"

"Not that we know of, and the wife's a pretty observant woman. In fact, she's said more than once it was a shame to leave the infant all alone in the house at night."

A car slid to a halt beyond the knot of people gathered at the street gate.

"How old was the baby?"

"Eleven weeks."

"You were on speaking terms with the mother, I suppose?"

"No more than that," Thring replied, adding: "Excepting that I've done her garden now and then. We know the baby's age because we knew when Mrs. Rockcliff went to hospital and when she came home."

A blind man could have told by the footsteps on the cement path that a doctor was walking it. Dr Nott was tall, large and dark. He wore no hat, and the leather bag appeared as having been tormented by rats.

"Spot of bother, Sergeant?" he surmised as though commenting on the weather.

"Mrs Rockcliff, Doctor, seems to be dead."

"H'm! And the baby?"

"No baby. Crib's empty. Looks crook to me."

"It will be crook . . . if the baby has been abducted. What'll it be? The fifth?"

Yoti went into the house, followed by the doctor. Essen planted himself in the doorway, and the constable stolidly regarded Mr Thring and continued to say nothing.

At the bedroom, Yoti stepped aside to permit Nott to enter. He watched the doctor release the spring blinds, turn to regard the cot. It seemed that the baby was of prior importance even to Doctor Nott, for he came back to the cot to peer into it and at the feeding bottle on the low table, having no apparent interest in the dead woman. He gained Yoti's approval by touching nothing . . . till he came to examine the body. Presently he said:

"Lower the blinds."

Yoti nodded, waited for the blinds to reduce the starkness of Death, withdrew before the doctor and crossed the hall to

9

the lounge. The doctor thumped his bag on the polished table, sat on the table-edge and produced cigarette-case and lighter.

"Been dead, I'd guess, about thirty-six hours," he stated. "Takes it back to last Monday night . . . sometime. Hit with something blunt and heavy. Could be a hammer, or the point of a walking-stick handle."

"Was done as she entered the bedroom, I suppose?"

"Looks like it. Merely the one blow was enough."

"Know anything about her?"

"A little. Came to me early in December. Wanted to book in at the hospital. Managed it all right, although she'd left it very late. She told me she had come up from Melbourne after her husband had been killed in a road accident."

"Why come to Mitford, d'you know?"

"Yes. Said she thought the dry conditions here would be better for her lungs. I agreed when I found that one was touched."

"Where did she live in Melbourne?"

"I don't know that, Yoti. She did say that her doctor was in practice in Glen Iris. Doctor Allan Browner."

"You contact him about her?"

"No reason to. Can't you get her background?"

"Haven't tried so far. Neighbours aren't helpful." Their eyes clashed. "If the baby isn't located we're going to have our backs bent."

"Can't go on," Nott said, sadly, and Yoti fancied he saw disapproval on the large white face. "What d'you think they're stealing babies for?"

"I've been asking myself that one. Can understand a woman pinching a baby because she had to have one, but no woman wanting a baby would pinch five, and commit murder. And don't sit there being superior. You ought to know why a lunatic pinches babies, lunatics being up your street, not mine."

The table rocked when Nott slid off.

"I can make four guesses, one for every infant," he said, his dark eyes wide and hard. "And each guess would make you shiver, tough as you have to be. You'll have the CID crowd out here again, I suppose?"

"Possibly, depends." Nott saw relief come to Yoti. "They're sending a detective-inspector to look into these baby cases, a man who boasts he has never fallen down on a job. He can have this one and welcome. As young George used to tell me when he couldn't do his home lessons, I've 'had' it."

"You have my sympathy, Yoti. Well, I'll be seeing you. I'll do the p.m. tonight. About nine do?"

"Yes."

The doctor took up his tattered bag. Footsteps in the hall halted his first step to the door. He looked at Yoti, and knew they were in agreement about the footsteps not being made by First Constable Essen, or one of Yoti's constables.

The sunlight shimmered upon the table, flowed across the linoleum, to frame in the illumined doorway a grey-suited figure carrying a velour hat. It was like looking at a framed portrait. They could see the faint stripe in the grey cloth of the creased trousers and the creaseless double-breasted coat, the sheen of the maroon-coloured tie about the spotless collar. They noted the straight black hair parted low to the left, the dark complexion of the face, the white teeth, and the whimsical smile. They could not evade the sea-blue eyes, or side-track the feeling that everything about themselves, inside and out, was being registered by those blue eyes.

"What the devil . . .!" thought Dr Nott.

Although Sergeant Yoti had never before seen this man, he experienced swift release from depression.

CHAPTER 2

'AM I CORRECT?'

"SERGEANT YOTI? I am Inspector Bonaparte."

Dr Nott, the practised observer, noted the evidence of physical and mental virility, how the light gleamed on the black hair like newly broken coal. Yoti, who stood with military stiffness, said:

"Glad to see you, sir. This is Doctor Nott."

Nott inclined his head, continuing to be intrigued by a name.

"The constable at the Station told me where to find you. Homicide?"

"Yes, sir."

"Oh! Of little concern to me . . . unless . . ." The blue eyes were abruptly masked. "Unless the absence of an infant is in question."

"The baby is missing," Yoti said. "It could be the Fifth Baby."

"Ah!" The grey velour was dropped on the table, and fascinated, Dr Nott watched slim fingers make the worst cigarette he had ever seen. "Could this murder be assumed to be an effect of the theft of a fifth infant?"

"Assumed, yes," replied Yoti.

"Then the murder is within the assignment given me to locate the thief or thieves of several infants. Do you agree?"

The senior police officer stationed at Mitford hesitated before nodding assent, for, being a civil servant by training and by nature, it was natural to avoid wherever possible the awful bugbear—responsibility.

"I am pleased you are willing to concede so much," Bony went on, and puffed out the match. "Four kidnappings, and not a lead gained by the CID, and now the fifth . . . assumed . . . supported by a murder which, also assumed, wasn't premeditated and thus should give a dozen leads. Having one lead in hand, I require but one more. You are about to leave, Doctor? Please delay a moment until I learn the meagre details from Sergeant Yoti."

It was Bony who first left the room, preceding the doctor and Yoti to the porch, where waited Essen with the constable and Thring.

"There is a point concerning which there must be no disagreement," he told them. "Mr Thring, to your knowledge the only persons who have been inside this house since Mrs Rockcliff was last seen alive are we five men?"

"That's so, Inspector."

"Thank you, Mr Thring." Mr Thring failed to understand what prompted the smile in and about the friendly blue eyes. "Now please return home. I shall be calling on you soon. Oblige me by ignoring the cement path leading to the gate and by walking on the bordering flower-bed."

The strip of cultivated ground between the path and the drought-stricken lawn was four feet wide, and the surface was dry and sandy. Mr Thring obliged, and Bony walked the cement path halfway to the gate, when he turned and called to Dr Nott to walk the flower-bed. Essen was asked to follow the doctor, and only Yoti was annoyed when requested to make his footprints to be studied by a man who never forgot footprints. The rubbernecks at the gate were entranced.

"Now Sergeant, you and I will re-enter the house, see what is to be seen and what is to be felt. I want no one else inside the house until we have done."

They stood in the hall, Yoti having closed the door and released the lock snib. Bony switched on the light.

"I detest wall-to-wall carpets," he said. "Harbours all manner of wogs . . . and cannot register footprints. Mrs Rockcliff was a wise woman when she selected linoleum, and a good housewife when she polished it, I should think, at least once a week. You might stay here while I look over the scene. Where is the body?"

Yoti indicated the bedroom and then, like those at the street gate, became an entranced spectator. He watched Bony sidle along the walls to reach the bedroom, noted how he placed his feet as close to the skirting as possible, and as closely to the door-frame when he sidled into the bedroom. The light went on, and he regretted he was unable to watch the man who had never failed to finish an assignment.

It seemed to Yoti that Bony was in the bedroom a long time, when he was surprised less by the identical manner of his return than by the pair of woman's shoes he carried.

"We will have to retain these," Bony told him, gazing upon the soles and heels. "I disliked the task of removing them."

The dark tan at the corners of Bony's mouth was oddly pale, and, having passed the morgue test in his training days and since being inured to death and violence, Sergeant Yoti felt a spasm of contempt for this man who betrayed fear of death. Bony said:

"I have to run about like an ant in search of a lead, and I'm not going to ruin my favourite suit."

Removing the creaseless coat, he passed it gravely to Sergeant Yoti, who was distinctly disturbed when Bony removed his trousers and proceeded to match the crease of one leg with that of the other. The trousers were carefully placed over the coat resting on the sergeant's forearm, but Yoti's attention could not be given to anything save the sky-blue silk underpants and the sock suspenders of the same hue.

"Open the door, please. I require more light."

Hoping that the crowd at the distant gate would be denied this spectacle, and that his staff wouldn't faint, Yoti obeyed.

Again turning, he found Bony on hands and knees, his face close to the floor as though trying to locate a small pin.

The blue-panted figure backed like a bull-ant before a thrusting twig, then forward again like the bull-ant determined to attack. It was not unlike a voodoo rite, but could have been more realistic were it not for the blue pants and the cream shirt. Quite abruptly, the figure moved with astonishing nimbleness to the front bedroom and disappeared.

Yoti heard the bedroom blinds snap up. The flies were persistent, the air heavy and dank with the odour of the dead. The little noises outside seemed too fearful to come in, and the sound of the flies within seemed hushed as though they flew with crêpe-draped wings. He could feel the presence of Essen and the constable on the porch, and wondered if they smiled at sight of him waiting like a well-trained valet.

Bony's reappearance was a relief. He came from the bedroom on all fours across the hall to the lounge. When again he appeared, he halted at the hat stand to make obeisance by bringing his forehead to the linoleum many times.

On his final reappearance from the rear of the house he was walking like a human being. Saying nothing, he donned his trousers. Perhaps he hoped Yoti would assist with the coat, but the sergeant wouldn't play. The coat on and the shirt-sleeves carefully pulled down, Bony smiled, for Yoti enigmatic-ally, and said:

"Bring in the constable, Essen I think, who found the body. We'll discuss the matter in the lounge."

They found him standing with his back to the window, engaged in rolling a cigarette.

"Permit me to transmit the picture I have studied with no little interest," he said, as though making a difficult request. "Circumstances sometimes favour the investigator, and on this occasion they have. When you, Constable Essen, entered the house by the unlocked front door, with Mr Thring follow-ing you, you first went into the lounge, having told Thring to remain in the hall. From the lounge you crossed to the bed-room opposite, pausing for a moment or two in the doorway. There you uttered an exclamation of horror, because Thring joined you there, standing behind you and seeing what you saw. You told Thring to stay in the hall, and he obeyed this time, while you went in, switched on the light, and stood looking down at the body. Then you moved to the baby's cot, and from the cot back to the door."

"You passed along the passage, opening the door to the left, then the next door on the right, and so to the kitchen, where you tried the back door. On returning to the hall, you and Thring went out to the porch. You closed the door, ordered Thring to remain and let no one inside, and you then left to telephone to Sergeant Yoti. Do I err in any detail?"

"No, you are all correct, sir."

"When Sergeant Yoti arrived, he followed you into the house, Thring and the constable being told to remain outside. Sergeant Yoti went at once to the bedroom, and you followed him to the door. As you had done, Sergeant Yoti stood on the threshold for a short period before entering the bedroom on tiptoe. All the time he was in the bedroom he walked on his toes, passing to the body, then to peer into the baby's cot, then back again to the door. You followed him from the bedroom door across the hall to the front door and went out after him to the porch. Again, do I err in any one detail?"

"In no detail, sir."

"When Doctor Nott reached the house," went on the soft, cool voice, "you, Sergeant Yoti, brought him in. He entered the bedroom . . . I incline to believe he went in first, not you . . . and it's the only point about which I am a little doubtful . . . and he crossed at once to the windows and released the blinds. Having examined the body, he drew down the blinds before joining you in the hall. Any error?"

"No," replied Yoti.

Bony chuckled.

"Were I Dictator I would prohibit the manufacture, sale, and/or use of any type of floor covering other than linoleum. Now, before I take the next step, do I have your co-operation?"

Receiving their assurance, he pointed out that when agreeing to investigate the disappearances of the babies he demanded no interference from the State CID. This murder, however, might upset the arrangement.

Yoti said, and Essen was astonished by his candour:

"We don't want the city fellers here, sir. We've had a stomach-full. Essen's had experience with the fingerprint section in Sydney, and he's a pretty good photographer. So we could manage without Sydney."

"Then we manage, and I will tell you what else the linoleum

has told me," Bony said, making no attempt to disguise his satisfaction. "I can reasonably assume that the dead woman polished her floors during the day preceding the night of her death, and as we know who entered this house after Thring called in the police, by eliminating known persons we have the prints of persons unknown.

"I find that two unknown persons have been inside this house after Mrs Rockcliff polished her floors. One was a man. A large man who wears shoes size eight which are worn along the outside edge beneath each toecap. He was drunk or he could be a sailor recently ashore after a long voyage. He entered by the scullery window, visited the lounge and stood against the wall behind the bedroom door, from which position he struck down his victim. He left the house by the scullery window.

"The other person is a woman. She entered by the front door. She stood for some time in the hall, possibly to be assured she was alone in the house. From there she entered the bedroom, where she crawled under the bed. She emerged on the far side, and stood by the cot. Her shoe size is six, wedge type, and she walks slightly forward on her toes as though habitually she wears high-heeled shoes. She left by the front door."

"With the baby," Essen supplemented.

"The baby not having left footprints, I am unable to be definite," Bony flashed. "The man could have taken the infant, for he, too, stood by the cot. It would seem that these two persons acted independently of each other. The fact that the woman crawled under the bed certainly supports the assumption that they did ; that the woman was under the bed when the man entered the bedroom, and when he killed Mrs Rockcliff. What d'you know about the victim?"

"Very little," replied Yoti. "And that from Dr Nott. She came to Mitford from Melbourne. Down there she was under the care of a Dr Browner of Glen Iris. She rented this house from Mitford Estate Agents."

"That's a beginning," Bony purred. "By the way, what is the number of your staff?"

"Two constables under Essen. Could draw another two from Albury."

"Could you spare Essen, and do a little yourself on this case?"

"Certainly."

"Good Have the body moved to the morgue, and meanwhile interview the estate agents for what they know of the dead woman. Murder trails quickly become worn, and this is now forty hours old. We don't want your CID tramping down tracks, frightening possible friendly witnesses, annoying me and irritating you. Therefore I will report this murder to Sydney, and you report to your Divisional Headquarters that I am in charge." To Essen he said: "Can you get on with the dusting and the pictures?"

"Yes, sir."

"Then I'll wait here for you. And, by the way, when we are alone, favour me by omitting the 'sir' and sticking to 'Bony'. I am Bony to all my friends."

Yoti chuckled, grimly amused.

"Now I know," he averred with emphasis. "Now I know why it is you've never failed to finish a case."

"Me too," agreed Essen, his wide face widening under pressure of subdued enthusiasm.

CHAPTER 3

A STRANGE PAIR

ALONE in the house, Bony brought a satin-covered cushion from the lounge to kneel on the hall floor and outline with chalk three sets of footprints: one made by a man and two by women.

Then he entered a second bedroom, but this was unfurnished, and he found in a linen cupboard the sheet he required and which he took to the front bedroom.

The golden shaft of sunlight had moved from the dead woman's hand to beribbon the cream wickerwork of the cot; otherwise nothing was altered. He switched on the light and deliberately studied the body, noting its position and finding nothing helpful excepting confirmation that she had been struck when clear inside the door.

The woman would be about thirty. She had been pretty rather than beautiful, the most attractive feature being the chestnut hair. The eyes were blue. The feet from which he had removed the shoes were shapely and the legs long and well moulded. She was wearing a tailored suit of blue gaberdine. Thirty years only had she lived; robbed of thirty years of life she might have enjoyed. With relief, he spread the sheet over her.

Now it was shut away from his eyes but not from his mind. The position of the wound and the stain on the linoleum proved she had been killed by a blow to the top of her head. He estimated she was five feet ten inches tall, and therefore the slayer must be a tall man. She wore no hat that last night of her life, and this wasn't remarkable in a town like Mitford in country like the Riverina in February.

The red-stained matted hair persisted in his memory, and he felt that hovering over the room and sprawled about him was an impalpable being with its lips pursed to direct an ice-cold breath upon the nape of his neck, its eyes unwinking like the eyes of the dead.

He gazed upon the infant's cot, noting the covers turned back, the imprint of the little head upon the pillow. The baby-linen and satin-bound blankets were of good quality and a small chest of drawers was filled with costly baby-clothes. These tiny garments Bony examined with that look of naïve astonishment common to all virile males.

A framed picture of the child stood on the dressing-table, and a miniature copy hung above the head of the bed. The puckish face was encircled by a shawl, and the subject, no doubt, would be unrecognisable a few months hence by him or any other policeman. A woman might recognise it. A woman would be able to tell a story from the cot, from the clothes in the chest, the clothes in the wardrobe, and from the things in the kitchen. A woman with experience in babies could perhaps tell a valuable story from the feeding bottle on the little table.

The wall behind the door might tell him a story. He removed the reading lamp attached to the head of the bed, to examine the wall behind the door, and the place immediately above where the murderer had stood to wait for his victim.

Yes, there was a story for him, but he had to bring a chair to stand on to read it. Not quickly did he distinguish the faint smear on the cream calsomine, a smear caused almost certainly by oil, the killer's hair-oil transmitted to the wall from the back of his head. The height of the mark would give the man's height in his shoes as over six feet. He could not detect any adhering hairs, but a magnifying glass might locate at least one.

He could hear the noise of a distant car, the shriek of a cocka-
too, the shout of a boy. About him was the Silence and the
Thing which kept its icy breath upon his neck. And as he stood
on the chair, holding the lamp and peering at the blemish, there
came a sound to make him jerk about to face the sheeted corpse.
It came again, the impact of a blowfly upon the drawn blind,
and somewhat hastily he stepped down from the chair, moved
it to open the door, and backed from the room as though from
the presence of royalty. It was royalty, too . . . in the raiment
of a winding sheet . . . to this man of aboriginal maternity, the
only king before whom he had to make obeisance.

Again in the hall, he remembered who and what he was and
walked briskly to the kitchen to study the feeding bottle on the
bench, and regard with puckered eyes the objects on the shelf
above the bench and on that above the fuel stove. He spent
time peering into cupboards, and left the scullery window to
Essen, who would find that the ordinary slip catch had been
opened, and eventually closed, with a knife.

There was washing on the line in the rear yard terminated by
a high board fence. The yard was cemented, and he could have
reached the front of the house by following the cement path.
The washing on the line was brittle dry and stained with
Murray Valley dust: it, too, might tell a story to an intelligent
woman. A woman would have been helpful . . . say, Marie, his
wife who ruled his home at Banyo, out of Brisbane, and his
heart no matter where he was.

When Essen came with his camera and other gear, Bony left
the house in his charge with orders to leave everything exactly
as it was. On the porch he asked the constable his name, said
he would leave the door ajar in case Essen wanted assistance,
and, putting on the grey velour, stepped into the sunglare.

The westering sun was the inescapable god ruling this land
of the River Murray. The people never gazed upon it, for it
was not to be looked at, being all about them, touching them
from the heated ground, from every near-by object, from the
cobalt sky. The shadows had no meaning, were merely rifts in
the prevailing golden glare.

The few remaining rubbernecks went unnoticed, and not
one could have named the colour of his eyes, so masked were
they in the presence of the god. They waited for something to
happen, and Bony was seated in the Things' front room when
the undertaker's van came and parked outside No 5.

In the front room of No 7, Bony could not avoid dislike of Mrs Thring, who was lean and hawkish and, metaphorically, asking to be murdered by her patient husband. She said it was ten minutes after eight on the Monday evening that Mrs Rockcliff left her house. She was watering her flowers in the gathering dusk and saw Mrs Rockcliff open her front gate and pass to the street. She was not wearing a hat, and she was not carrying her baby. No, she didn't have a pram for the child. Yes, she went out quite often at night . . . in fact, it was mostly at night. She couldn't have been up to any good.

"Aw, steady on!" complained her husband. "No doubt Mrs Rockcliff went to the pictures or a dance or to see friends. Nothing against that."

"Suppose not, if you don't take into account that she never had any friends calling on her. Even the Methodist parson gave up calling," opposed the wife, a disfiguring sneer writhing on her thin lips. "But she did leave the child alone in the house . . . like a canary in a cage with a cloth round it. I heard it crying once when she was gallivanting about, and when I told her about it she as good as told me to mind my own business."

"She didn't actually neglect the child, did she?"

"No, not in other ways," replied Mrs Thring. "It was clean enough," she went on with a sniff.

"And you have the impression that Mrs Rockcliff had no friends?"

"That's what I think. And further, Inspector, I've always thought she didn't have a husband, either."

"Might have been a widow," soothed Mr Thring.

"Never told me, if she was. She lived too quiet, if you ask me. Not natural for a young woman like her. She must have spent most of the daylight hours reading. I've seen her taking armfuls of books to change at the Municipal Library. D'you think the child was kidnapped, Inspector? Like those others?"

"Too early to decide," countered Bony. "Mrs Rockcliff could have taken the baby out in the afternoon, and left it with an acquaintance . . . perhaps at the hospital. We'll find out."

"She didn't leave it anywhere but in the house," declared Mrs Thring. "She went out at ten past eight, as I told you. At half past seven she took the baby in from the crib on the front veranda. It was in the house all right when she went out that night."

Bony stood, saying:

"I am glad we are able to establish that, Mrs Thring. Tell me, did you notice what Mrs Rockcliff was wearing?"

"Yes. She was wearing her blue suit. I'm not positive, mind you, but I think she was carrying her library books."

"Quite so. Mr Thring, you stood in the hall when Constable Essen entered the bedroom. Can you recall if the bedroom light was on?"

"No, Inspector. Constable Essen switched it on."

"You then crossed the hall to stand just behind Constable Essen, who stood in the bedroom doorway. Can you recall if the blinds were drawn or not?"

"They were drawn," Thring replied without hesitation.

"It would appear that Mrs Rockcliff drew the blinds before she left the house that evening," Bony persisted. "It was then ten minutes past eight and it wasn't dark enough to warrant switching on the light and lowering the blinds. She didn't lower the lounge blinds before leaving. When previously she left the baby alone in the house at night, did she draw the blinds?"

"Oh, yes," replied Mrs Thring. "And the light on, too."

"H'm! A point having perhaps no importance," Bony purred.

"I think she left the light on when she went out to give people the idea she was in," said Mrs Thring. "It looks like that to me. Not putting on the light this last time seems to hint she thought she wouldn't be away more than half an hour. What time was it she was murdered, do you know?"

Bony warded her probing questions. Thring accompanied him to the front gate, where he apologised for his wife, who, he said, suffered from an ulcer.

The rubbernecks had gone, and a constable strange to Bony sat on a chair before the door of No 5. Bony, once again conscious of the sun-god, passed along the street of these middle-class homes to arrive at another street which would take him to Main Street. Here the houses were larger and the gardens more spacious. The still air imprisoned the odours of tar and of street dust, the scent of roses and the tang of grapes and peaches. Only such as he could have detected the fragrance of the vast untamed land beyond the extremities of the irrigation channels, the fragrance of the real, the eternal Australia where dwell, and will for ever, the spirits of the Ancient Aclhuringa.

He was wondering how he would react did Mr Thring

confess to having sliced his wife's throat with a table knife, when he became conscious of a voice containing nothing of gall and venom.

"Where do you come from?" demanded the voice.

Bony glanced to his left. The voice could have proceeded from the stout woman standing inside a wicket-gate into a thick hedge of lambertiana. She was shapeless in a sun frock, and from her wide shoulders a large straw sun hat was suspended by the ribbon about her neck. Her face was large and round. Her eyes were small and brown. At the corners of her mouth was a humorous quirk.

"Was there something?" asked Bony, who was an admirer of a famous radio comedian.

"Yes. Where do you come from? You're not a River Murray contact. An oddity, yet true. A rarity, and yet not so rare. I find you most interesting. Where do you come from?"

"Madam, your interest is reciprocated," Bony said, bowing slightly. "How much money have you in the bank?"

"What? . . . Er . . . Oh! I didn't intend to be rude. Good education, eh! Good job, by your clothes."

"Your continued interest, Madam, is still reciprocated. What is all this about? Who are you? What are you? How are you?"

The round and weathered face expanded into a smile. The large brown hands expressively gripped the points of the pickets. From behind her in the secluded garden a man said:

"Come here, dear. I wish to show you the pictures of bottle-trees in the Kimberleys. The magazine is very good this month."

"A moment, Henry. I am confronted by a remarkable specimen not possibly belonging to the Murray Valley tribes." To Bony: "Who am I? I am Mrs Marlo-Jones, Dip. Ed. What am I? A damned nuisance. How am I? Delighted to meet you. Come in and meet Professor Marlo-Jones. Chair of Anthropology, you know. Ex, or now retired."

The gate was swung wide in invitation. When the invitation was wordlessly declined, the gate was swung shut. Behind this somewhat original woman appeared a giant of a man, a decided personage. Possibly seventy, he stood and acted as a man of forty. The grey eyes were young and full of light. Above the high, tanned forehead the thick hair was more dark than grey.

"Great Scott!" he said, loudly. "Good heavens! Where did you get it?"

Genuine curiosity kept Bony standing before these unusual people. He was startled that they could see him, know him as the branch he was from the maternal vine whose roots are deeper far than the deepest artesian bore in Australia.

"Lizbeth, you have offended this man," rumbled the aged youth.

"Hope not, Henry. I want to be friends with him."

"Of course, Lizbeth." To Bony: "Please tell us who you are."

"I am Napoleon Bonaparte," conceded Bony.

"To repeat one of the questions you put to me, Mr Bonaparte, what are you?" asked the woman less belligerently.

"I am a detective."

"You had to be," she agreed. "Tracking would come naturally, like breathing. And your third question, I ask you. How are you?"

"Somewhat doubtful," admitted Bony. "Since a moment or two ago. Now, if you will pardon me, I will attend to my own business."

"Oh, don't go yet," urged the woman. "We're quite sane, really."

"I have never doubted that," was the gravely uttered falsehood.

"Then do come in for a few minutes. I'll make you a billy of tea, and I have some real brownie."

Bony heard the car slide to a stop at the moment when he was undecided whether to be amused or angry by these persons' persistent attitude of superiority. He saw the man look beyond him and gaily wave a hand to whoever opened the car door. Then he heard Sergeant Yoti say:

"Thought you'd like the car, sir."

Amusedly Bony witnessed dawning astonishment in the woman's eyes. The man said loudly:

"Please present us, Sergeant."

Yoti regarded Bony, caught his slight nod of assent.

"Professor Marlo-Jones and Mrs Jones. Detective-Inspector Napoleon Bonaparte, of the Queensland Police."

Bony bowed. The Marlo-Joneses automatically copied him. They said nothing, and when they regained balance Bony was smiling.

23

"Strange pair, Sergeant," remarked Bony when the car was moving.

"Harmless enough," replied Yoti. "They say he's a clever old bird, she does a lot of good at one thing and another."

"A real Prof.?"

"Too right! Retired, of course. Lives here to be near the aboriginal settlement up-river. Writing a book about them. She teaches botany."

Softly Bony laughed.

"Thought I was a new flower, I believe. Wanted me to stay for a billy of tea and a slice of brownie . . . her idea of a smoko tea suitable for a half-caste." The laughter ran before bitterness. "Guess to what I owe my self-respect, and my rank."

"Haven't a clue," declined the now cautious Yoti.

"The facility with which I thumb my nose at superior people. Stop at the Post Office, please. I wish to telegraph a request to Superintendent Bolt, down in Melbourne."

CHAPTER 4

ALICE McGORR

SUPERINTENDENT BOLT, Chief of the Criminal Investigation Branch of the Victoria Police, was verging on sixty and hated the thought of compulsory retirement. He had many friends and admirers in the Department, and one of them was First Constable Alice McGorr.

Bony had never met Alice McGorr, and he had not heard her story from Superintendent Bolt, although aware of Bolt's warm regard for her.

It appeared that old man McGorr was the finest 'can opener' of his generation, having served an apprenticeship with an English firm of safe makers and kept his knowledge up-to-date. Bolt was a sergeant when he came in contact with McGorr, who at the time was on vacation from gaol, and was chiefly instrumental in terminating the 'can opener's' holiday.

McGorr died in durance vile, and it happened that Mrs Bolt heard through her church association that Mrs McGorr and the children were facing the rocks. She visited the house owned by the widow to see what was what, and arrived an hour after Mrs McGorr had been taken to hospital with a fatal complaint.

Mrs Bolt was invited into the front room by Alice, a thin slab of a girl of fifteen who explained that her mother had been desperately ill for a long time. There was no animosity towards the visitor and Mrs Bolt learned that the eldest son was nineteen and in steady work, the eldest girl was eighteen and still in her first job as a stenographer. Next to this girl came Alice, who was followed by a girl of six and finally twin boys aged two and a fraction. She learned as well, from other sources, that Alice McGorr had been running the home for eighteen months, nursing the mother, caring for the small sister and the twin baby brothers.

The Bolts, having no family, became the parents of that one, when the mother died soon after entering hospital, and not one member of the family took the slightest interest in safes and the problem of opening them without keys.

Alice McGorr went to night school, and when Alice looked at Superintendent Bolt she was beautiful to see. She studied between making beds, sweeping rooms, even as she cooked, and Alice passed the Intermediate. They lived in an inner industrial suburb, and Alice took a keen interest in the people of the district, becoming the social worker of the church . . . and something more. She had the knack of spinning threads of information into patterns, and the bread Bolt launched upon the water was returned to him by the baker's batch.

When the twins left school and went to work, and the eldest son's wife took over the home, Alice joined the Force. She had all the gifts the job demanded. She could fight like a tiger before she entered the training school for women, and when she passed for duty she could master the instructors in ju-jitsu. They put her into the worst districts, and she was never hurt. Attempts to cripple her were made by thugs, and the thugs were crippled by their own. A gunman shot at her, and the gunman had his face slashed. A low type once told her what he'd do to her, and the bad man's wife bided her time and emptied a potful of boiling cabbage over him. No one seemed to know why, save Bolt and the church minister.

The evening came when Alice was instructed by the Senior Officer of her district to report to Superintendent Bolt at his private house. Bolt said:

"Alice, will you do me a favour?"

"Of course. Anything," she replied with quiet earnestness.

"I got a pal," Bolt went on. "He's the most conceited man in Australia. The most aggravating cuss in the world. He thinks he knows everything . . . sometimes. I've known him for years, and we're still pals. He's half-abo but whiter than me. He's . . ."

"Couldn't be, Pop."

"He is, so don't argue. The name's Napoleon Bonaparte."

"I've heard things, Pop. Go on."

"Bony . . . he's Bony to all his friends . . . seems to have been persuaded to investigate the abduction of those four babies at Mitford. Bit out of his line, 'cos he concentrates on difficult homicides. Anyway, he's up at Mitford, and has asked me to send you up to off-side for him. You know, just like that. No thought of us being in the Victoria Force and him working for New South Wales. Oh, no! Such matters as State boundaries and inter-State jealousies wouldn't register with Bony. Just asks . . . just expects. Will you go?"

"I'd like to."

"Good! I've arranged it. You'll have no authority in Mitford, of course . . . being Bony's private assistant. There's a plane for Broken Hill in the morning at ten which will put you down at Mitford. Catch the bus leaving Airways House at nine-thirty. Apply there for your ticket, which will be paid for."

"All right! No uniform, of course." Alice rose. "Thanks, Pop! I'll not let you down, or your pal. Those vanished babies will be right in my handbag in no time. I've read all about them . . . poor little mites."

At eleven the next morning Alice McGorr landed at Mitford and was welcomed by First Constable Essen.

"Ordered to meet you, Miss McGorr, and told to take you straight home. You're staying with us, and we have to make you take morning tea before you join up with the Big Boss. Give me your case."

Alice McGorr liked Essen and his wife. She liked her room. She fell in love with the baby. She liked Main Street. She liked the smell of the town itself, of fruit ripening, fruit drying, fruit cooking, fruit rotting, and could not name that other smell, the indefinable, the haunting essence of the untamed hinterland of saltbush plain and mulga forest.

She liked No 5 Elgin Street, although she had read about

the murder in the paper when on the plane. Essen conducted her to the lounge.

"Miss McGorr, sir," he said, and withdrew.

"Ah, Miss McGorr! I'm delighted that you were able to come. Please sit down, and smoke if you wish." Bony set the chair for her, smiled at her, the shock she gave him never rising to his eyes. He held a match to her cigarette, sat down and asked after Superintendent and Mrs Bolt.

She liked Napoleon Bonaparte.

He listened . . . and wondered. The face was a tragedy and yet heroic. The tragedy lay in the almost entire absence of chin. The eyes were softly brown, large, beautiful when she was telling of Superintendent Bolt. Her hands were beautiful, too, and well kept. Later, on suggesting she removed her hat, he marked the wide forehead, and disapproved of the blonde hair-do, drawn hard back to a tight roll. The hat was low-crowned and of white straw. It was better off than on. Her clothes . . . there was something the matter with them . . . and before he could make up his mind where, she gave him a letter from Superintendent Bolt.

Dear Bony. Now you have it. Think yourself in luck. Remember what I told you about her. She will serve you well, for she has the most extraordinary variety of capabilities I've ever come across. You can unload your secrets, confess all your low sins, and she won't tell . . . excepting to me. Yet be warned. There's no weakness anywhere, save with children and sick people, and you may take my word for that.

Attached to the letter was a report by a detective who had interviewed Dr Browner of Glen Iris. Dr Browner declared he had no knowledge of a Mrs Rockcliff, and during the last eighteen months had had no case of an expectant mother which had not been completed by the birth of the child.

Having dropped the letter on a pile of papers, he found her eyes directed to him, and they didn't waver, but held in the mutual summing-up. She was, perhaps, thirty-five, tall and angular, with good shoulders and well-developed arms. When Bony smiled, her look of appraisal vanished.

"The Biblical writer stated that there is a time to be born and a time to die; he should have included a time to be frank," he said. "I will be frank with you now. When I want photographs, I apply to an expert. When I want to know why a man died in convulsions, I apply to a pathologist. I want to know more about babies, which is why I asked especially for you. You do know something about babies?"

"I was thirteen when Mother fell ill, sir. There were twins as well as a little sister. Yes, I know something about babies."

"And learned more when you joined the Force."

"More about parents, sir."

"I have agreed to investigate the disappearance of five babies in this town, Miss McGorr. You would like to work with me?"

The eyes only betrayed eagerness.

"I would indeed, sir."

"We will work in harness. Later I'll want you to study the Official Summaries on the four missing infants, and will outline what is known of the fifth child, who was, almost certainly, stolen at the time the mother was murdered in this house last Monday night. Those Summaries were compiled by men—mark—by men who when glancing into a pram couldn't tell the sex of the child. Could you?"

"With very young babies, it would mean guessing, but I wouldn't often be wrong."

"H'm! Wait there. I have something to show you."

The brown eyes watched him leave the room. She sat with remarkable passivity, her shapely hands resting on the table and in sharp contrast to the hard and muscular forearms. A smile hovered about her unfortunate mouth, but it had vanished on his return with two feeding bottles, which he placed side by side on the table.

"Tell me what difference you find in those bottles," he asked. "You may touch them, they have been tested for prints."

Alice McGorr viewed the contents of each bottle against the window light. The liquid in each was a coagulated mass of seeming solids and bluish water. She took up each bottle to examine closely the teat, and then, arranging them as he had done, she sat down.

"Although of different makes, sir, both bottles are of standard size," she began. "This bottle contains a preparatory food, and this one contains cow's milk. The teat of the bottle of preparatory food has been in use for some time, it's soft from constant sterilisation. The teat on this bottle of cow's milk is quite new. It has been sterilised, but very seldom

28

used, if at all. There's another difference, too. The hole in the old teat has been enlarged with a hot needle, but this other one, the new one, hasn't been treated like that."

"Well done, Miss McGorr. The teats when bought would have a standard-sized hole in them, no doubt."

"Yes, sir. You see, the makers say the size of the hole is just right for the average baby, and that it induces the baby to exercise its mouth and throat muscles when getting its food. Much more often than not, though, a baby isn't strong enough, or too lazy. It's like drawing at a cigarette that's too tightly packed. So the mother enlarges the hole with a needle."

"And then the baby is content?"

"Yes. But the hole mustn't be too large or else the baby will have hiccoughs," Alice continued gravely.

"H'm, reminds me of the beer swill," said Bony, not daring to smile. "I'll replace these bottles. Wait there, please." On returning, he went on: "Mrs Rockcliff leased this house, but furnished it herself. Last Monday evening she went out at shortly after eight o'clock, leaving the baby in the cot at the foot of her bed. It appears that she often went out at night, leaving the infant unattended.

"I will not tell you more than that now, and before we go to lunch I want you to do what you like with the place to find the answers to these questions. One: What was Mrs Rockcliff's character? Two: What were her habits in the house? Three: Why does the bottle in the bedroom contain cow's milk, and the bottle on the kitchen bench preparatory food? And any other information you may glean."

For a full hour Bony silently watched Alice McGorr at work, effacing himself. She examined the bedclothes, the interior of the baby's cot, and the clothes in the wardrobe. She rummaged into drawers and cupboards, removed the contents of shelves and expertly looked at cooking utensils. She brought the washing in from the line. She fingered the curtains, examined the backs of the few pictures, lifted the linoleum along the edges. She glanced through the magazines and opened the covers of the few books. And when she was done, her hair was wispy with dampness and her hands were dirty.

"That woman was proud of her baby," she said, when seated at the lounge table and smoking the cigarette from Bony's special case. "The baby's clothes are hand-made, and

29

expensive material. The needlework is simply glorious. I can see her making those little garments, every stitch a beautiful thought for the baby."

"And yet Mrs Rockcliff left the infant alone for hours at night," murmured Bony.

"It doesn't square," Alice McGorr admitted, her eyes puckered, three vertical lines between her brows. "What did the woman do for a living?"

"We don't know."

"No money . . . handbag?"

"No handbag, money or bank-book. Her picture has been shown at every bank and no one can identify her."

"She must have had money to live, and she lived well. She knew how to cook, and wasn't satisfied with plain ingredients. She hated dirt and untidiness. She took an interest in geographical subjects and read travel books in preference to novels. Her taste in clothes was beyond what I understand, but then I never had a hope. Her clothes were expensive. She must have had money . . . more than I earn."

"I haven't omitted the matter from my calculations," Bony said. "Go on, please."

"Things don't square, sir," she reiterated. "She had to go out at night and leave the baby alone in the house. She wasn't hard up. The baby's clothes are all made with the most expensive materials. It lacked for nothing. She didn't entertain, for no one entertains these days without having empty bottles in the back yard. But she had to draw money from some place or person. D'you know what place or what person?"

"No."

"I think she lived here under an assumed name," Alice proceeded, her eyes almost closed. "There's something here I don't catch. You said her name was Pearl Rockcliff, but on some of her clothes is a name tag with the initials P.R. overlaid on others which could be J.O. or J.U. And she didn't buy her clothes second-hand, I'll bet a pound."

Because he hadn't observed her taking special interest in clothes' tags, Bony secretly gave her a hundred marks. He was rather liking the rôle of maestro encouraging a pupil.

"Go on," he said softly.

"Mrs Rockcliff took care to rub out all evidence of her life before she came to Mitford. She came here to escape the consequences of a crime, or because she feared someone. Her

Christian name wasn't Pearl. It was Jean or Joan . . . for preference."

"Why Jean or Joan for preference?"

"The paper said the woman's age was about thirty, and thirty years ago it was the fashion to name baby girls Joan or Jean or Jessica."

"There are, then, fashions in Christian names?"

"Oh yes. Read the death notices and compare names with ages."

"I should do so, but . . . What do the feeding bottles tell you?"

"Before Mrs Rockcliff went out that night, she fed the baby. The baby didn't take all the food, and she took the bottle to the kitchen, where she should have washed it. She didn't wash it because she must have been in a hurry. The steriliser is still on the stove, face powder is spilt in the bathroom cabinet and two dresses have fallen from their hangers. Everything else is tidy, so she would have replaced them. The baby was being fed on a preparatory food; I found a large tin partly used, so the bottle on the kitchen bench is the baby's real bottle.

"The person who came to steal the baby brought the other one, the one near the cot. It was brought to keep the baby from crying while it was being taken away. It was a man who stole the baby."

Alice McGorr fell silent, flushing slightly as though suddenly conscious of talking too much, assuming too much to this man Bolt had often told her was the finest investigator in Australia. Quietly, Bony pressed her.

"Why do you vote for a man? It should have been a woman."

"A woman would not have risked a bottle having a teat with a hole so small. A tiny baby might not have been able to draw the milk and would have yelled, which would be the last thing she would want to happen. A woman would have been sure about that teat. A woman, in any case, wouldn't have brought the milk at all. She'd have brought an ordinary dummy and dipped it in malt extract or honey, which she could have carried in a small jar. That would keep any baby quiet for ten minutes at least . . . all the time she needed to take it out of the house."

Bony rose, smiling.

"Put on your hat," he ordered. "We are going to lunch."

He watched her putting on the absurd hat without bothering to stand before the mirror over the mantel. As she was flushing when she joined him in the hall, he said:

"I've known Superintendent Bolt for many years. Bolt calls me Bony. Even my Chief in Brisbane invariably does so. All my friends so address me. It would be nice if you could make yourself believe you are one of my friends."

She said wistfully that it would not be difficult, and added that she would be very happy to call him Bony on the condition that he called her Alice.

As his illustrious namesake is said to have done when pleased, he pinched her ear, laughed outright at her startled face, and opened the front door. Bolt would have been astounded that he got away with that pinch.

CHAPTER 5

BABY NUMBER ONE

ACROSS THE luncheon table in a quiet restaurant, Bony departed from practice by taking Alice McGorr further into his confidence.

"You know, Alice, your theory that it was a man who took the bottle of cow's milk to the house, that it was a man who stole the baby, is not a little upsetting," he said, as though it were a reluctant admission. "It doesn't support what I read on the linoleum, yet still could be the truth. The story I read begins with the entry of a woman by the front door when Mrs Rockcliff was out. She was in the bedroom when she heard the man climbing in through the scullery window, and she crawled under the bed. The woman had a good look through the house. The man didn't. It would seem that the man was familiar with the house and the woman was not. He heard Mrs Rockcliff open the front door on her return, and he slipped to the bedroom to stand behind the door, where he waited to strike her down. He departed via the scullery window; the woman left by the front door. As Essen found the front door snibbed back, and the door closed merely by the catch, either the strange woman forgot to release the snib, having a key or a strip of celluloid, or Mrs Rockcliff herself forgot to release the lock. We can assume that the man and the woman were not accomplices, and also that the woman was under the bed when the murder was committed."

The end of this statement found Alice frowning, and Bony hastened to smooth away the perplexity.

"We will not permit this divergence of opinion to bother us just now. It will work out in the light of subsequent investigation. There is a point we must keep in mind, which is not to give homicide preference over abduction. The five babies may still be alive. We must proceed on the assumption that one or two, if not all, are alive, whereas Mrs Rockcliff is dead and her murderer cannot escape me. Therefore we give priority to the babies and hope that the murder of Mrs Rockcliff will assist us in locating them, or establishing their fate."

The frown had vanished now, and the brown eyes were full of unmistakable approval. With absorbed attention she watched the intent face, forgetful of the food she ate, conscious of the power in her host, power generated by intelligence teamed with something she couldn't fathom.

"The story you read from Mrs Rockcliff's possessions is accurate," Bony went on. "We cannot find a lead to her past life and we cannot find the source of her income. She told Dr Nott that her previous doctor was Dr Browner, of Glen Iris. She told the Rev Baxter, as well as Nott, that her husband had been killed in a road accident, but there is no record of a man of that name having been killed on the roads anywhere in the Commonwealth.

"The letters taken from her mail-box tell us nothing. Two were bills from local stores, one a charitable fund appeal, and the other a lottery ticket. So far we haven't found anyone in Mitford with whom she was on friendly terms . . . but we will.

"A neighbour told us she thought Mrs Rockcliff was headed for the Library when she left the house last Monday evening. It was dusk and, according to the neighbour, Mrs Rockcliff was a great reader. However, Mrs Rockliff didn't change her books at the Library, and the last batch of books she borrowed are still in the house. Where she went, whom she met, what time she returned home, we don't know.

"We have very few clues . . . as yet. We know that the unknown man stood six feet one or two inches, in his shoes, that he was slightly drunk, or is a sailor accustomed to long voyages. He wore gloves, and Essen is sure they were rubber

33

gloves. His shoe size is eight. He weighs only a little more than I do, so that in view of his height he must be a lean man. The unknown woman wears a shoe size six, is heavier than I, and is accustomed to wearing high heels instead of the wedge shoes she wore that night. She too wore gloves, the first finger of the left hand being repaired. I incline to the belief that she is left-handed.

"We may gain further clues from the sweepings sent to the lab in Sydney, as well as from the clothes' tags bearing those initials. Mrs Rockcliff's dresses may be traced to the shops where she bought them. All in good time. This routine work we leave to the experts in such matters. Do you recall reading about a newspaper magnate, Lord Northcliffe?"

"Yes. He was out here when I was a small kid."

"When someone asked him why he never learned to write shorthand, he replied: 'Why should I have spent valuable time on such a task? I had always more important things to do.' I am like Lord Northcliffe."

Alice McGorr forbore to smile at this, to her, first sample of Bony's vanity.

"So, having put the experts to work, you and I will continue placidly to browse and delve into the souls of men and women. This afternoon we visit the parents of the stolen babies, putting out of mind everything those Official Summaries have to tell us. Do you think you will be happy with Constable and Mrs Essen?"

"Yes, of course. They are both very kind."

"I thought they would make you comfortable. I have been made warmly welcome by Mrs and Sergeant Yoti, and I am additionally pleased by not having to stay at a hotel where my movements can be so easily checked."

When in the taxi which Bony hired for the afternoon, he said:

"The first of the abductions took place on October 20th. The parents are a Doctor and Mrs Delph. The Delphs employed a nurse girl, and the girl was told to call for a parcel at a frock shop on Main Street. It was a busy shopping afternoon. The shop is narrow and long, carpeted and crowded with racks, dress stands and that kind of thing. As the girl explained later, it isn't a shop into which to push a pram. So she left the baby in the pram braked against the shop fronts. She had to wait several minutes before being attended to, and

34

when she went out to the pram it was empty. No one came forward to say they had seen anyone interfering with any pram."

"Pretty slick, wasn't it?" observed Alice, powdering her nose, and Bony was suddenly grateful that she didn't use lipstick.

"As you say, slick. We will now call on Dr and Mrs Delph. You concentrate on the reactions of the parents to my questions. Unless a pertinent point should arise which you think I have missed, say nothing. You are my cousin, interested in crime investigation."

"Very well," Alice assented demurely.

Their taxi entered a wide boulevard fronting the tree-lined river and backed by the residences of the élite of this localised community. Dr Delph's house was of colonial architecture, its veranda masked by striped blinds, the main door being reached via three wide stone steps guarded by stone lions.

The glass-panelled door was opened by a woman, sharp-featured and angular, of the type who speak loudly in the belief that it is socially impressive. On Bony announcing himself and his business, her face became momentarily vacuous, but she asked them to enter and invited them to be seated in the Tudor-furnished lounge. Mrs Delph herself did not sit down. She waited, examining them alternately with disfavour, waiting for the scum to make known their wants.

"I am hoping it's possible to glean further information concerning the abduction of your child, Mrs Delph," Bony opened smoothly. "Exactly how old was the baby when it vanished from its pram?"

Mrs Delph uttered a cry of anguish, sank to a settee and closed her eyes. Instantly Bony was regretful of having spoken so abruptly. Glancing helplessly at Alice, he was astonished to encounter contempt. Presently Mrs Delph was able to say:

"The little darling was just four weeks and two days when that fiend took him from his pram. Oh, why come to torture me in my loneliness?"

Sobs shook her body, and were partly muffled by the cushion into which her face was buried. Bony patiently waited for her grief to subside. Alice McGorr crossed her long nyloned legs, and the window light gleamed on the smart brown shoes. The upper shoe began to wag as though the owner was intolerant of grief, and that shoe displeased Bony.

35

Eventually Mrs Delph regained composure to launch into details of the abduction as given by the nursemaid, and Bony listened with attentive sympathy.

"Tell me, Mrs Delph," he requested, "was he a healthy little fellow?"

"Naturally, Inspector. He was a beautiful baby. I ought not to have allowed that wretched fool of a girl to take him for his airing, but I was so tired after my return from hospital."

"A tragic blow," murmured Bony, again noting the impatient shoe. "Believe me, Mrs Delph, I regret opening the wound, as it were, but please be assured that we are doing and shall continue to do all in our power to restore the infant to you."

"Oh no! You'll never find him after all this time," wailed the unhappy mother. "They've killed him most likely. I've given up all hope."

"How long had you been home from the hospital when it happened?"

"How long? I must think. Oh, my poor heart!"

It was a question not previously put to Mrs Delph, and therefore her hesitancy was excused.

"Eleven days, to be exact. I wasn't at all well, and my husband agreed to engaging that girl, that awful fool of a girl. She produced excellent references, too."

"Pardon my next question, please. Was the child bottle-fed?"

"Oh yes. I . . . I couldn't, you know. I was too ill."

"Was the child raised on cow's milk?"

Mrs Delph was now emphatic.

"No, of course not. It wouldn't do, what with cows feeding off the same grass as myxomatised rabbits and things. The little mite was doing splendidly on a preparatory food."

"Who was your doctor?' "

"My doctor . . . at the hospital, you mean? Dr Nott. I was at his private hospital, of course, not the Public." Mrs Delph sat up and mopped her eyes with a useless lacy item. "Dr Nott specialises with babies, Inspector, and he even takes the babies at the Public Hospital, too. He and my husband have an agreement permitting my husband to do the outside work, which he prefers."

"Who fed the baby, Mrs Delph?" interjected Alice.

"I . . . oh! What was that?"

One visible eye pinned Alice like a butterfly to a board.

"Who really fed the baby?" Alice repeated firmly.

"My cook actually did that," replied the doctor's wife. "She has had several children and is an excellent woman with babies. As I said, I was not well at the time."

"Yes, of course," interposed Bony. "The nurse girl was employed only to look after the child in a general manner, I assume."

"That was so, Inspector. She didn't live in, you see. She came every day."

"Have you ever met Mrs Rockcliff?"

"That poor woman!" Mrs Delph again collapsed to the cushion. "I don't know what will happen next. No, I never met her. She didn't belong in our set."

"Have you met the mothers of those other stolen babies?"

"Only Mrs Bulford and Mrs Coutts. I wouldn't know the others, socially. Why are you asking all these questions, Inspector?"

"In order to find your missing baby and return him to you. You have not received a demand for ransom?"

"No." Mrs Delph again won composure. "I . . . we would have paid it, if it had been demanded." She added sharply: "Did any of those other women receive a ransom demand?"

"No. How long has Dr Delph been in practice here?"

"Almost seven years now. But we've been married only two years, and although I'm not young I wanted a baby of my own."

"Was it customary for the nurse girl to collect parcels when the baby was in her charge?"

"It was not. The chauffeur-gardener does that. But that day he had to take my husband to four outlying cases, and I wanted that dress. I never dreamed she would leave the child outside the shop."

"You know the shop, of course?"

"Certainly."

"It was a busy afternoon, and the shop too crowded to accommodate a pram. Because of this the girl left the pram outside. Don't you think too much blame is attached to the girl?"

"No, I certainly do not," replied Mrs Delph, grey eyes granite-hard. "She could have wheeled the pram just inside the door. It would have been all right there. Madame Clare wouldn't have minded, knowing it was my baby. There was no excuse for leaving the pram outside . . . unless the girl was an accomplice of the thief . . . which wouldn't surprise me."

Bony rose.

"Beyond your family circle, you know no person who took an inordinate interest in the child?"

"No one. Please, no more questions. It is all so terrible, and I can't bear to talk about it."

"Thank you for being so co-operative under such tragic circumstances," murmured Bony, and Mrs Delph again closed her eyes and sighed. "Au revoir! And do permit yourself to hope."

The sound of Mrs Delph's sobbing accompanied them to the front door. Together they walked the gravelled path to the street gate, where Alice turned quickly to look back at the house. In the taxi, Bony gave an address to the driver and to Alice said:

"Why were you so intolerant of Mrs Delph's natural grief?"

"Because she was putting it on," Alice replied bitterly. "I know that kind. She's tough, heartless, selfish to the backbone. And a dirty snob."

"You don't mean that Mrs Delph was pretending to be grieved?"

"Over to you. We left her flat on the settee: she watched us walk to the gate, from behind the window curtain. They will touch the curtains when they're watching. I could never understand why."

Alice sat bolt upright when it was easy to relax, and the straw hat angled severely over her brow as if to emphasise her mood.

"Where are we going now?" she asked, hopefully.

"To interview the nurse girl."

"Good! We'll get something out of her."

"You will soft-pedal," Bony said quietly.

She looked at him, then her anger subsided and she said, as soft as a whisper:

"I'm sorry, Bony. I . . . that woman infuriated me. I'll play poker."

"Good girl."

After that neither spoke till the taxi stopped outside a small house in a sun-heated street appearing to have no beginning and no end.

"I will enquire if the nursemaid is home," Bony said. "Should I beckon, please come to my aid."

The door was opened to him by a matronly woman who said her daughter was working at the cannery, and so followed a further journey of fifteen minutes to reach the huge iron structure which swallowed fruit by the truck-load. The manager conducted them through the maze within.

Here a hundred people were working. From a distant point gleaming tins were conveyed by belt and wire guides to the benches where girls were de-stoning peaches and other fruit. Seven semi-nude men tended the fires beneath the vats cooking jam. Above the rattle of machinery was the hammering of the 'casers', and case after filled case was being added to the mountain along one wall.

Amid this ordered chaos, they were presented to Miss Betty Morse.

CHAPTER 6

PEACHES AND BULLION

BETTY MORSE quickened a man's eyes, which is different from stirring his pulses. She was wearing a light-blue smock, and her hair had caught the bronze of the sky and held it fast. Her arms were bare, and the knife she put down was the wickedest-looking weapon Bony had seen outside the police museum. The manager having left them, he said in his easy manner:

"I understand, Miss Morse, that you work here on contract rates, so perhaps you could talk as you work. Think you could? I don't want to hinder you."

"You won't, Inspector," she told him, and, selecting a peach, sliced it at once, plucked out the stone and dropped the halved peach into a tin. The knife was razor-sharp, the operation complete in two seconds.

"You are sure you won't be distracted and cut yourself?" persisted the doubtful Bony, and turning to him she laughed, and the horrible knife appeared to do its work of its own volition. Beyond her, other girls were displaying equal dexterity; some were gossiping to their neighbours, their hands working automatically, their minds busy with boy friends.

"I've told over and over again all about Mrs Delph's baby," asserted Betty Morse a trifle edgedly. "The baby simply vanished from the pram outside the shop when I was inside getting a parcel."

"You must be bored, Miss Morse," Bony soothed. "Personally I'd rather talk about peaches, and how many tins you fill in a day, and what is the highest money you've earned in a week. My cousin here, who wants to be a detective, is more interested in babies than I am at the moment, but, like you, I have to work for my living. When you took Mrs Delph's baby out in the pram did anyone stop and show interest in it?"

"No. It was just an ordinary kid. It wasn't really my fault it was stolen. Plenty of women leave a baby in a pram outside a shop. Mrs Delph had no cause to yell and scream for the police, and tell them to arrest me."

"Bit of an old bitch," remarked Alice, and the indignation on Betty's face gave way to astonishment, followed by obvious gratitude that here at last was someone who sympathised.

"You're telling me," she vowed warmly. "Screamed the place down. Said rotten things about me. Yelled for cook to ring for the police, and told the policeman that I'd sold the baby and he was to search me for the money."

"Excitable woman," observed Bony, but Betty Morse was no longer interested in him. The knife flashed, the peaches fell apart and their stones dropped into a pail at her feet. For only a tenth of every second did she look at what her hands were doing as she poured out her story of martyrdom to Alice, who energetically nodded and oh-ed and ah-ed, occasionally inserting a diversionary question and revealing to Bony that she had mastered the art of arriving via the roundabout.

Thenceforth he was kept in his box to listen and watch with prolonged aversion the gleaming knife attacking the fruit with seemingly ever-increasing speed as Betty Morse became really warmed up. A boy came to empty peaches into her tray. A man came to remove the filled tins and make a note on her pad, and when there should have been a gallon of spilt blood there wasn't a speck. Bony was forgotten, but was entranced.

It came out that Mrs Delph's cook knew more about the Delphs than they could possibly know about each other. The husband managed a very extensive practice. He was working himself to death, and only kept on his feet with the aid of whisky 'planted' in the garage. There was no reason to hide booze in the garage as there was plenty of it in the house. He was 'a nice old thing', although Bony was aware that Dr Delph was not turned forty. His wife was the daughter of a parson, had married 'somewhat late in life'. Bony knew she wasn't more than thirty-five. She was 'stuck up', a delicate type, was given to 'turns' to get her way with her husband. And, they didn't sleep together. When she found she was going to have a baby, she sacked the cook four times in the one day, screamed at her husband, and moaned for a week.

After that, Mrs Delph went on as before, going to cocktail parties and giving them, and to musical do's where morons played five-fingered exercises on the piano. Although perfectly well, she insisted that Dr Nott call at the house once a week, and when he missed on two occasions she threatened her husband that she would drown herself, as no one cared what became of her.

In view of the fact that Betty Morse had been employed by Mrs Delph for only ten days, the amount of background information she poured into Alice's receptive ears was remarkable. Only once did she pause, when Alice adroitly spurred her to renewed efforts. Once Bony interjected, but wasn't heard.

Did Mrs Delph really love the baby? Of course she didn't. She could only love Mrs Delph. Yes, cook fed the baby. Poor little devil! More nights than not cook had the baby's cot in her own room. But didn't Mrs Delph have anything to do with the child? Damn little. Only when there were visitors, then she'd wheel the cot into the lounge and ooze the loving mother stuff all over it. And the guests, too.

And so it went on and on.

Bony wanted to smoke and was defeated by the large and numerous notices ordering him to forget it. Looking at his watch, he saw it was afternoon tea time, and then felt on the verge of collapse from thirst. He learned that Mrs Delph's eldest brother was the organist at a city church, that her second brother was being groomed to take over their father's church when the 'old bloke' retired. The third brother was a doctor specialising in 'psycho something' down in Melbourne, and the only sister had married a jeweller and at the moment was in a home for inebriates. He learned, too, that Betty Morse had several boy friends, but wasn't going to marry one of them. Men were essential in any girl's life. He was hearing about the virtues and vices of these boy friends when he surrendered and retired to the taxi.

"Are you married?" he asked the driver.

"No ruddy fear," replied the man, as though the very idea was an insult.

Time was slain.

"Shall I go in and break it up?" suggested the clairvoyant driver.

"Better give her five minutes. My cousin may be difficult."

The driver sighed. Bony smoked. Ten minutes drifted before Alice appeared at the gate in the tall iron fence. She was looking cool, energised, and when she settled herself on the seat beside Bony she sighed with enormous satisfaction.

"As a mark of my commendation, Alice, you shall have cream cakes with your tea this afternoon," Bony told her, and she glanced swiftly at him, to confirm the pleasure she detected in his voice.

Again in the car after refreshment, Bony said zestfully:

"We shall now delve into the abduction of the next baby, which took place on November 29th, five weeks after the Delph baby vanished. The name of the parents is Bulford. He is the manager of a bank and they live over the bank chamber. They have been there six years."

"How long married?"

"I don't know yet. As they have two sons at boarding-school we will assume that the period covers several years."

"I was only wondering," Alice claimed, a little abashed.

"As I mentioned," went on Bony, "the Bulfords live over the bank. They have a private entrance to a ground-floor hall. On November 29th the bank closed as usual at three-thirty, and, as often he did, the manager worked in the office until five-thirty.

"At five-forty-five he had an appointment in the town, and, having locked the rear door to the bank, he went upstairs to wash. He knew his wife had left the building some time previously as he had heard the door of the private entrance being opened and closed, and on reaching the first-floor landing, where stood the baby's cot, he assumed that his wife had taken the child with her. She had not. Between the time she left the building and he went upstairs to wash, the baby was stolen from its cot on the landing."

"No leads?" Alice asked.

"None. Here we are to see the place for ourselves and to draw our own inferences and conclusions."

To reach the bank's private entrance meant following a lane between the building and a high board fence, and whilst Alice pressed the doorbell, Bony needed to jump to see over the fence the rear part of unoccupied business premises. The doorbell could be heard ringing somewhere on the first floor. Alice, becoming impatient of delay because the lane was a sun trap, was about to ring again when from closer at hand a telephone shrilled.

A full minute lapsed, when the door was opened by a man in his shirtsleeves, rimless glasses aiding tired hazel eyes having soft brown flecks, and a toothbrush moustache suiting his square face. On Bony announcing their names and business, he explained that his wife was dressing to go out, and that the telephone had delayed him in answering the bell.

They were invited inside, passing the door to the rear of the bank chamber, and mounting carpeted stairs to be shown into a sitting-room. The manager withdrew to fetch his wife, and Alice began pricing the furniture, beginning with the carpet.

Mrs Bulford was Alice McGorr's opposite number: the brow high and narrow, the eyes small and dark, the chin a warning to any man having an ounce of experience. She greeted the callers frostily and, when seated, posed like Queen Victoria giving Gladstone a piece of her mind.

"It was the most mystifying thing that ever happened, Inspector," said precise Mr Bulford.

"Allow me to deal with the matter, John," objected his wife. "My husband, Inspector, was working in the parlour, the bank being closed for the day. After I left to keep an engagement, there was no one in the building except my husband, and had the child wakened and cried he couldn't help but hear it."

"I heard nothing, not a sound."

"Please, John."

"Very well."

Bony cut in:

"The private entrance was locked after you left that afternoon, and the rear door to a small yard at the back was also locked. The only windows left open were those fronting the street, and only by using a ladder could anyone have entered

43

through one of them. The ladder isn't feasible, and we are left with two theories. Either the kidnapper was concealed inside the building, or he was in possession of a duplicate key of the side door, the back door being secured by a bolt in addition to the ordinary lock. The side door would automatically lock when you pulled it shut on leaving. You are sure you did that, Mrs Bulford?"

"Quite, Inspector."

"I heard my wife close the door and the lock snap," added Mr. Bulford.

"What would be the odds favouring anyone hiding in the building before the bank was closed to the public?"

"Odds in favour! A million to one against. There is nowhere to hide. You shall see for yourself."

"I was hoping to. When is the bank chamber cleaned?"

"Every morning. A man comes at seven-forty-five. I let him in, and he leaves when the bank is opened for business."

"Does he ever use the back door?"

"Yes. The kitchen, you see, is on the ground floor. There's a door from the kitchen to the back yard, but it is fitted with a Yale lock and never left open. The kitchen window is protected with iron bars. The cleaner couldn't have had anything to do with it. He's been engaged here for over twenty years."

"You have other children?"

"Two boys," replied Mrs Bulford. "They are at boarding-school in Melbourne."

"Mrs Bulford. The baby was born at the local hospital?"

"Yes, it was."

"Your doctor?"

"Dr Nott. Whatever ..."

"Pardon me, was the infant bottle-fed?"

"It was," answered Mrs Bulford, frowning.

"Healthy?"

"Naturally," came the echo of Mrs Delph's reply.

"Do you entertain much?"

"No. We give a sherry party on the third Tuesday in every month."

"Er, the bank pays," interrupted the manager. "Usual thing, you know. Important clients and others who cannot be overlooked. And, of course, our personal friends."

"These parties ... the usual time?"

"From four-thirty to six."

44

"Where are we going?" asked Mrs Bulford, and Bony presented the next question as though he hadn't heard her.

"Do the same people come to your house every month?"

"The majority, yes. All known very well to us, of course."

"Mrs Delph . . . is she one of your guests?"

"Yes. So is her husband when he can get away from his practice."

"Does Mrs Rockcliff have an account here?"

The question probed. The eyes behind the rimless glasses flickered, and the shutters fell.

"No, Inspector. We never heard the name before we read about it in the paper, and the staff couldn't recognise a client from the picture brought by a constable."

"Is it true that the woman's baby has vanished?" asked Mrs. Bulford.

"Unfortunately, yes. Forgive me if thought impertinent. On that afternoon your baby was stolen, what was the nature of your engagement?"

"Oh! A cocktail party given by Mr and Mrs Reynolds."

"Our best clients, Inspector," interposed the manager. "I was supposed to be at their house before six that day. I left the chamber at five-thirty to brush up before leaving. It was then I found the cot empty. It was on the landing outside this room."

"What time did you leave?" Alice asked, and Bony frowned, for he had already told her this detail, and it was the question he was about to put. Mrs Bulford glared at Alice.

"At about half past four," she snapped.

"Then it was intended that the baby be left alone for something like an hour and a half?" persisted Alice.

"The child was quite all right, and, we thought, quite safe," replied Mrs Bulford firmly and frigidly.

"When investigating these cases," Bony said, suavely, "it's necessary to explore every avenue to ascertain whether the thief's success was due to chance circumstances or to close knowledge of the parents' habits. And so these questions which may seem too personal. How often prior to the date the child was stolen was it left alone in the building?"

Mr Bulford's face slowly reddened, but no change came to the face of his wife, who replied with some asperity:

"That I cannot recall, Inspector. Several times, probably. It has happened when my husband and I have visited together, or he had to go out on business or play tennis when I, too, had an engagement."

"You said that you give a sherry party every third Tuesday in the month. Do Mr and Mrs Reynolds also have a set day every month?"

"Oh, yes. It's always on the second Wednesday."

"You meet there the same people who come to your parties?"

"Yes, everyone in our social circle, you know."

"Of course. Do you employ a domestic?"

"That's impossible," replied Mrs Bulford, indicating that lack of domestic assistance was her major cross.

Bony stood, bowed his leave to Mrs Bulford and followed Alice and the manager down the stairs to the hall, where he said he would like to glance into the banking chamber

It was quite small, the wide counter crossing the width of the partitioned offices behind it. They were shown the strong-room, and finally the manager's office ornately furnished with a large table desk commanded by a swivel chair, and several well-upholstered chairs for the clients.

"Very snug," Bony observed. "A client should find it a pleasure to ask for an overdraft, and you, Mr Bulford, to grant it."

Mr Bulford chuckled . . . suddenly a different man.

"As a matter of fact, Inspector, every bank likes to accommodate a client, and always finds refusal distasteful."

"Ah! I shall remember that when next I interview my bank," Bony vowed. "I've always thought my bank manager to be an ogre."

When Mr Bulford had opened the side door and Bony was about to leave, the manager said, hesitantly:

"That poor woman, Mrs Rockcliff . . . did it happen that she disturbed the baby-thief, d'you think?"

"It could have been like that, Mr Bulford. She had habitu-ally left the baby alone in the house. Indicates a pattern, doesn't it?"

The telephone in the parlour called the manager, who closed the door after them with a slight show of haste. Alice walked on to the street. Bony leaned against the door with an ear to the keyhole, where he could hear the manager's voice, but could not distinguish the words.

On joining Alice in the taxi, he said:

"I think that will do for this afternoon. It's nearly five."

"I want a drink," Alice stated.

"Pardon!"

"Drink, please."

"Nearest milk bar, driver," ordered Bony.

"The River Hotel," firmly countermanded Alice.

CHAPTER 7

A DRINK FOR ALICE

THE CAR slipped through a wide avenue of date palms which laid bars of black shadow across the road so that it was like traversing a tiger's back, and ultimately the palms gave place to ancient red gums framing the River Hotel. The green roof and the cream-painted front, the wide verandas festooned with passion fruit vines, and the shining spaces of the broad river beyond combined to welcome with cool relaxation.

The driver said he would like to take the opportunity for a word with a pal in the public bar, which, of course, suited Bony and his lady friend. They mounted the few steps to the front entrance, and Alice paused to note with disapproval the several prams and pushers parked in an alcove where they certainly wouldn't cause an obstruction. Bony waited whilst she peeped at the infants, and could not evade the glint in her eyes when they entered the building. In the lounge the mothers were joined in a school for inebriates.

"Same old tale," Alice remarked, sipping ice-cold lager. "Eleven women drinking their heads off, and nine kids parked outside because it's against the law to bring them into a pub. I'd make it illegal to leave babies outside a place like this."

"It's shady and cool on the veranda," murmured Bony, rolling a cigarette. "So open, too. So safe . . . perhaps."

"Tell me about the baby stolen from here," Alice pleaded. "It's why I asked you to bring me."

"I read your mind, Alice, and I agreed to your wish because you have earned a drink." Bony gallantly applied a match to her cigarette. "It was on the afternoon of December 27th, a Mrs Ecks brought her new baby here and left it out there on the veranda.

"When she arrived, there were already two prams on the veranda. It was then about a quarter past four. At twenty minutes to five, or thereabouts, another woman arrived, leaving her child outside to make the fourth. This woman said she remembered seeing Mrs Ecks's baby in the pram.

"Mrs Ecks says she was the first to leave at five-twenty-five, so that it was between four-forty and five-twenty-five when the child was stolen. Mrs Ecks states that she had three gin squashes, but the steward amends that by adding another four. Anyway, Mrs Ecks, according to several women present who knew her, left this lounge moderately sober. She withdrew her infant's vehicle from the rank, bumped it gently down the steps, and set off home to cook her husband's dinner. On the way she met a friend she hadn't seen for a long time and who wanted to see the new baby. It was then that Mrs Ecks found the pram empty."

"Seven gins . . . stinko . . . no wonder," Alice almost hissed.

"Mrs Ecks acted automatically on leaving the hotel. She was sufficiently sober to avoid taking another woman's pram, but sufficiently hazy not to make sure that her baby was all right for the journey home."

"Must have been slick to pinch a baby off the veranda here, unless, being the day after Boxing Day, the public had run out of money and trade was slack."

"Trade wasn't slack. The licensee says they were very busy."

"And no one reported having seen anyone interfering with the prams?"

"No one has done so."

"The husband put her into hospital, didn't he?"

"Mr Ecks is a fruit-packer. He said he lost his temper because he had long disapproved of his wife going to the hotel every Friday afternoon. Personally, I do not approve of a husband hitting his wife with a chair."

"No? I do," Alice said severely. "What happened to poor Mr Ecks?"

"In view of the circumstances, the magistrates let him off with a fine."

Alice stubbed her cigarette and glared across the large room at the women who were seated at the far side. She said:

"A doctor's wife, a banker's wife, a fruit-packer's wife, and a supposed widow. What about the last one, mother number four?"

48

"She is the wife of the Town Engineer."

"Oh!" Alice pondered and Bony asked the steward for refills. The steward having obliged, Alice said:

"That banker's wife keeps him screwed down."

"She looks hard," Bony agreed.

"Too right, she does. I . . . I hope you don't mind."

"What?"

"Being too free with you, an inspector. Throwing my weight around, aren't I?"

"No. Should you do so you will recall Humpty Dumpty. You were going to say?"

"About Mrs Bulford. I can see how it is with her. Two boys away at boarding-school . . . youngest not less than ten. Then the baby comes . . . late in life. It isn't decent. It interferes with the social jag, the plonk parties. It's beginning to add up, isn't it?"

"Is it?" smiled Bony.

"Of course, and don't tease."

"Very well. How does it add up?"

"Well, Baby Number One vanishes from a pram in Main Street. Mother's a social drone. Couldn't be bothered with a baby. Interfered with her figure and her plonk parties. Baby Number Two is pinched from a bank. Mother has it late in life. Thinks people are sniggering at her, and again it interferes with the plonk parties. Baby Number Three taken from pram outside this hotel. Mother thinks more of gin and gossip than her baby. All this adds up: plonk plus plonk plus gin totals— neglect."

"And Mrs Rockcliff?"

"Mrs Rockcliff doesn't drink, but she left her baby alone at night when she went out. Neglect caused by something we have to nail. What about the Town Engineer's baby? What happened there?"

"His wife says her baby was taken from its cot on the front veranda when she was busy in the house." Bony regarded Alice with impish interest. "There may be no booze there, Alice. No neglect."

"We don't know yet. When do we get into that case?"

"Tomorrow."

"We'll get neglect there again, I'll bet on it."

"And if we do?"

"The grand total will be neglect. Someone prefers neglected babies."

"Someone certainly chooses male infants. All the vanished babies were boys."

"That could add up to another sum."

"Perhaps it could," agreed Bony. "You have a 'penchant' for mathematics. Another drink?"

"No, thanks, Bony. Two drinks a year is my limit. I have my career to think of."

"A fine career, too," he said, but she would not agree. Regarding him steadily with faintly wistful eyes, she confessed:

"My career isn't the Police Department. My career is making Superintendent Bolt pleased that he helped the McGorrs. I'm telling you that because you're a friend of his. D'you know that my father was a 'can opener'?"

Bony inclined his head.

"My dad never got a fair go. A can found opened, and they rushed for Pat McGorr. More than once he did time when he was cold." The soft brown eyes lit momentarily the smile about the tragic mouth. "Mother never blamed the police, and I didn't either, because Pat McGorr was the greatest can opener of the century, and every time the police got him cold made up for times they didn't get him. Mother was the wife of Pat McGorr, and I was his daughter, and Sergeant Bolt was Sergeant Bolt, now Superintendent. You understand?"

"Swift and complete understanding is natural to me, Alice."

"Then you won't find it difficult to forgive me when I show off like just now, will you? Only Superintendent Bolt and his wife have been kind, truly kind to me, so when I meet kindness it sort of goes to my head. And that's not the beer talking."

She rose from her chair and Bony accompanied her across the lounge to the door. As they passed down the steps to the waiting taxi neither spoke, and silently Bony held the door open for her. Only when the taxi was speeding back to Main Street and the Police Station did he ask encouragingly:

"What did you think of Mr Bulford?"

"A worm, Bony. The wife boosted him up to his present position, and she never lets him forget it. She'll grow worse and worse as the hairs grow on her lip. Could be that the worm will turn and bump her off and sink the bits in the river. It's deep enough."

"He doesn't look the type," objected Bony.

"Type enough to Crippenise her."

"Did you notice his eyes?" persisted Bony.

"Looked tired to me. Working too hard to provide the social background of this Mitford Hole in the Wall. Have you worked out how the thief got into the bank?"

"I am beginning to formulate ideas."

"I'd like to go over the building by myself and without interference," she went on. "Perhaps the baby wasn't stolen after all. Perhaps the husband got so sick of hearing his wife moaning about having it that he strangled it and buried the body in the back yard."

After this observation Alice became pensive, and Bony made no effort to rouse her. His emotions were mixed. He was pleased that she had not noticed the shutters fall before Bulford's eyes when he mentioned Mrs Rockcliff, and he was feeling distinctly entertained by the company of Policewoman Alice McGorr.

The Celestial Furnace was still blasting when they left the taxi at the Police Station and walked into the driveway separating the offices and the police residence, and leading to the rear area off which were the cells, the stables, now used as a garage, and the outbuildings. Essen met them, saying he was going home for dinner, and Bony suggested to Alice that she accompany Essen in his car and go to bed early after what must have been a trying day.

"Tired of me, eh?" she asked.

Nodding, he opened the car door for her, and said:

"We must not overwork Alice, Essen. You understand?" Essen grinned broadly, let out the clutch, and Alice McGorr departed with a picture of a smiling dark face and laughing blue eyes.

From watching the car reach the street, Bony turned about, intending to enter the police residence by the rear door, and so came face to face with a young aborigine wheeling a barrow.

"Hullo! Who are you?" he asked.

The aborigine lowered the barrow handles and straightened to examine this stranger so elegantly dressed and so well spoken. He took his time in answering, first producing a half cigarette from the pocket of his shirt and a wax match from a trouser pocket. Having lit his cigarette, he said:

"My name's Fred Wilmot. What's yours?"

51

"Napoleon Bonaparte. What are you doing here?"

"I'm the tracker, the car washer, and the wood chopper. What are you doing here?"

The black eyes were insolent, the full mouth pouted with subdued anger. Black eyes encountering blue eyes began to falter and finally looked down at the barrow, anywhere to avoid those blue eyes. He was a well-conditioned man in his early twenties, handsome by aboriginal standards. The open neck of the blue shirt revealed the cicatrices of the full initiated male, a fact arousing interest in Bony, who said:

"I am a detective-inspector, Fred Wilmot . . . in other words, a big-feller policeman. Where's your camp?"

No answer. The voice which had been purely accented drew ice from thin air.

"Where is your camp?"

"Up the river."

"How far?"

"Three miles and a bit."

"Which side?"

"This side."

"You stay here at night or go back to camp?"

"Go back. I got a bike."

"And how long have you been working for Sergeant Yoti?"

"This time since last Tuesday. Time before about three months. I been away for a spell."

"Oh! How many people in your camp?"

Black eyes now lifted to encounter blue eyes, and the blue eyes were no longer extraordinarily large and menacing.

"Round about seventy to eighty," replied Fred. "It's a Mission Station. The minister is Mr Beamer, Methodist."

"I've heard of him," purred Bony, and produced his case containing tailor-mades. Fred accepted a smoke, and the ice began to melt, but still he tried to avoid as much as possible the blue eyes. He began to lift the barrow handles when Bony's next question stopped him.

"How long have you been at the Mission?"

"'Bout five years. The Ole Man's there and the rest of us. We're Darling River abos, from up Menindee way. You been to Menindee?"

"Several times. I knew old Pluto."

"He's dead. Died long time ago."

"So I heard. Well, I see you have a job to do before sundown. You can carry on."

Black eyes were swiftly shuttered, and Bony felt amusement that the little lesson in discipline wasn't appreciated. Too much money, and too much spoiling by government and societies interested in aboriginal welfare, produced too many Frederick Wilmots.

CHAPTER 8

BONY WAITS

THE ROOM occupied by Bony at the police residence possessed the advantage of ready access from the garden. It was small, plainly furnished, and, being on the south side, cool and airy. Formerly it had been the room occupied by young George Yoti now in the Traffic Branch, Sydney, but Bony was urged to make full use of the desk and, did he wish, young George's portable typewriter and the shelves of novels.

Bony, showered and changed, was seated at the desk when from the garden door Yoti asked if he might come in. He was welcomed and offered young George's rocking chair.

"Still half an hour to dinner," he said. "How's your day gone?"

"Full of promise," replied Bony, swinging sideways and crooking a leg over the chair arm. "Haven't achieved much other than atmosphere and backgrounds."

"Your Alice McGorr any good?"

"She pleases me, yes. I sent her home with Essen and, I think, she departed with rebellion in her heart, so I rang Essen's house and gave her an assignment for this evening. As Essen was just leaving, I didn't delay him. Did he raise anything, d'you know?"

"Yes and no. He visited all the banks and none had an account in Mrs Rockcliff's name. I went over to see the Postmaster, he and I being sort of friends and belonging to the same Lodge, and he promised to question his staff and examine his records to find if Mrs Rockcliff had an account at the Commonwealth Bank or received money through the Post Office. Said he would drop over this evening to give us the results.

"Returning to Essen, he visited the woman's butcher, milkman and baker, and also the grocer. She ran monthly accounts, and there's a peculiarity about this which might be significant. She paid all her monthly accounts on the 12th of the month . . . in cash. Seems that she drew money, or was paid money, regularly once a month, doesn't it?"

"It would seem so," agreed Bony. "Anything on her associations here?"

"Nothing, or next to it. She didn't belong to any women's guild, or to any sports club, or reading circle. She was a regular borrower from the Municipal Library, and seems to have spent a good deal of her time in the reading room. If she had a friend or friends here, Essen can't locate any as yet. His sister and her husband say she never had visitors excepting the Rev Baxter, and Baxter says she went to church every Sunday evening, but would not join in church activities. He christened the child at church, but she never took the child there afterwards."

"What about the agent who let the house to her . . . references?"

"The boss, named Martin, wasn't at the office this afternoon, but the clerk told Essen the house was let to Mrs Rockcliff on a year's lease, and she paid three months rent in advance in lieu of a reference. She took the house on October 12th. Before living there she stayed at the River Hotel, and according to the Lodgers' Book she arrived at that hotel on October 9th. In a taxi. We dug up the driver of the taxi, and he says she stopped him in Main Street about eleven in the morning and asked him to recommend a hotel. That's as far back in her history as we've gone."

"H'm! Eleven in the morning. Does that time coincide with the arrival of a train or plane?"

"No. The first train gets in at 2.20 pm, and the first plane arrives at 9.45 am. Seems likely that she came to Mitford by car. Police at Albury up-river and Mildura down-river are going into that angle. Course, she could have come down from a station up north, or from a farm down south. Could have arrived here in a hired car or a friend's car."

The old pipe had gone out, and Yoti applied another match, the while regarding Bony with moody eyes, and suddenly Bony smiled and then watched the Sergeant's face register annoyance.

"We should keep in mind salient facts: some material, others abstract," he said. "Before I came to Mitford four babies were abducted, and the four crimes were thoroughly investigated. About the time I arrived here you discovered a fifth abduction and a murder. Nothing emerged from the first four baby abductions to give us a lead in our investigation of the fifth. We start with nothing relative to those five babies, yet we must combine those five abductions and attack the problems as one.

"The person or persons who abducted those five children live here in Mitford. They move about as we do. They are, naturally, greatly interested in what we may be doing. Almost certainly they know by now that Detective-Inspector Napoleon Bonaparte is in charge, and they will be specially interested in me. Without doubt, if one person is responsible for those abductions, he, or she, is extremely versatile. When we go back in criminal investigation, we find that circumstances, co-incidence, and what may be termed luck have been vital to the success of the investigators or of the criminal. To date, the baby-thief has had the luck, and the investigators have missed out. So what have we?

"A person, acting alone or in collaboration with others, believing he, or she, is extremely clever, but, none the less, must be a little anxious to know what D-I Napoleon Bonaparte is doing and is likely to do. As I've often said, if a criminal would be still after the commission of his crime, he would more often escape retribution, but, fortunately for law and order, he cannot be still.

"I've no license as yet to say so, Yoti, but I am inclined to think that the murder of Mrs Rockcliff is the first sign that the baby-thief's luck has ended, and ours has begun. I've known men who have robbed a bank, burgled a house, won a confidence trick, men who have pitted their intelligence against scientific investigation, and in doing so proved themselves to be driven by the same sporting urge that drives most of us to back a horse. To these people murder is as alien as it is to you and me. It is the criminal in this class who stole the five babies . . . or so I incline to think. What therefore is his present state of mind when a murder charge can be directed against him? He must be all hot and bothered. Assuming that he did murder Mrs Rockcliff, say because she recognised him, what would be the natural effect on his accomplice? Recriminations, fear, treachery, all stem from murder. As I said, murder is a spur giving no rest, no peace, no confidence in anyone or anything."

Yoti, who had not once looked directly at the speaker, continued to stare beyond Bony at a picture of his son in swimming togs. Bony said:

"The effect of murder will affect the minds of those concerned in stealing babies. It must do. Was that your wife calling us?"

Yoti nodded. He wanted to express some thoughts, and subject others to analysis, but he was looking into Bony's smiling eyes and hearing the pleasant voice say:

"Inevitably, the enemy will make a wrong move, and meanwhile let us not disturb our gastric juices. Now you will apologise to your wife for both of us. We were late for dinner yesterday, remember, and I apologised."

Yoti grunted opposition, but he made amends and dinner passed off happily. After the meal they crossed to the Sergeant's office to wait the coming of the Postmaster, but Essen arrived first, saying that Alice McGorr had left his house on what she said was her case.

"Her case!" murmured Bony, and the large policeman smiled, and vowed those were the words she had used while nursing his small son and his wife was serving dinner.

The night had brought no cooling zephyrs, and the three men seated at the table desk wore sports shirts and slacks. To his reports Essen was adding impressions and theories, when voices in the outer office preceded the entry of a man about fifty, greying, energetic, a cheerful smile about his lean mouth and a cast in his left eye. The damp silk shirt clung to his back, and from the waistline where shirt was tucked into trousers he produced four bottles of beer. Having vigorously shaken hands with Bony, he said in the unmistakable drawl of the inlander:

"There's no hobby as satisfying as beer-drinking, Inspector, and no better place to indulge than Mitford. It's why I've refused promotion to a bigger office. I like a beery climate. Look at Essen. He wasn't a he-man when he came to Mitford although he did have to shave every day."

"I was never much good as a policeman after I met you," Essen countered, returning from a wall cupboard with four glasses and a bottle opener. "Worst thing I ever did was to join your Bowling Club."

"Don't believe it," protested the Postmaster. "Mrs Essen's as keen on the Club as I am, and Yoti. How's the baby?"

"Where does he come in?"

"H'm! Bit of muck on the liver, eh? No matter. Take a gulp of that." To Bony he said: "Hope you play bowls, Inspector. You must join our show. Make you an honorary member. Good crowd. Got a licence, too. Make more money outer the bar trade than the subs." He eased himself into a chair, raised his glass and drank with appreciation. "Well, now for this Rockcliff woman. Can't stop long, as I've got the Lodge books to get ready for tomorrow night."

The Postmaster refilled his glass and glared at the other three glasses, in which the tide had only begun to ebb.

"Went back to the office after dinner," he said. "Place shut up, of course, so I had a free go. Went through the registration books for four months. No registered letter in or out for Mrs Rockcliff. Went through the Money Order section: same result. Finally I made sure my memory wasn't at fault with the Commonwealth Bank part of the joint, and proved I was correct. No account with the Commonwealth."

"That's generous of you, and positively helpful," Bony said.

"That's okay, Inspector. Always ready to lend the police a hand. You know, diplomacy, and all that. Police can be damned narks. Let me top your glass. Stiffen the crows! Haven't any of you fellers learned to drink properly? I went a bit further. Telephoned the manager of the State Bank here. No good. No Mrs Rockcliff on his books. He's a friend of mine. In the same boat."

"Bowling Club boat?"

"Right."

"And the Lodge boat?"

"Right again." The Postmaster drained his glass, filled it and did the trick once more. "Well, so long, Inspector. Bring him out for a game Sat'day afternoon, Yoti. Plenty of beer floating around, and the green's in good nick, too."

"I shall look forward to a game or two before leaving Mitford," Bony assured this cheerful man who loved a beery climate.

"It's a go, Inspector. So long. Me for the Lodge books. What about proposing the Inspector, Yoti?"

Essen accompanied the Postmaster to the outer door, returned to pour drinks and light a pipe.

"Should have the report on those name tags by midday

57

tomorrow," he said. "Damn funny that woman always paid her accounts on the 12th of each month."

"An interesting point," agreed Bony. "My assistant put forward the idea that the money came from a local boy friend."

"No man ever visited her, according to the Thrings," Essen argued.

"She could have visited the man . . . at night."

"M'yes, that's true."

"Who belongs to your Bowling Club?"

It was Yoti who replied that the membership was round about eighty and included business people, civil servants, the Stationmaster, the Town Engineer and most of the Councillors.

"What of the managers of the private banks?"

Yoti grinned without mirth.

"They think they're a cut above our crowd."

"The doctors?"

"With the private bank managers."

The telephone shrilled and Essen went out to the duty constable.

"I'd like to get the point clear, Yoti," Bony went on. "Do the managers of the private banks, the doctors and others on the social summit have a club or association of their own?"

"Yes, bowling green, tennis-courts and golf courses all in one. What prompts the point?"

"That baby theft from the Olympic Bank was the most difficult to carry through, and was dependent on timing and intimate knowledge of the habits of both parents. How many old-time wall telephones are there in Mitford? I notice you have one here."

"We've been promised hand sets when they go over to automatic. Why?"

Essen came in.

"Bloke named Wyatt, No 17 Ukas Street, reports a badly injured aborigine outside his front gate," he said. "Abo says he was attacked by three men. I rang the ambulance. They'll be calling here to pick me up."

"All right!" grumbled Yoti. "Find out what that blackfeller's doing in town after sundown. If he isn't a hospital case lock him up for the night."

Essen went out to wait for the ambulance, and Yoti said:

"That Bank case?"

"Probably carried through by people familiar with parents'

habits and knowledge of interior of bank living quarters as well as the banking chamber. Three persons needed. One walked to the lane way leading to the private door. Another rang the manager from a near-by call-box. Manager in his office had to leave his desk, from which he could see his private hall, and stand at the telephone, when his back would be turned. First person opened private door with duplicate key, went upstairs, brought down baby and, leaving by the same door, handed infant to third person waiting on the other side of the board fence. Could have been in the vacant building next to the bank whilst the uproar went on, and stayed there till it was dark."

"Very neat," agreed Yoti. "Didn't Bulford tell you who rang him that afternoon after his wife went out?"

"I did not ask him about that," replied Bony. "It is stated in the Official Summary that Bulford said no one rang him that afternoon after his wife left."

"All right, but how did second person know first person was talking to Bulford on the telephone? There's no call-box in sight of that door."

"From outside the door the second person could hear the manager at the parlour telephone." Bony glanced at his watch. "H'm! Almost eleven. Time Policewoman McGorr reported. Remarkable woman, that."

"Brains, or to look at?"

"She thinks all the infants were stolen because they were neglected. Could be right."

"Neglected! How the hell does she make that out?"

"Neglected while mother drinks gin in a pub. Neglected while mother gallivants about to plonk parties . . . plonk being Alice McGorr's designation of a sherry party. Neglected baby left to cook to rear so that mother can rush off to plonk party. Neglected baby left alone while mother goes out to the library, or to meet a boy friend. Something of a pattern, isn't there?"

"Could be," Yoti conceded.

"As we progress other patterns will emerge," Bony continued. "Time itself will provide coincidences joining events, coincidences which, it is said, never occur in real police work."

"Don't agree. I can name a few for a start."

"Of course. I was thinking of my biographer's difficulties with the critics. . . . Ah, sounds like Alice McGorr."

Alice appeared in the doorway, came striding to the desk.

She was carrying that straw hat. The frilly collar of her blouse was torn, and when she tossed the hat upon the desk they saw that something tragic had happened to the crown. Something had happened, too, to her brown eyes, and there was a mark on her negligent chin which could be the beginning of a bruise. Bony placed the chair Essen had vacated, and she flopped into it as though her legs were wired.

"Did you meet with an accident?" Bony asked.

"An incident, not an accident," she snorted. "I thought I was being tailed before I reached Betty Morse's house. When we were walking to the Delphs' place I was sure. He was still tailing when we left the Delphs, and he was hanging on when I left Betty at her house. So I waited in the dark under a tree. As he went by I grabbed him and marched him to the nearest street light for a look at him. I didn't like him, and he wouldn't say what he was after."

"Awkward, Alice. Did you break anything?"

"Had to," Alice confessed. "He was twice my weight, and he fell hard. I heard him complaining to a man that his arm was broken, he had a crick in his neck, a sort of concussion and a sprained ankle."

CHAPTER 9

BONY VISITS THE SICK

BEFORE BREAKFAST the next morning Bony made additional notes covering the results of Alice McGorr's visit to the Delph's cook. These notes were supplementary rather than additions to the build-up of the background against which five infants had been stolen and a mother of one murdered.

Having breakfasted, he rang Essen to pass the order to Alice that she was not to report to him until after lunch, when they would interview Mrs Coutts concerning the abduction of her baby, and at nine o'clock he set out for the Public Hospital to chat with the man who had tailed Alice the previous evening.

Permitting himself to hope that the shadowing of Betty Morse and Alice was evidence of the first move made by his opponents, Bony sauntered along Main Street as the shops were being opened, and then took the cross-street to reach the river boulevard and the hospital. A hot north wind was threatening to raise the dust, and to bring the indefinable scent of the Inland which was to become so significant. The river gums already were spraying their perfume of eucalyptus.

Following an interview with the Matron, a wardsman conducted him to a single bed ward.

There was nothing clear-cut about the patient, a veritable League of Nations having subscribed to his pedigree. Bony dissected him in a flash of time: two parts Australian aborigine, three parts Malay, one part Chinese, three parts European, and one part Brazilian gorilla.

The name on the hospital chart above the head of the bed was Bertrand Marcus Clark, which might have annoyed that pioneer Australian author.

The bed was a heavy iron one, and a pair of handcuffs anchored the patient's left foot. Otherwise he was as comfortable as medical science could make him, despite the right foot being in plaster, the left arm in splints, and the top of the cranium being bandaged. Small dark eyes regarded the visitor balefully, and Bóny kept out of reach of the uninjured right arm.

"How are you this morning?" Bony gravely asked.

"What's it to do with you?"

"I . . . er represent the police," Bony said soothingly. "It would seem that you erred in your assessment of the situation in which you ultimately found yourself last night. Foot-cuffed to the bed, too."

"I didn't do no 'arm," vowed Bertrand Marcus Clark, adding a rider, however. "Only being in town after sundown. Met an old bloke I knew years ago. Camped down the river a bit, he was, and I went with him for a bit of a yabber. He had a bottle of gin, and that sort of mucked up the time.

"When I got going from the Settlement, it was dark, but not dark enough to go straight through the town. I 'ad to keep to quiet streets, not wanting to be grabbed by the police. Then all of a sudden three blokes jumped me. I clouted one flat and booted another in the stomach, but the last one got me arm over a shoulder and snapped the bone. Then I got slogged in the ankle, and me head bashed in."

"What a fight, Bertrand. What happened then?"

"Passed out, of course. I comes to and there's a bloke bending over me what lives in the nearest house. The ambulance comes, and Constable Essen gets rough 'cos I'm in town after dark. When I won't tell no lies about it, he gets properly nasty, and I remembers I still got one good fist left."

"Quite a beano, Bertrand," sympathised Bony. "Still, you'll receive only six months. One for resisting arrest, one for bad language, another for being in town after sunset, and three for following two young women with intent to molest. We could, in fact, work it up for three years."

"I'm telling you's the truth. Don't I look like the flamin' truth?"

"You look terrible to me," admitted Bony. "Did I not know the truth, I would believe the number of your assailants was thirty, not three. The picture you present this morning must read: Aboriginal thug, intending to molest defenceless white girl, inadvertently mistook his mark, as intended victim is expert in the art of judo and the Australian Science of Boots-and-All-In. Too bad . . . for you, Bertrand."

The patient was able to turn his face to the wall, and kept it there.

"Further, Bertrand, you are a liar, as was proved later last night when Constable Essen found no friend camped down-river at the place you said you visited him and enjoyed his hospitality. Gin you said it was which delayed you. I'm glad you chose gin, Bertrand. Never indulge in plonk. Leave plonk to the élite of the allegedly superior race."

The patient continued to gaze at the blank wall.

"For you the prospect is indeed gloomy," Bony went on. "And yet, in your grave extremity, you have a friend. None other than Detective-Inspector Napoleon Bonaparte . . . otherwise me. Come clean and tell me why you tailed that innocent young woman, and I will persuade her to withdraw the charges against you of assault, battery, doing grievous bodily harm, and making a hell of a bad mistake. Then you would have only to spend one week in the jug for being in town between sunset and sunrise."

The silence of the patient continued whilst Bony rolled and lit a cigarette. There might be something in the third degree system of the American police, even in the methods of the Hungarian police. But then, no. British methods, if slower, do produce greater obstacles to crime investigation, and so prolong the interest of the investigator.

The interest provided by Bertrand Marcus Clark lay in Alice McGorr's opinion that he tailed her not for the purpose of assault but for the purpose of learning her actions in company with Betty Morse. Was that intention to satisfy his own curiosity or the curiosity of another who employed him? Eventually, Bony was satisfied that Bertrand Marcus Clark was not going to enlighten him, and so politely he wished him well, for the time being, and departed.

The morning sun was now really hot when he strolled from the hospital grounds to the boulevard, where he appreciated the black shadows under the trees. And then a car slid to a halt at the kerb and Dr Nott called:

"Hullo there, Inspector! Did the Sister turn you away because it wasn't visiting hours?"

"Morning, Doctor!" Bony leaned on the door of the smart coupé. "I've been visiting Mr Marcus Clark, and Matron was most charmingly co-operative."

"You interested in that inky blackguard? Done over properly, wasn't he?"

"From appearances, yes. Mitford must be a rough place. Poor fellow."

"Peaceful enough generally, Inspector. We have our baby-thieves, our occasional murderer, but hoodlum stuff in respectable streets is rare enough to be news."

"Perhaps Clark fell into a drain or something. People are always digging holes in unlikely places. You look tired."

"I am. Four additions to the population last night. Expect four more between now and tomorrow." The tired eyes were illumined with enthusiasm. "Two of a kind last night. Seven pounds apiece . . . twin boys." Bony could see the doctor's chest expand. "Only lost one baby in the last six months, and that was the fault of the fool mother."

"Fool mothers are rare?"

"Happily so, Inspector. But neglectful mothers are not. Some women don't deserve to be blessed with a baby, and many oughtn't to be allowed to keep the child."

"What, in your opinion, is the greatest factor causing a mother to neglect her child?"

"Booze," was the swift answer.

"So! And the next factor?"

"Writing novels."

"Is that so?"

"Both are forms of escapism, and a normal woman should be happily content with the responsibility of a baby. Mrs Ecks drank to excess and, to my mind, deserved to lose her child. Mrs Coutts writes rubbishy novels. You met her, I suppose?"

"Not yet. I may call on her this afternoon."

"When you do you will agree. How's the investigation going?"

"The baby-thieves are a little slow in announcing themselves, but they will. Criminals invariably call on me, some quickly, others a trifle reluctantly. I have but to wait. You know, I pride myself on being the most patient man in Australia."

Dr Nott chuckled, but Bony's face remained calm.

"Once upon a time," Bony said, "I was with a murderer in an unfurnished house from which the light had been disconnected. All I did was to sit on the floor with my back to the front door and wait. And I had to wait only three hours for the murderer's nerve to break, when he came to me with the request to be taken into custody. Subsequently he said he could see my eyes glowing in the darkness, and that I had a hundred pairs of eyes which closely hemmed him into a corner. Imagination, of course, Doctor. My eyes are quite normal."

Nott, who had listened without movement, abruptly pushed out the clutch and shifted from neutral to low gear.

"Normal, eh! I wonder! Well, I must get along to see my babies. See you sometime, I hope."

"Oh yes. I may be lolling about Mitford for ten years. Au revoir!"

The gleaming car passed through the hospital gates, and Bony sauntered along the boulevard and eventually entered the offices of Martin & Martin, Estate Agents, Auctioneers and Valuers, on Main Street. He asked to see the senior partner.

"What is the nature of your business?" asked the clerk, his eyes superciliously registering this client.

"My business is to unmask murderers . . . and other incidentals." Bony witnessed the superciliousness fade. "I am a detective-inspector. The name is Bonaparte."

Mr Cyril Martin was sixtyish, looked like an undertaker on duty, and spoke like a saw eating into the heart of a red-gum log.

"Sit down, Inspector. What can we do for you?"

"The subject interesting me at the moment is the late Mrs Rockcliff," opened the seated Bony as he crossed one creased trouser leg over the other. "You rented her the house in Elgin Street, I understand."

"Yes, that's correct. We gave the particulars yesterday to the constable."

"You let the house to Mrs Rockcliff for a period of twelve months?"

"Yes."

"At the monthly rental of ten pounds?"

"Yes."

"Calendar months?"

"Yes. The constable obtained all . . ."

Bony smiled. "I like my information first-hand," he said. Mr Martin did not smile.

"The rent was paid promptly?"

"Oh, yes. On the 12th of every month."

"Was that rent date a term of the lease?"

For the first time Mr Martin evinced hesitation.

"Er, no. It was an arrangement Mrs Rockcliff herself made with us. She offered to pay the first three months' rent in advance in lieu of a reference, which normally we would insist on having."

"How did she pay the rent?"

"In cash."

"To whom?"

"To my clerk in the outer office."

Bony produced his cigarette-case, and Mr Martin hastened to forestall him.

"Most extraordinary affair, Inspector. I met Mrs Rockcliff only twice. She seemed to be quite a nice woman, too."

"The victim of homicide isn't necessarily not nice, Mr Martin," and the estate agent chuckled as Bony's observation was smilingly made. "Could you be more precise in your impressions of Mrs Rockcliff?"

"Yes, I think so. I should say she was well educated. She spoke well, culturally, if you know what I mean."

"Australian or English?"

"I'm doubtful on that point. She had no pronounced English accent. And, like you, she didn't have the Cockney-Australian accent, either."

"Who owns No 5 Elgin Street?"

The timing of this question was well chosen . . . when Mr Martin was looking directly at the questioner. The shutters fell.

"A Miss Mary Cowdry who lives in Scotland," he replied with less spontaneity.

"What is Miss Cowdry's address?"

"Well, the last time we heard from her she was living at a hotel in Edinburgh. She travels a good deal, and we send the rent along when she writes for it." Mr Martin again chuckled. "She's what we call one of the floating owners. We have several clients in that category."

"How do you transmit the money to Miss Cowdry?"

"Oh, through the bank."

"What bank?"

"The Olympic."

Mr Martin flicked a handkerchief from his breast pocket, cursorily wiped his nose, furtively mopped his forehead. Despite the fan, it certainly was close in the office. Bony rose to leave, glancing at his wrist-watch.

"When could we expect to have the house released by the police?" asked the Estate Agent, also on his feet. "Rental houses are few in Mitford, as elsewhere, Inspector, and the demand for them is heavy."

"Possibly in a week, Mr Martin. It could be later. Well, I won't take up any more of your time. Thank you for your co-operation."

"You are welcome."

Bony doubted it as he passed from the offices to Main Street and the hot sunshine. It was ten minutes after eleven, and morning-tea time, and he was passing Madame Clare's Hat and Frock Salon when Alice McGorr almost collided with him.

"Such haste," he admonished her. "In Mitford, too."

"I've spent all my money," she said.

"I can easily believe that, Alice. The hat suits you very well."

The soft brown eyes searched his face for irony, and, as she was beginning to expect, saw nothing of it.

"My, it's hot, isn't it!" she exclaimed. "Were you going to ask me to morning tea?"

"Your perspicacity is astonishing, Alice. I thought of it the moment you bumped into me."

"Only way to make you notice me."

"Most unseemly, such was your haste to read my mind on the subject of morning tea. Here we are."

At the table inside the comparatively cool café, she asked:

"What have you been doing this morning behind my back?"

"I visited the hospital and did my best to comfort the sick. Poor unfortunate little man. You did ill-use him." Alice was examining her recent purchase with the aid of a small mirror. "You appear to be quite unconcerned about your victim."

"He's lucky that his neck's not broken."

"Generous of you. What have you been doing this morning?"

"Off duty. You told Essen to tell me. I bathed their baby, and then decided to buy a hat. On the way, I thought I'd call at the Station for you . . . thought you'd like to choose the new hat. The duty constable told me you had gone for a walk, and Sergeant Yoti had his office full of reporters. They were badgering him with questions and he was snarling. I asked the desk constable where Essen was, and he said down at the Municipal Library . . . there's been a robbery."

"Robbery at the Public Library?" exclaimed Bony. "Well, I expected it, you know. People will read books, and now that the government has cut down on the importation of books, people are bound to rob the libraries to get them. It's a crime which I acclaim. May I have another cup of tea?"

CHAPTER 10

DEGREES OF NEGLECT

THEY WERE about to visit Mrs Norman Coutts, when Bony asked:

"Yesterday, when returning from the River Hotel, you did a sum in mental arithmetic and arrived at Neglect causated in Booze. Pardon the verb. To what else could child neglect be attributed?"

"I'd say bargain-hunting at the store sales. A lot of women leave everything, desert anything for the chance of a bargain."

"Of our five babies, we have examined the background of four, and in no case have we found physical neglect. D'you know anything about writing novels?"

"Do I look as though I wrote novels?"

"Yes."

"You're kidding."

"Now I have to pardon your verb. And myself for using it. I never kid. My reason for asking you is that Mrs Norman Coutts writes novels. In Dr Nott's opinion, that is another cause of child neglect."

For fifty yards Alice pondered on this angle, her stride matching her companion's, head straight, shoulders back, mouth grim and tight. Unless she fell in love and married, she was doomed to become a replica of the lady novelist whose picture was menacing the readers of current magazines and was at the moment occupying a corner of Bony's mind.

"D'you want me to keep to the subject of infant neglect or to argue about verbs?" she asked, as they turned into a side road.

"The subject of neglect, that we might arrive at the degree of neglect. After calling on Mrs Coutts, we shall probably know that she merely forgot about her baby when in the throes of inspiration, not neglected it to the extent of physical distress. We can then consider whether the degree of neglect covering the five babies has anything to do with their abduction."

The house occupied by the Town Engineer stood well back from the street and was seemingly built on a well-tended lawn which successfully defied sun and heat. The house was of the bungalow type, having a spacious front veranda, now shaded by coloured blinds.

The front door was opened by a tall blonde, arrayed in a gay Japanese kimono and armed with a foot-long cigarette-holder, and instantly Bony was reminded of Mrs Thring and the lady novelist in the magazines. She was obviously displeased, and ungraciously conducted them to what could be the lounge. Here the furniture was good enough, but the carpet felt lumpy beneath their feet, the hearth was strewn with cigarette-ends, and the one table by the window was littered with books and writing materials. The close, fuggy odours of food, cigarettes and lemons were at least authentic.

"Well, Inspector, what is it?" asked Mrs Coutts, seating

herself before the writing materials. "Have the police found my baby?"

"Regretfully, no, Mrs Coutts," replied Bony, who was unaware that Alice, although seated demurely, was again pricing everything visible. "I've been assigned to the investigation into the kidnapping of your baby, and the others, and I'm trying to get the general picture clear. Tell me, what was the weather like that afternoon your baby was stolen from the front veranda?"

"The weather! What an extraordinary question." Mrs Coutts fitted a fresh cigarette to the long ebony holder, and Bony presented the match. "You know, the suspect is often caught out when asked where he was on the night of the crime, isn't he? I write, as you may know, straight novels, not these beastly thrillers." Carelessly, she indicated the partially filled sheet of foolscap on the pad, the pile of covered sheets to her right hand and the wad of virgin paper on her left. "The weather that day. Why, it was hot and thundery. In fact, it did thunder now and then, but as usual I was busy with my writing, and the baby was asleep."

"Your husband saw the child sleeping in the cot when he left for his office. At what time did your husband leave?"

"Ten minutes to two. He always leaves at that time."

"And you found the cot empty at half past three, did you not?"

"Yes."

"Was there a particular reason to visit the cot at that time?"

"My husband and I rose from lunch at about a quarter to two. He went to his room for something and then, as I told you, he left the house by the front veranda. I came here to write as the inspiration was very strong. I worked until half past three, and then remembered I hadn't cleared away or fed baby. So I went to the cot, and found him gone."

"Then what did you do?"

"Rang my husband, of course. I thought that he had taken the child with him to his office. A moment after he said he hadn't done anything of the kind and would ring the police, I flew to the front gate, hoping I might see the person who must have taken it."

"You saw a car outside a house towards Main Street, an elderly woman on the far side of the road who was carrying a suitcase, and two boys running away as though to escape the thunderstorm?"

"That is right, Inspector. That is the scene I gave the police."

"You said then that you could not recognise the elderly woman with the suitcase. Since then, Mrs Coutts, has memory of that woman reminded you, say in general, of anyone you know?"

"I wasn't able to see her face as she was hurrying away from me. The police thought those two boys might have noticed her, but they hadn't. You know all that, of course. You don't think that woman stole my baby, do you?"

"No. But if she could be found she might tell us of something she saw which could assist us. Your description of her to the police was rather vague, understandably, naturally, in view of your distress. I was hoping that since then memory of her might have recalled to mind someone you do know, someone with whom we can make a comparison."

"I see what you mean. Well, she was not unlike Mrs Peel, or Mrs Nott, the doctor's wife, or even Mrs Marlo-Jones . . . shortish, stoutish, quick in movement. But it wasn't one of those women."

"Why are you so definite?"

"Because that woman was wearing bright blue, so unkind to the elderly woman, Inspector. The other women I have mentioned usually wear pastel colours. And when they forget their age they wear dizzy florals."

"H'm!" Bony rose to go. "The baby was only seven weeks old. Was he a healthy child?"

"He never had a day's illness," replied Mrs Coutts, remaining seated. "He hardly ever cried, and he slept well, too. That's why I didn't bother about him immediately after lunch that day."

Mrs Coutts nodded to Alice, and, on glancing at Alice, Bony found her nodding in reply . . . or in sympathy. Alice departed, and Mrs Coutts hastened to say:

"I find my writing so very absorbing, Inspector. I become quite lost in it, and very often the characters take full possession of me."

"It must be absorbing."

"Yes. I hope to succeed as a novelist. I've written several

short stories, you know. I gained first prize at our Mitford Literary Society."

"Congratulations! How many have you had published?"

"None, as yet, Inspector. Our President, James Nyall, the well-known Australian novelist, says I have to master the art of writing down to please editors. One has to learn to commercialise one's talents. Not that I really want to do that, but I must be practical. My husband, who is very practical, insists that if a story isn't acceptable to an editor it's worth nothing. So silly of him."

"Perhaps one oughtn't to be too practical in any of the arts," Bony suavely agreed. "Er . . . The Mitford Literary Society, by the way. Do Mrs Peel and Mrs Nott and Mrs Marlo-Jones belong?"

"No. Mrs Marlo-Jones has given talks, but, as she says, she's far too busy to undertake another interest."

"You have met these ladies, socially?"

"Oh yes. At sherry parties, and that sort of thing."

"During the vital period of time, after your husband returned to his office and you found the baby missing, were you called to the telephone?"

"No. I mightn't have heard it if it did ring. I was barely conscious of the thunder."

"What led you to think your husband had taken the infant with him to the office?"

Shutters fell before the green eyes, and Mrs Coutts almost hurriedly pushed back her chair and rose from the table. Alice appeared in the doorway, and Mrs Coutts looked at her and would have spoken had not Bony remained with obvious expectancy of being answered.

"Oh, I don't really know, Inspector. Sometimes my husband teases me about my writing. Says it takes me away from everything."

"Including the baby?"

"Of course not." The green eyes were hardening. "He came in for lunch one day when the child was whimpering and I was in the kitchen. I couldn't leave what I was doing, preparing something, and he accused me of neglecting the baby and said he'd take it with him to the office and let his fool of a secretary mind it. More in fun than not, naturally."

"Quite." Bony expressed the hope of ultimately recovering

71

the child, and Mrs Coutts accompanied them to the front gate. Again in Main Street, he said:

"Well, give, Alice."

"Filthy house," Alice stated as though in the witness-box. "You said I wasn't to ask the woman questions, and I didn't . . . out loud. She's balmy on her writing, and everything else rots. She didn't give a damn about the baby, and she deserved to lose it. I know the type. Baby probably died of sheer neglect, and she buried it in the garden."

"What a prognostication! Why were you and Mrs Coutts making faces at each other?"

"Oh that! I was making excuses so that I could see the rest of her house."

"So that now we know. . . ."

"The pattern, Bony. Five babies kidnapped. Five tiny babies. Five boy babies. Five healthy babies. Five neglected babies. Sounds like a horrible nursery rhyme," Alice recited grimly. "Three mothers in the same social set: two mothers outside. Three mothers drink sherry, one mother drinks gin, and one is thought to drink nothing worse than tea."

"It's possible that the infants were not chosen for abduction because they were superficially neglected by the mothers, but because that superficial neglect made easy the abductions."

"You don't think that, Bony."

"No, I do not believe it, because the abduction from the bank was not easy, and the abduction from the pram outside the shop and the pram outside the hotel was decidedly risky. Let us go into the Library and make a few discoveries about Mrs Rockcliff."

"Has it occurred to you that the abductions began after Mrs Rockcliff came to Mitford?" Alice asked when they stood in the portico of the Grecian front of the Municipal Library.

"Yes, I have considered that point. Now, leave me to interview the librarian. If Essen is still here, interest yourself in the robbery."

Essen was no longer in the building, which, being a museum as well as a library, entertained Alice. For a while they remained together, examining cases of aboriginal relics, photographic sections of the Murray River, the bridge nearby, of the local fruit and wine industries. There were models of the paddle-wheel steamers, now almost extinct, models of water-wheels, pictures in oils, etchings, water-colours, and displays of native weapons.

For a few moments, Bony studied a large-scale map of the district, showing Mitford to be the hub of radiating roads. Including the river, there were sixteen exits from the town, and through one of those exits five small infants had surely passed.

Other than a young woman at a bench rebinding a book, and an elderly man seated within a glass-fronted office, the place was empty. Bony strolled into the Reference Room, where he found a Who's Who and looked up Marlo-Jones. Born 1881, making him 71. DSc., Adelaide. Dip. Anthropology. Research Fellow in Anthropology, Adelaide. H'm! Well up in his field. Publications: 'Ceremonial Exchange Cycle of the Warramunga Nation'. Married Elizabeth Wise. No mention of children. Recreations: gardening and walking. Knowledgeable old bean. Full of sting at 71. Would live beyond a hundred.

Bony spent a further ten minutes with the famous, looking up one who ought to have been hanged four years previously, three who should be serving gaol sentences, and one concerning whom he was slightly doubtful. Then he studied the insect specimens in glass cases, and wondered who had classified the case of mollusca found in the Darling and Murray Rivers Basin. Alice was looking at a journal in the Reading Room when he entered the glass-fronted office.

"I am Detective-Inspector Bonaparte," he said to the scholarly-looking man, and as usual noted the flash of astonishment, disbelief, caution, reserve. "You may wish to telephone to Sergeant Yoti. I am investigating the circumstances surrounding the death of Mrs Rockcliff, and I understand she was a regular borrower from this library."

Interest now predominated in the pale grey eyes.

"Yes, Inspector Bonaparte, Mrs Rockcliff was a regular borrower. In fact, there are three of her books not yet returned to us. They are, presumably, still at her house."

"Do you happen to know her taste in literature? One of the books at her house is a biography, and two are classics."

"I do know that her taste wasn't the usual run of the mill," replied the librarian. "She liked biographies, having a special preference for world-famous authors. Her novels could be only the best. I was decidedly grieved about her."

"Was she interested in writing, or any of the arts?"

"Not to the extent of practising one of them. She wasn't very communicative about herself." The librarian smiled, and Bony liked that smile. "So many women are, you know. They seem to think this is a Gossip House, and my assistants sometimes chide me with being too friendly. But I like to be helpful, especially with earnest people and students."

"Tell me, was Mrs Rockcliff aloof? I mean, did she give the impression of being without interest in other people?"

"Well, hardly that, Inspector. She often talked to me. About literature, of course. I found her rather intelligent, and not objectionably so. Her interest in famous writers is shared by one of our bank managers. They became acquainted here, actually, and would often retire and talk for twenty minutes or half an hour. I'm sure Mr Bulford will miss her. He has a passion for Joseph Conrad, and she almost worshipped the Brontës."

"And the Library is open in the evenings?"

"Until ten o'clock. We have discussion groups, and neither my daughter nor I regret the extra time we give."

"Your work must be more engrossing than mine," Bony said. "I have to keep to one world, that of abnormal psychology; you may live in other worlds far more wholesome. You have had a robbery, I hear. Lose much . . . books . . . pictures?"

"Nothing like that, Inspector. It's most peculiar. The object stolen was an aboriginal rock drawing. I've only been in charge here for six months, having previously lived in Sydney, and I don't know much about its history. I must dig up the records."

"A painting of the original rock drawing, I assume?"

"No. It was actually the section or stratum of the rock on which the drawing had been done in white and yellow ochre. It must have weighed a hundred pounds, and it was supported by a special stand in the Reading Room."

"H'm! Peculiar thing to steal. Valuable?"

"As a museum or collector's piece, without doubt."

"And what did the drawing portray?"

"No one knows. My predecessor might have known, but he died shortly after I took over. It even baffled Professor Marlo-Jones. He thinks the drawing might have something to do with the rain-making ceremonies of the Arunta Nation."

"As you say, an extraordinary thing to steal from a

Library," Bony agreed. "Well, thank you very much for your co-operation. I will see that the books are returned from Mrs Rockcliff's house. Goodbye."

Alice was waiting for him in the main room, her interest being captured by the ceiling.

"I like it, don't you?"

"The colour, yes."

"I think I'll do our lounge ceiling in that colour . . . duck-egg blue ceiling and ivory matt walls for the lounge at least."

"You decorate?"

"Too right. Get the brother to give a hand. Can't afford to employ house decorators these days. Nice place this Library. I could spend a lot of time here."

"Alas, Alice, our time is spent."

CHAPTER 11

THE CHIEFS ARE WORRIED

THE 'BOYS' room' at the police residence, now occupied by Bony, faced the south and therefore was on the coolest side of the house . . . a distinct advantage in February. In addition to the open door and the raised window, one end of the room was merely fly-netted, and could be shuttered were the wind too unfavourable. Thus the 'boys' room' was ideal in which to work on a hot afternoon.

When Alice knocked on the open door and was bidden to enter, Bony was seated at the desk, minus his coat and arrayed in tussore silk shirt, the rolled sleeves showing the smooth texture of dark skin and deceptively flaccid muscles. He smiled at Alice and indicated the chair opposite himself.

"Essen still busy?" he asked.

"Yes. Rushed back to his lab., as he calls his darkroom, immediately after lunch. He's got something cooking in that rathole. He says he's on an important lead in that Library job, but I think he's brewing something."

"It could be the heat, Alice, but it does sound involved. Something cooking . . . we think . . . brewing something."

"Must be," Alice agreed, removing her hat and gently mopping her forehead. The short-sleeved dress revealed the almost masculine arms, and the plunging neck-line mocked the scrawny neck supporting the large head so ill served by the full blonde hair drawn so tightly back.

"So Essen is excited," murmured Bony. "It's possible that that Library theft might concern us, and what you say of Essen's speed from lunch table to darkroom tends to promote possibility to probability. You know what was stolen?"

"Yes, although you didn't tell me."

"You distracted my mind by discussing interior decoration. Anyway, we must wait for Essen. He has made an excellent job of these pictures."

Alice accepted the copies made of the picture of Mrs Rockcliff and her baby, and the manner in which she studied them almost convinced Bony that her primary interest was in the infant and remained so. Without doubt, the mother instinct in Policewoman Alice McGorr was exceedingly strong.

"As you say, a good job," conceded Alice. "You ought to see Essen's pictures of his wife and baby. Just perfect. What did you have these done for?"

"Chiefly for the newspapers. Yoti has been complaining about the reporters from both Melbourne and Sydney, and we must give them something. Someone might recognise the dead woman under another name." Alice sniffed, and Bony detected the thought it expressed. "You dislike my methods?"

"It's not for me to say."

"You are thinking I am being too deliberate, too slow. You are remembering that the murder was forty hours old when discovered and that it's now seventy-odd hours later . . . with nothing to show."

"Perhaps I am. Murder is a job for a team."

"Two teams are working on it: one in Melbourne, the other in Sydney. A good team would have telephoned me last night or this morning the examination results of those clothes' tags, that wall section containing the hair grease of the murderer, the analysis of the floor sweepings. I am still waiting. Teams of experts rushed to Mitford to investigate the abductions of Babies 2, 3 and 4. Teams rushed about, wearing out Sergeant Yoti, annoying Essen, drawing their salaries and expenses and achieving precisely nothing.

"Now you just browse through these Summaries on the four stolen babies prepared by Inspector Janes, who conducted the three investigations. Note anything contradictory, abnormal,

76

even absurd when applied to your own knowledge of back-grounds, and finally give me your opinion of Inspector Janes's team work."

As Alice accepted the closely-typed documents there was faint resentment in her brown eyes, for even now she was unable to be sure if Bony mocked her, was being sarcastic or merely teasing. She read the first Official Summary and made a note. The second Summary produced two notes written in a sprawling hand and with the deliberation of the poorly educated. Once she looked up at Bony to see him completely relaxed, eyes closed, and in her own was something akin to wonderment, for Alice McGorr had been brought up in a world of cynicism and distrust.

She was engaged on the last Summary when voices without upset concentration, and again looking at Bony, found him in the same position but with one eye open.

"Hi, get up out of that and polish my car," roared Essen. "It's no time for sleeping, and if you don't want to work get back to the Settlement." Mumble . . . mumble. "I'm just telling you, Fred, that's all."

Essen came in, broadly smiling. Bony's second eye opened, and he nodded to a vacant chair, saying:

"Your tracker loafing on the job?"

"Does little else but sleep on the job. Got a favourite shrub just beyond your door. Don't blame the coot really. It's hot enough to make anyone go on strike."

"Catch your burglar?" Bony asked.

"No. What a fool thing to achieve. Slab of rock four by five feet and about three inches thick. Got in through a back window, easing the catch with a knife. Left glove smudges on the window glass. One smudge on the inside of the window tallies with the glove print we found under Mrs Rockcliff's bed, the mended glove."

"I hate to express doubt, but are you sure?"

"Camera proves it," answered the enormously satisfied Essen.

"Go on," commanded Bony. "You have my attention, I assure you."

"There was more than two in this robbery, but how many I don't know. The windows open over a cement path encircling the entire building. There must have been more than two because the object stolen was carried out via the back door, round

77

the side of the building to the front, where they must have had a utility or truck waiting."

"Right on Main Street! In full glare of street lights!"

"Street lights are switched off at one am. Constable Robins made his last round at 2.15 am. There was then no vehicle outside the Library. Near-by residents don't recall hearing a motor arrive or start up, but as Main Street is on a slight slope, the vehicle could have coasted from the west end, stopped at the Library, and then pushed off down to the other end. It could have travelled a full half mile without the engine running.

"What is certain is that they went to the Library to pinch that rock drawing, and that one of them was the woman who crept under Mrs Rockcliff's bed at the time she was murdered."

"The librarian told me he doesn't know the meaning of the drawing, and, further, that old Professor Marlo-Jones doesn't know what it means, either," Bony added. "It would appear that the meaning has no significance, that it was stolen for its value as a museum piece, or stolen at the behest of an unscrupulous collector. Marlo-Jones may be able to help. He might know of such a collector. Being busy with the burglary, you were unable to interview Mrs Ecks on the lines I suggested?"

"I was, but the Sergeant agreed to let Robins do it. Found out that when Mrs Ecks's baby was pinched there were altogether four prams, as we know. Of the five babies outside the pub, Mrs Ecks's baby was the only boy."

"Good. Substantive evidence that the abductor wanted only male children." Bony made a note. "I think we ought to do something about the hospital, see that every precaution is taken that a baby boy or two isn't stolen from the infants' ward. There were male twins born there last night."

"Be hell and damnation if those twins were pinched," Essen said. "What d'you reckon is behind these abductions? I don't get it."

"You will, eventually. Patience, Essen, patience. The enemy is on the move. They made a slip when putting Mr Bertrand Marcus Clark to tail Alice. They . . . now, as Alice would say, what's brewing?"

Voices, deep and loud, drew near. Heavy feet clomped on the cement outside the door, and then the door was filled by a mighty man having short, straight, grey hair, a ponderous paunch, and the feet of a dancer. After him came Yoti.

Essen jumped to attention. Alice, observing the movement, also stood. Bony stepped forward, a smile on his face, but no smile in his eyes.

"Why, it's Superintendent Canno, and all the way from Sydney."

"Good day, Bonaparte. How are you?"

"Excellent. But, being among friends, Bony to you. Permit me to present my cousin, Alice McGorr. Miss McGorr is studying my methods. Hopes to set up a private school for third-rate detectives."

"Haw! How do, Miss McGorr?" Canno sank gracefully into Essen's chair. Yoti said something and went out. Alice and Bony sat. And Canno added: "Friend of mine, name of Bolt, mentioned something about you assisting Bony. You must find him very trying at times. Everyone else does."

"I find him always original, and so nothing else matters," replied Alice, who then thought that association with Bony had destroyed all discipline in her. "Shal I go along and ask Mrs Yoti for some tea?"

The Chief of the Sydney CID chuckled like rumbling thunder.

"Damn good idea, Miss McGorr. And I'm not going to argue with you over our mutual friend." He stood when Alice got up, chuckled again, and sat when she had gone.

"That lass has a hell of a reputation," he announced. "What are you up to with her, Bony?"

Bony washed his hands, saying:

"You ask her that, Super, and then find out how it feels to be bounced out of the room and on the path outside. Anyway, I am pleased to be seeing you. Why come?"

"Just for the pleasure of seeeing you." Canno loaded a large pipe and applied a match, Bony waiting. Essen, now seated, waiting as he had not been dismissed. "Had to run down to Albury, so decided to come over here to see how you're going. How are you going?"

"I am satisfied."

"Yes, I know that, Bony. But what progress?"

"Decidedly more and decidedly faster than that made on three cases undertaken by your best men, Super."

"Yes, but . . . Look, Bony, my 'Commish' is getting windy over press opinion sent from here. They aren't so hostile to us over this Rockcliff murder as over the baby series. I know

Janes and all his men fell down, but we have public opinion to cope with. The 'Commish' said last night if there's another baby bust up in Mitford we'll all be kicked out of our jobs."

"And what does your Chief Commissioner suggest is to be done about it?"

"That every man jack of us rush to Mitford and tear the town to shreds."

"Do you agree with your Chief Commissioner?"

"Well, I think we ought. . . ."

"Relax, Super." Bony slowly rolled a cigarette, and the large CID Chief smoked a shade too vigorously, thereby betraying perturbation. "I will run over with you these Summaries, and then say that which will enable you to tell your Chief Commissioner to take a running jump at himself. Tell me, first, could you or Janes, or any other senior officer in your Department, look at a six-weeks'-old baby in a pram and tell its sex?"

Canno pursed his lips and spurted a thin shaft of smoke at the ceiling.

"Go on, answer me," urged Bony. "You're the father of a family of six. Janes has a son and a daughter. Both family men, like me. You answer my question."

Superintendent Canno slowly complied.

"I don't think I could say with certainty. I'm no chicken sexer."

"Of course you couldn't. Yet what happened? Among your experts there wasn't one woman. How, then, could you expect teams of men to dig successfully into this series of abductions? I had Alice McGorr in mind when I accepted this assignment. I want prints photographed, I call on Essen here who is an expert photographer and who is wasted in a small town like this. And when I want to know about babies, do I ask a policeman? I ask a policewoman.

"Now for these fool Official Summaries. There's no mention that the other babies outside the pub where Mrs Ecks's baby was stolen were females, proving that the abductors wanted a male child, as were the babies previously stolen. There's no mention that the child belonging to Mrs Delph was reared, nursed and minded by the cook while Mrs Delph ran around Mitford attending plonk parties. There is no mention in the relative Summary that the telephone in the manager's office at the Olympic Bank is an old-fashioned contraption nailed to a wall, and not one theory put forward concerning the theft of the child from that bank.

"So I could go on and on, but to do so would weary you with the crass stupidity of your teams of alleged experts. I've been assigned to this case only three days, and you want the murderer and the abductors handed in right away. Essen, step outside and make sure your tracker isn't listening. Not once but fifty times I've been given an assignment when the great white investigators have fallen on their big fat . . yet I'm to be bullied into producing the criminal from a hat within three days. That's why I cock a snook at you now, at your Commissioner, at my own, at every detective officer in the country. You can take it or leave it. I will produce the murderer of Mrs Rockcliff, and the abductor of her baby, when it suits me, and with or without your leave."

"Now, now, Bony old friend," rumbled Canno. "There's no argument, only a spot of worry over what the blasted papers are stirring up. All we want to do is to help as much as possible."

"Then why the devil didn't you chase the reports on that stuff we sent to your lab? Why haven't those reports been flown to me if they were too revealing to be telegraphed or telephoned?"

"Surely you have received them?"

"Of course not. I'll tell you what you can do. Arrange with District Headquarters to let Yoti have another four constables out of uniform, when Yoti will assign two or more to Essen. We have to guard the infants at the hospital, and keep an eye on the babies of fool women who still leave them outside pubs. Was that tracker lounging about outside, Essen?"

"No, sir."

"Why not agree to my men coming in?" Canno asked.

"Because, Super, your men had their opportunity here, and seemingly preferred to play 'two-up'."

"Insulting little pal, aren't you?"

"I could do better."

Alice was there with a large tray, which she placed on the desk. She began to arrange plates and cups in their saucers, and Bony went on:

"There is a traffic in babies as you know. Doubtless you have covered all the ins and outs of such traffic where you suspected it, and Bolt will have done the same. Now make your men work, Super, on another angle of the same traffic. You will remember

Davos in Vienna, and Lumsdon in Argentina. The same horrors could be practised in our own cities, in a hideout anywhere; even in a supposedly respectable house."

"What?" Canno almost shouted. A cup clattered, spilled some of its hot tea over the tray. Then Alice was gripping Bony's shoulders, her hands rigid and her face frozen.

"Davos! You don't think . . . Devil worship . . . black mass . . . babies being crucified upside down . . . babies . . . not here in Australia. . . ."

"Steady, Alice McGorr," Bony quietly urged, and Alice stood stiffly while one could count four, and then proceeded to serve them with afternoon tea.

CHAPTER 12

THE STOLEN MASTERPIECE

OF COURSE, Bony did the honours, escorting the great man to the airport, and only when he was airborne did Superintendent Canno feel like the mother-in-law who has been diplomatically evacuated.

Alice McGorr was doing something to a hat with needle and cotton when Bony returned to his office-bedroom and immediately asked if the reports had arrived from Sydney. Instead of betraying exasperation with the delay, he left no doubt in his assistant's mind that he was immensely pleased with life in general.

"We haven't been working hard enough," he told Alice when rolling one of his absurd cigarettes. "Great Whitefeller Chief not satisfied with what we, of the lower orders, have done in Mitford."

Alice tried to smile, gave up the attempt, saying:

"I'm sorry that I made such a fool of myself."

"But you didn't, Alice. You supplied just the right touch of drama to my idea put forward to rock the Great Whitefeller Chief on his throne. He was on the verge of knocking me for a sixer so that he could tell his Commissioner that he had 'fixed that Bony feller' and the alleged experts could return to Mitford."

The girl's hands resting on the desk expressed her mood.

"Do'you really think that those tiny babies were done to death like you said?"

"It's a possibility, Alice. The fact that the five babies were all healthy boys tends to make me uneasy, as does the fact that prior to our coming to Mitford the abductors did not make one mistake. You have been thinking that those babies were stolen for what . . . and why?"

"To sell, the same as stolen cars," she replied. "Foundling homes have long waiting lists for adoption and many people can't wait too long. They'd be too old. Properly organised the racket pays well. There was the case of Nurse Quigly who ran a very private hospital in Melbourne. She was in cahoots with a doctor, and an unmarried girl expecting a baby could have it safely at her hospital, never see the infant, walk out and back to her job. The babies were sold to people aching to adopt one. Quigly and her doctor received as much as five hundred pounds for a baby and never less than fifty pounds."

"The variation of price dependent on the purse, of course. Would male children fetch more than females?"

"No. The Matrons of the Homes say that as many people want a girl as want a boy."

"And so we return to the fact that all our five babies were boys. If our baby-thieves were running a racket similar to your Nurse Quigly they would steal easy babies, steal a baby girl from a pram rather than take the risk of stealing a boy from the Olympic Bank. Did you ever hear of the Satanics?"

"No," Alice said as though she didn't want to hear.

"I know very little about them. A few years ago in Sydney the remains of three male babies were dug up in a garden at the rear of a large house. The investigation stopped when bogged down by official impatience, but there was reason to believe that the people who occupied the house at the time the children died were Satanics, a particularly virulent organisation of Satan Worshippers. Therefore, we must accept the possibility of such practices.

"What you need just now, Alice, is sunshine in your mind. Put on your hat and stroll along to the hospital and see the Matron; I'll phone her you are coming. I want you to look over the Infants' Ward and find what is the routine at night for their welfare and take note of the general plan of the building."

Alice left, obviously glad to be up and doing, and Bony used

83

the house telephone to talk with the Matron. On returning to his room he found Essen waiting.

"Mail just delivered," Essen said, expectancy and impatience writ plain on his large face. He had placed on Bony's blotter several letters and one large official envelope. He was invited to sit and, having glanced at the envelopes, Bony selected the large one for first opening.

"Under the initials P.R. on the clothes' tags are J.Q.," Bony eventually told Essen. "Coincidence, I expect, but Alice mentioned less than an hour ago having known a Nurse Quigly who was in the baby-adoption racket."

"I remember the case," Essen said. "Four years ago. Quigly was said to be fifty-two years old and she got eighteen months. Our Mrs Rockcliff isn't Nurse Quigly."

"The section of wall plaster tells us nothing excepting that the mark left upon it is of a well-known hair dressing which is free from gum and contains ingredients not included in any other formula. You will see a jar of it on my dressing-table behind you."

"The sweepings from the bedroom floor gave better results. Two male hairs, dark brown, and having other attributes which need not concern us until we find that murderer. There are several hairs from the head of the dead woman, and no less than five hairs from another woman's head. You will recall that you found one long hair caught in the spring mattress and obviously pulled from the head of the woman who crawled under the bed. This is one of the five hairs from the woman not Mrs Rockcliff. They are black, like mine. But they haven't been treated with any hair dressing.

"The section of the report dealing with fingerprints is disappointing, or would be had you not dusted and photographed. Only the prints left by the dead woman are clear. The prints of the unknown woman's gloves show they were made of a cotton material and the enlargement of the mended tear will surely interest Alice McGorr. The unknown man's prints prove he was wearing rubber surgical gloves. You may examine the report at your leisure."

"Thank you, and thanks, too, for that remark you made about me to the Superintendent," Essen said. "That right, we're to have reinforcements?"

"From Albury Divisional HQ. Five are being sent. I'm going to suggest to Yoti that he assign you and at least three of the men for prevention of further infant abductions. Alice has gone to the hospital to see what opportunities a baby-thief has there, and it will be up to you to place your men. If you will take care of the babies left in Mitford, that matter will be lifted from me."

"I'll certainly do everything possible."

"I know you will. How is friend Marcus Clark?"

"Dr Nott had him shifted to the hospital at the Settlement this morning. Said he'd be all right out there, as Dr Delph takes in the Settlement and visits there every other day."

"I haven't met Delph. What's your opinion of him?"

"One of those men who seems to be too energetic on a hot day. Always on the go. Well liked by men. The women say he's a dear."

Essen departed and Bony passed to his dressing-table and pensively unwound a hair from the bristles of his hairbrush. Taking it to a shaft of sunlight, he studied it for a full moment before putting on his hat and also departing.

Despite Alice McGorr's private opinion of his rate of progress, and despite the visit to Mitford by the Chief of the CID, who held the same opinion, Bony was wholly satisfied with his methods. As with many an assignment he had undertaken only when the police team work had bogged, so with this one. He had begun with an unobtrusive study of the people concerned by this series of baby thefts, and was now at the stage when the criminals were beginning to unmask themselves. Presently, and it might well be soon, he would prod the nest and watch the infuriated ants unmask a little faster.

Team work, Alice had suggested, was always good. It wasn't, always. It was often very good when applied to a city crime bearing the hallmark of the criminal's methods, or the criminal's fingerprints, and assisted by informers. It was when a crime yielded no such leads that team work folded up and he, the half-caste detective, was asked to investigate by officials who secretly hoped he would fail, that in his failure they themselves would be excused.

When Bony entered the Library he felt almost gay, a mood not generated by the prospect of success but by the many little facts and clues already garnered. He was, too, delighted by the latest item, the fact that Fred Wilmot, the official Police Tracker, had been following him from the Police Station, and was idling behind a remover's van as he stepped into the Library.

Mr Oats, the librarian, welcomed him with friendly naïveté.

"Sit down, Inspector. What is it this time?"

"Well, chiefly your recent robbery, Mr Oats. Constable Essen who is looking into it has run against several difficulties, and I thought I might be able to help him out. I don't suppose you know, by repute, of course, any art collector who would be tempted to buy your stolen aboriginal picture?"

The librarian gently shook his silvered head.

"An art collector would be less likely to be interested in that rock slab than, say, the curator of a museum, and I know no curator so unscrupulous, even if he had the money, which, recalling my own salary, I'm sure he wouldn't have to spend!"

"Can you recall the picture to mind? Do you think you could sketch it, from memory?"

"I'll try, but don't expect to see the work of an artist." Mr Oats drew a pad forward and took up a pencil. "Let me see, now. There was a general line near the bottom, a horizontal line running like this. Wait a bit, I'm wrong. The line wasn't exactly horizontal but slightly curved, and on the line was a figure carrying something like a bag, something like . . . You remember the boys' comics? Pictures of Bill Sykes carrying away a huge bag of swag? Peculiar figure, too. It had an emu's head and tail. Well, that seemed to be what the figure was doing in the picture. At the top of the drawing were lines bending downwards which could be meant as clouds, and between these clouds and the ground there's what looks like a tree. The tree is in front of the striding man, and at the foot of the tree are little things, I could never make out what."

Mr Oats passed the sketch to Bony, who thought he could draw much better.

"Professor Marlo-Jones," went on the librarian, "says it is his opinion that the clouds above are heavy with rain, and that the figure represents an old man who, in the far days of the Alchuringa, came up out of the ground and threw rain-stones all about to make the clouds drop the rain."

Bony studied the sketch.

"May I keep it?" he asked.

"Yes, of course."

"It was drawn in ochre . . . white and yellow?"

"Yes."

86

ROUGH SKETCH MADE BY LIBRARIAN OATS

"Not gypsum?"

"Well, that I could not be sure about. It looked like white ochre, I think."

"It needn't be important, Mr Oats." Bony lit a cigarette. "I'll have the sketch copied and circularised, and someone might report having seen the slab of rock. By the way, what was the colour of the rock?"

"Purple brown, Inspector. Desert sandstone, I think Professor Marlo-Jones said it was. It comes from a very wide area of Central Australia. I suppose the colour of the rock is why red ochre wasn't used in the drawing."

"Probably. I would like to know why it was stolen. The theft might have been a cover-up for something more valuable. Have you checked over the other museum pieces?"

"Nothing else was taken," replied Mr Oats. "We haven't very much here, as you know, and it didn't take us long to be sure on that point. Like you, I can't understand it."

Standing, Bony looked down upon the rough sketch. Mr Oats couldn't be sure, but he felt rather than saw that Bony was smiling.

CHAPTER 13

A CHAT WITH MR BULFORD

THE BELL at the private entrance to the Olympic Bank was rung at seven minutes after four, and on opening the door Mr Bulford found Bony standing on the wire mat. Revealing no surprise he smiled his greeting and retreated in invitation to enter.

"Please go on up, Inspector. I must lock the parlour door."

"That is where I would like to chat, Mr Bulford," Bony countered, and turned to enter the bank chamber and thence to the manager's office. Mr Bulford might have been a junior clerk, when he sat diffidently in his managerial chair behind the ornate desk.

"Are you aware that anyone outside your private entrance can hear when you are engaged on the telephone in this room?" Bony asked.

Mr Bulford was instantly alarmed.

"No, I didn't know it," he replied. "I am apt to speak loudly because the damned instrument has had it and ought to have been axed long ago. That's just too bad."

"It isn't possible to distinguish words, Mr Bulford. The point concerning this fact is that, knowing when you were engaged on your telephone, the people who stole your infant son were able to carry through a simple plan."

The manager paused in the act of lighting a cigarette, his brows raised above hazel eyes now brightly alert.

"There were three people engaged in abducting your son," proceeded Bony, who then outlined the actions of each participant to conform to pre-arranged timing. "You can see for yourself that when you stand before your antique telephone your back is to your office door. Seated now at your desk, you can see clearly to that side door or private entrance. Only when you were at the telephone could anyone enter the hall unseen and mount the stairs, descend with the child and leave the building while the confederate continued to engage you in conversation. You agree that this theory is feasible?"

"Feasible, yes," Mr Bulford stroked his clipped moustache with the end of the cigarette, and the lazily friendly voice had the pleasing quality of the tiger's purr.

"Mrs Bulford told us that on the afternoon the infant was stolen she left the bank for a sherry party at four-thirty. You went upstairs about five-thirty. It must have been during that hour the kidnapper entered your hall. Using a duplicate key, or as seems more likely a stiff ribbon of celluloid, that operation from start to finish would occupy, say, ninety seconds. Correct?"

"Yes. Or it would if anyone had rung me. No one did during the period from the time my wife left to the time I went upstairs."

"I'd like you to be sure, Mr Bulford."

"Very well." The manager produced a black book from a desk drawer and swiftly turned the pages. "Here's the record for that day . . . November 29th. The last call was at two-fifty-six, made by a client named Rawson."

"No friend rang you during the period vital to us, a friendly call not to be recorded."

"No, no one, Inspector."

"Did you ring anyone?"

"I cannot remember having done so."

Mr Bulford had answered frankly. His eyes had remained frank if alert. Bony's opinion of this bank manager was confirmed: he could be tough in business under a suave and friendly exterior, always sure of his facts and completely reliant on his figures.

Bony stubbed his cigarette and pensively regarded his fingernails. His attitude, his facial expression were both indicative of disappointment.

"During that vital hour, Mr Bulford, did you remain in this office all the time?"

"All the time, Inspector."

"Think back, please. I want you to be very sure. Remember, your infant son's life could be at stake."

"You needn't apply the spur, Inspector."

"It's not to my liking, I assure you, Mr Bulford. Let us start from another point. On that afternoon, your wife attended a cocktail party given by people named Reynolds. It was a monthly engagement, and these people are important clients. Babies in arms would not be taken to such a party, I assume?"

"No, decidedly not."

"In the report by Detective-Sergeant Moss it is stated that you said, on finding the cot empty, that you assumed Mrs Bulford had taken the child with her. The other day you told me you assumed that your wife had taken the child to the cocktail party."

"Well . . . Now wouldn't that be natural?" countered the manager. "I went upstairs, and I found the baby's cot empty, and naturally I assumed that my wife had taken it with her."

"Neither to Detective-Sergeant Moss nor to me did you say that, finding the cot empty, you rushed to the bedroom where your wife might well have put the infant before going out."

"But she always left it in the cot and, I repeat, it was natural for me to assume she had taken it, even though I knew she was going to a cocktail party, and even though I knew she had never done so before."

With deliberation which even Mr Bulford realised was due to mental activity, Bony rolled another cigarette and then, as deliberately, tamped the tobacco into the paper with a match. He ignited the match, placed it to the tip of the cigarette, held the flame and gazed at the bank manager. Deliberately, he gave

Mr Bulford time to organise his mind to meet an attack. It was delivered.

"The other day you said that Mrs Rockcliff did not have an account with your bank."

The shutters fell before the hazel eyes, which never wavered.

"That is true. Mrs Rockcliff did not bank with us."

"You said, too, that prior to seeing her name in the local newspaper as the victim of homicide you had never heard of her."

"That is so, Inspector."

"I recall that I asked you that question when we were upstairs and your wife was present. Mrs Bulford is not now present."

The hazel eyes moved to focus their gaze on the cigarette-box. A white pudgy hand hovered over the box and took a cigarette, and when the match was struck the sound was distinct. The match was blown out and dropped on to the tray. And the hazel eyes again met the ice-cold blue ones watching him.

"I had met Mrs Rockcliff," he admitted quietly.

"You met her in the Library?" asked Bony, and subsequently often remembered a bad mistake.

"Apparently you know that."

"Were you with Mrs Rockcliff at the Library during the period or part of the period when your son was stolen?"

"I'm afraid so. I left here ten minutes after my wife, and I returned at half past five. Obviously I couldn't mention the matter before my wife."

"What were the circumstances of your first meeting with Mrs Rockcliff?"

"It was in late October. I was in the Library and overheard her discussing books with the librarian. The subject also interested me . . . and the librarian, well, made the introduction easy. I found her intelligent and pleasant to talk to, and often after that we met and talked. About books I can assure you."

"Not about herself?"

"No, other than that her husband had been killed in an accident, and that she had lived in Melbourne for several years."

"And you felt that your wife would disapprove?"

"You have met Mrs Bulford, Inspector."

"Mrs Rockcliff had no place in your social crowd?"

"There were reasons barring Mrs Rockcliff from our set. Stupid, of course. Worse, they were snobbish reasons. Ye Gods! Humanity makes me sick. With the exception of Mrs Marlo-Jones, there isn't a woman in Mitford the equal of Mrs Rockcliff in intelligence." The manager waited for the next question, and when it did not come, he said:

"Being the manager of a country branch is very safe and respectable, but I have for years had moments of rebellion. I mentioned Mrs Marlo-Jones. She and her husband, a retired professor of anthropology, are both charming and clever. Yet their range of subjects is sadly narrow, and after a time they become boring. Outside those two, the rest are mean-spirited, unaware of the world beyond their social rope. I belong with them. The bank says I must. My wife says I must. And what the bank says I must not do, must not know, my wife prohibits, too. For me there is only one road to mental freedom, the road paved with books telling of people who are free, or were free when they lived. Yes, I came to know Mrs Rockcliff very well. She was never inquisitive about my personal affairs, and I never attempted to probe into hers."

"I appreciate your frankness," Bony murmured and lit another cigarette. "I appreciate, too, your moments of rebellion. We are all slaves to one master or another: you to convention, I to a power much stronger. Were you in love with Mrs Rockcliff?"

"Yes. I knew that only after she was murdered."

"You would not like your friendship with her to become known, of course."

"I would not. And yet . . ."

"Well?"

"If it did become known, and the worst happened that I was reprimanded by the bank and threatened with eternal nagging by my wife, I might walk out on everything and carry a swag into the bush. If I did that, went looking for a bush job, I believe I would know greater content."

"H'm! When your two boys have grown to independent manhood, you may be able to do just that . . . and perhaps be very wise. Now for a direct question. Did you have any affection for your baby?"

"No. It wasn't permitted."

"Was not permitted by your wife?"

Bulford nodded, seeing himself as Bony was seeing him, writhing with self-contempt, being roasted by a damned half-caste.

"Did your wife have any affection for the baby?"

The picture of himself vanished and was replaced by that of his wife, and the simmering anger of years erupted.

"None," he replied loudly. "None whatever. It came late, unwanted. She said everyone was laughing at her, and she hated the baby because of that, and she hated me, too. And now I hate her . . . for all of it."

Mr Bulford buried his face in his hands, and Bony rolled and smoked another cigarette before Bulford regained composure, himself swayed by sympathy, his patience unaffected.

"Let us go back to Mrs Rockcliff," he said, coldly, and thus succeeded in assisting Mr Bulford back to normal poise. "Mrs Rockcliff leased the house from Martin & Martin, to whom she paid the rent. Who actually owns the property?"

"The bank does."

"Not a Miss Cowdry?"

"Miss Cowdry would own it if she paid off her overdraft. Before she left for Europe last year she agreed to let the bank have full control of the property, meet its interest on the OD, and apply the balance to the reduction of the OD."

"You did not know Mrs Rockcliff before she rented the house, I think you said."

"No, I did not. Mr Martin recommended her, and I agreed to the rental when she offered three months' rent in advance."

"She always paid the rent in cash. She always paid her bills in cash also, Mr Bulford. She never drew money from a Mitford bank or the Post Office. Did she have an account here?"

"I've answered that question before . . . in the negative."

Bony sighed, and settled himself as though prepared to stay for a week. He said, slowly:

"All other things being equal, I have the idea I could forget to include in my final reports your platonic friendship with Mrs Rockcliff. If, Mr Bulford, you could forget that you are the manager of a bank . . . out of business hours."

Mr Bulford regarded Bony steadily.

"I would like to know what you want me to do, Inspector."

"Does the firm of Martin & Martin bank with you?"

"Yes."

"Does Mr Martin have his private account here, too?"

93

"Yes."

"Would you examine those two accounts for any abnormality?"

"Yes. Give me half an hour."

Bony nodded agreement and the manager passed from the parlour to the banking chamber. Thereafter occasional sounds reached Bony, who relaxed in this comfortable parlour where so many money problems had been discussed. Outside the bank, the world passed by, even the little world of Mitford, a community of hurrying ants, each carrying its load, but, unlike the ant, trying to drop its load to take up another.

There was Bulford trying to escape life, and knowing he never would. There was Alice McGorr trying to run away from her feminine instincts, and heavily laden with inhibitions created by adolescent environment.

Inhibitions have sunk more human craft than any other agency. Inane ambition has sunk countless others. Only a Napoleon Bonaparte, by sheer will power and determinedly trained intelligence, has the strength to fear nothing, not even death, and no one save himself.

Could Bulford really drop his load and escape to the bushlands without having to take up another? Could he, Napoleon Bonaparte, jettison his career and be swallowed by the vast interior of this continent, and be free of the load he carried?

The manager came back and thus terminated these somewhat pointless cogitations.

"I think I might have what you want, Inspector," he said, having seated himself in his chair of importance. "On the 11th of every month, beginning last October, Mr Cyril Martin cashed a cheque for fifty pounds. The money was paid by the cashier in one-pound notes. On February 11th, that is this month, the cheque for fifty pounds was not presented."

"So?" mused Bony. "Mr Martin cashed a cheque for fifty pounds on the day before Mrs Rockcliff rented the house, and after she was murdered, on February 7th, Mr Martin did not cash the usual monthly cheque for fifty pounds."

Mr Bulford sat quite still, waiting. Bony rose.

"Thank you, Mr Bulford," he said. "I hope our little trade will lighten your load."

The manager didn't move. He gave no evidence that the load was eased.

CHAPTER 14

THE ENEMY STRIKES

ALICE MCGORR and Essen tapped for admittance to Bony's room shortly after seven, when the sun-god was losing his grip on the world and showing his anger by splashing the sky with blood. Indoors, room corners were beginning to melt into shadow and the mosquito that had forced an entry during the day was now lusting.

They found Bony slumped in his chair, on the desk his notes and reports. He was minus his coat and the white linen shirt looked as though recently donned.

"Come and sit down, both of you. After such a hot day you must be tired. Light up and relax."

"I came in after I got back from the hospital, and you weren't here," Alice said, and proceeded to remove her gloves and produce a cigarette-case and lighter from her handbag.

"I was calling on the élite."

"A woman?" she asked, suspiciously. Essen chuckled.

"Free and easy, aren't we?" he mocked. "We could be reminded about our place."

"I don't need to be reminded," snapped Alice. "We were both told to call him Bony. He said all his friends call him Bony, and that we were his friends. Now, didn't he?"

"He did," agreed Essen, lighting his pipe. "Still, we are lowly constables and he's a DI. Wonder if he ever wears all the doings ... braided peak hat, striped pants, gold-mounted tunic, etc."

"The wife has the lot, including a sword, wrapped in tissue paper and in her treasure chest," Bony said proudly, and then joined in the laughter against himself.

"And now, my friends, with your permission, a few questions."

Alice and Essen looked at each other, challengingly.

Bony spoke: "Competitor Number One. What did you think of the hospital, Alice?"

"Hospital first-rate. Got everything, from what I could judge. Nine babies in the Infants' Ward. Those boy twins!

Gorgeous kids . . . well worth the effort. But, anyone could sneak in at midnight and pinch the lot. Ward is wide-open to a fly-netted veranda, and the door in the veranda's never locked. I told Constable Essen about it at dinnertime."

"Sister on duty all night through?"

"Yes, but she has other duties which take her away from the Infants' Ward, although not so far that she couldn't hear a baby cry."

"And you, Essen? What have you done?"

"I spent a couple of hours with the Registrar of Births and Deaths and obtained the addresses of all parents with children under three months."

"Did you make a note of the sex of the children?"

"Yes."

"Concentrate on the safety of the male children. Have you plans?"

"Yes, I think I can cover it. The reinforcements from Albury are due in at half-past eight. The Sergeant says I can have Robins, who knows the town, and two of the Albury men. Robins is now visiting the homes of all the male infants to warn the parents. We'll guard the infants at the hospital and, with the other men, take general duty in the town. You got a hunch the kidnappers will try again?"

"History has produced one kidnapping per month," replied Bony. "I am taking these measures to satisfy Superintendent Canno, and to rid myself of mental distraction created by the possibility of another kidnapping. Do you think it possible that Sergeant Yoti instructed your tracker, Fred Wilmot, to trail me today?"

"Trail you! Lord, no."

"How long has he been employed by the Department?"

"Oh, some three years, I think."

"Mrs Rockcliff was murdered last Monday night. The next morning Wilmot came here to work. I am wondering if that were coincidence or arrangement made by Yoti or yourself."

"Don't think. I'll ask the Sergeant."

Essen departed in some haste, and Bony slid over the desk top a print made by a glove finger which had been repaired.

"Would you say that sewing was done by an expert or by a woman not really proficient?" he asked Alice, and then silently watched her.

She took the print to the window, wasn't satisfied and switched on the light, standing directly beneath the globe.

"Finely darned and evenly spaced," she said. "Yes, the person who did the mending is an expert."

"Would you be able to recognise her work on another garment . . . from memory of that print?"

"I might, but I wouldn't guarantee it. Alice continued to study the print. "I'd say that the person who mended the glove was used to doing a lot of sewing, and also that she was used to making her things last as long as possible, not being one of the idle rich."

Essen came back to report that Sergeant Yoti had certainly not put Fred to shadow Inspector Bonaparte, and further that the arrangement made with Fred to act as police tracker had been elastic. Fred often failed to come to work for days and even weeks unless sent for. He had not been sent for when he came to work on the previous Tuesday. His job was to keep the yard tidy, scrub out the cells, cut the wood for Mrs Yoti, and accompany an officer when required.

"You sure he was tailing you?" asked Essen, and Bony replied at zero.

"Of course. Marcus Clark tailed Alice. Now Frederick Wilmot tails me. There is the robbery from the Library, a large slab of rock on which an aborigine has made a crude drawing. It would not surprise me if the rock drawing was stolen to prevent me seeing it."

"No one seems to know what the drawing means, according to Oats, the librarian," Essen said. "Not even old Marlo-Jones, and being a professor of anthropology he'd know most things about the abos."

"Mr Oats told me that the Professor believes the drawing has something to do with rain-making," Bony continued. "Oats knows nothing about the drawing, where it came from, or who gave it to the Library Museum. I must pay a visit to the Mission Station tomorrow." Bony lit a cigarette he had been toying with for several minutes. "There is in these baby thefts something of the aborigine, and, so far, nothing of the whites. And by the way, Alice, you and I have been invited to a sherry party tomorrow afternoon. What is a good antidote for Australian sherry, d'you know?"

"A drop of battery acid, my old man used to say," replied Alice.

"H'm! I remember hearing that one before," Bony said, faintly disapproving. "I have a less drastic formula. Well, here is the invitation. Reads: 'Sherry at five. Marlo-Jones. Do come. Inspector Bonapart and Cousin.' The last written in green ink in a style rarely seen these days. Cousin! Knowledge from gossip, Alice. You cannot escape."

"I'm not going," Alice declared. "I won't drink plonk."

"You will accompany me, Alice," Bony ordered, the smile leavening the flat evenness of authority. "You will drink plonk with me. I will have at hand an efficient antidote so that neither will suffer . . . much . . . in performance of duty."

"There's nothing in the Oath of Allegiance about having to drink plonk," argued Alice, tossing her head and having to re-tighten the roll of hair.

"You won't drink plonk for a reason other than to please me," soothed Bony. "I must accept the invitation. I must be supported by someone, decidedly you for preference, and if eventually we swing down Main Street arm in arm and minus decorum, well . . ."

"I don't like it," Alice continued to protest. "Could I take a bottle of gin or something?"

"I fear not," Bony gravely told her. "Our hosts would feel insulted. So, sherry it must be."

"I hate the filthy stuff."

"They say you get to acquire a taste for it," Essen observed. "Don't mind it myself."

"You're not going; I am," announced Alice . . . all objection banished by the thought that Bony might substitute Essen for her.

A few minutes later Bony dismissed them for the day and, having gathered his papers and locked them in his case, he strolled into the warm and balmy night to call on the Reverend Mr Baxter, who received him with smiling friendliness and kept him talking for an hour.

Nothing came of that interview additional to the sparse information already obtained from the Methodist Minister, and for a further hour and a half Bony walked the streets of Mitford, feeling within his mind a growing restlesness, which sprang from intuitive promptings that forces were gathering against him rather than from impatience with the progress and speed of his investigations.

He could think of nothing left undone, no avenue left

unexplored. There was no Pearl Rockcliff on any Electoral Roll in the States of New South Wales and Victoria, and the Income Tax authorities knew of no tax payer of that name. Teams of patient men were delving into the background of all persons whose name began with Q on the chance of finding a woman absent from her usual abode . . . a gigantic task seemingly without end and without prospect of success.

People were leaving the cinema when he passed down Main Street to reach the Police Station. The police residence was in darkness, but there was a light in the office across the way, and there Bony found a constable on duty. He had nothing to report.

With thought of a shower before bed, Bony entered his room physically and mentally tired. Switching on the light, he sat on the bedside chair to remove his shoes for slippers, when bodily movement abruptly ceased.

Something was wrong with the room.

Standing, his eyes registered this pleasant interior, accepting every item with suspicion and finding no fault. The suitcase against the wall was as he had left it when brushing his hair before dinner. The chest of drawers was normal, and things upon it unmoved. The desk was neat and almost bare, the ashtray littered with cigarette-ends. But numerically less than when he had gone out. The ends were of cigarettes smoked by Alice McGorr. All the ends of his own self-made cigarettes had vanished.

Oh yes, something was wrong. He sniffed, without sound and without cease, like a hound silently hunting a scent. He lowered the blinds and prowled like a cat suspicious of danger, often bringing his nose close to the furniture, and sometimes to the linoleum covering the floor. The linoleum was old and the light was of little use to show tracks.

The bed was as when expertly made by Mrs Yoti, the upper sheet folded down over the blankets, his pyjamas neatly folded and lying upon the pillow. He sniffed at the pyjamas, the pillows. He studied the bed again, and again sniffed at the pillows, and the pyjamas. The coarse cream linen bedspread was without a rumple anywhere.

He looked under the bed. Nothing. He opened the wardrobe and burrowed among the clothes there. He opened the suitcase and carefully examined every item. Still nothing. But the prickling at the nape of his neck, the reaction to danger which had never yet fooled him, continued to warn, warn insistently.

Back again at the bed, he sniffed it all over and now with loud vigour. He fancied he detected a strange odour, could not be positive, and the doubt put springs to his shoeless feet and magnified sensitivity at his fingertips. Gingerly he took up the pyjamas and dropped them on the chair. The top pillow he lifted as carefully, and then the second pillow. Deliberately cautious, he rolled down the bedclothes, over and over to the foot of the bed.

And then he leapt to the dressing-table for his hairbrush to smash five red-back spiders which had been lying in wait to inject their poison into his feet.

Lurking under cover, often in colonies, this insect's attack is to be countered by swift medical attention, or surely culminates in long illness if not death.

CHAPTER 15

THE DOOMED RACE

IT WAS not a pleasing day, and Alice decided that if people liked living in the bush in preference to the salubrious cities, they could stay in their damned bush. Once away from the vineyards and the orchards nurtured by the network of water channels webbed about Mitford, the Murray Valley in summer presents a picture of flat barrenness, a suntrap masked by dark grey dust raised by the wind.

Constable Robins drove his own car, with Bony and Alice as passengers, and a mile out of town the macadamised road gave place to the natural earth track of the outback . . . the road to Albury. This was followed for two miles, over the barren flats, under the occasional gum or box tree, until, when the track was about to cross a creek, a branch track took them to the Aboriginal Settlement.

Compared with the river flats, the site of the Settlement was a surprisingly pleasant change. Several acres occupied an elbow of the tree-lined creek, and guarding the elbow stood the Superintendent's house, with the store on one side and the church on the other. Behind this first rampart were the trade shops, the school and the hospital, and beyond these buildings, in the elbow itself, were streets of one-room shacks capable of housing a family.

It was shortly before eleven, and the 'streets' were empty of children, who were now packed into the school and singing their lessons. Those aborigines to be seen were dressed in white fashion, the women in gaily coloured clothes.

The Superintendent, the Reverend Mr Beamer, received the visitors in his office, occupying a part of the store. He was young, obviously enthusiastic and not averse to cigarettes. Further, he was brisk, frank, dressed in white duck, and re-minded Bony of a successful peanut farmer.

"As Sergeant Yoti explained on the telephone," Bony opened, "I've come to interview Bertrand Marcus Clark. I brought my cousin, Miss McGorr, with me because she wishes to see your work with the aborigines."

"Then, Inspector, Miss McGorr is more welcome than you," Mr Beamer said decisively. "We are always delighted to meet those who are interested in our efforts and, perhaps excusably, less delighted to receive anyone representing the law. Clark appears to have been more sinned against than sinning . . . by the look of him." Mr Beamer chuckled. "Quite a sound thrashing for being in town during prohibited hours."

"That's the view taken by Sergeant Yoti, I believe," returned Bony. "However, my interest in him lies in the reason for his being in town. There is no restriction on these people by you?"

"Regarding their freedom, none at all. They may come and go off on walkabout at will, but we do persuade the children to stay during school terms. Everyone knows, of course, that they must not be in town between sunset and sunrise unless with official permission. And they have to keep the rules govern-ing their conduct when in the Settlement."

"And white people are not permitted to enter the Settlement without your sanction?"

"Correct. Actually they want for nothing, being provided with rations, from flour to tobacco. They are also provided with straw-filled mattresses and blankets. Reverting to Marcus Clark, his real reason for being in town late that night was to visit Ellen Smith. He wants her to marry him, but, I understand, the courtship isn't running smoothly."

"And Ellen Smith is . . .?"

"The domestic employed by Mrs. Marlo-Jones. Ellen is a

full-blood lubra. Mrs Marlo-Jones told me that Ellen won't make up her mind about Clark, and that as he was pestering Ellen, she ordered Clark away from the house and told him not to go there again."

"Ellen Smith is probably being wise," Bony said, smilingly. "I cannot sense the romantic in Clark's makeup. How long have you been in charge here, Mr Beamer?"

"A little over three years," replied the Superintendent, who, Alice guessed, was wondering what really lay behind these questions.

"During your service here, have there been upsets among them?"

"At the beginning of my term, yes, quite a number. Then I knew very little about these people . . . from personal contact, but . . ." The minister smiled and Alice liked that . . . "but I was very willing to learn and I readily admit that Professor and Mrs Marlo-Jones were towers of strength.

"I found that these people had come a very long journey from the tribal discipline enjoyed by their ancestors. They had become too closely associated with white civilisation, and because our civilisation will not or cannot assimilate them, for I refuse to believe the Australian aborigine cannot himself be assimilated, they were fallen into a condition of racial chaos.

"We came to this country and conquered with guns and poison. What a basis for national pride today! From the aborigine we took his land and the food the land provided. Worse, we took his spirit and trod it into the dust, leaving him with nothing excepting the pitiful voice crying: 'Gibbit tucker.' When plain murder was no longer tolerated, we tossed the starving aborigine a hunk of meat and a pound of flour and told him to get to hell out of it. A wonderful Christian nation, are we not?

"Forgive me for becoming heated," pleaded Mr Beamer. "I had never placed the aborigine on a pedestal, but I have sought ways and means of helping him to help himself back to his former independence of mind and spirit. I roused the head men from their indifference to exert again their old influence and power . . . of course, under my general supervision. Thus the people were brought under the kind of discipline they can understand, and they became keenly interested in the least obnoxious of the corroborees and the folk-dancing. This in turn has enhanced the tribal and community spirit, and that pride in themselves without which no people can exist, let alone flourish."

"Good work, Padre," warmly complimented Bony, and Alice wanted to add 'Hear! Hear!' "Thereafter you have had less and less upsets?"

"Yes. But the credit must go largely to the Marlo-Joneses. They are both knowledgeable and understanding."

"You must have the vision and the energy to translate it to reality," softly insisted Bony. "You have been able to gather the head men into conference?"

"Yes, they meet in council. Often I am invited to attend, and still more often I ask them to attend on me. One great advantage is that delinquents like Marcus Clark are tried by the head men and, if they persist in misbehaving, are banished from the Settlement. Very seldom do I participate.

"We insist that the adults attend church service twice on Sunday and find we need to use no coercion. The children . . . you shall see them at work . . . give pleasure to their teachers, not worry. The point to be determined with the children, and here Professor Marlo-Jones has been of enormous assistance, is how to give them the best education to occupy the tragically limited spheres in which white civilisation will permit them to live. You know how it is. Other than stockmen and domestics, they are not wanted."

"Yes, I know how it is," admitted Bony, and Alice caught the note of bitterness. "What staff have you?"

"My wife runs the school with aboriginal women of Intermediate standard. We have an aborigine who is an excellent store-keeper and he helps me with the books. I received my medical degree shortly before coming here and so, with the assistance of Dr Delph, manage the hospital. We have an aboriginal butcher, and aboriginal carpenter, another a blacksmith, and an old fellow who actually repairs watches for a Mitford jeweller."

"Excellent, Mr Beamer." Bony stood. "Well, we won't keep you longer than can be avoided. Thank you for being so patient."

"Thanks are due to you, Inspector, and to you, Miss McGorr. Would you like to look round now?"

"Yes, very much."

At the school they were presented to Mrs Beamer and her assistants, where they examined the children's work and listened to their singing. They were shown over the church, and greatly admired the tapestry done by the senior girls. They looked into the neat and well stocked store, and found the watch-mender at his bench in the blacksmith's shop, an ancient man with a scraggy white beard, scraggy white hair and scraggy white eyebrows. He amused Bony, talking and joking while displaying his fine tools, and Bony wondered if the metal filings on the bench were likely to be blown into the mechanism of the watches. Alice was completely absorbed when in the hospital she found two new babies not yet old enough to have lost their red skins.

Bertrand Marcus Clark had a ward to himself and failed to appreciate the honour. He was surly and replied evasively only to the Superintendent. When again in the hot sunlight, the minister said:

"One of the few I neither like nor trust, Inspector."

"I can understand your failure to like him," agreed Bony. "Why do you distrust him?"

"I have no proof, but I think he is at the bottom of many little upsets. For some time I've felt undercurrents antagonistic to my work and hopes, and have suspected they emanated from Clark. I try not to be uncharitable, but . . ."

The Superintendent and his wife walked with them to the car, and invited them to come again.

"Friendly people, weren't they?" Alice said when on the road back to town. "And those cuddly little babies. Is it true they will turn black in a few days?"

"Yes. I think it will be an improvement."

"I don't. I just love them as they are."

He glanced at her profile, saw by the set of her mouth that she was in her rebellious mood, and again glancing at her he felt pity for this woman to whom a career was merely an opiate, and he was momentarily concerned by what inhibited instincts might do with her.

"They reminded me of newly hatched birds in a nest," he said, and swiftly and sharply she exclaimed:

"Shut up."

They came to the green belt of fruit trees and vines, of lucerne plots and lawns about the brightly painted houses, and presently to the lower end of Main Street. Here Alice spoke softly, and gently touched his hand.

"I'm sorry I was snappy. It was your fault, as usual. You will make me forget you're an inspector and I'm a nobody."

"I shall continue to make you forget, Alice. As my wife sometimes admits, I'm the most understanding man in the world."

For the third time he glanced at her, and now she was looking at him, and her eyes were misty.

CHAPTER 16

THE PLONK PARTY

AMID THE lower Australian peck order where Alice McGorr had been born and reared, wines are imbibed from the bottle or thick china cups or tumblers. Of course, in the particular section of Australian society to which she was now to be presented, wines are sipped or swilled from fragile crystal. There is no difference in the quality or potency of the liquor.

For people like Bony this sherry-quaffing was unfortunate when, as in this instance, he was forced to drink it in the course of duty. Any other type of wine would have been less obnoxious, because Australia can produce wines the equal of overseas products . . . all wines excepting sherry, which has a digestive reaction similar to the oil in sardine cans.

As Alice told him when they were being driven to the home of Professor and Mrs Marlo-Jones, she wasn't a wowser, and was not averse to a drink provided she could choose her drink and say when. Far more than Bony had she seen the ill effects of alcohol from good honest Scotch down the ladder to methylated spirits and, still lower, battery acid. Alcohol had ruined her father, had blurred his brain and thickened his fingers. He had been extremely successful on rum; the beginning of the end was plonk.

She was still mutinous at having to accompany Bony to this social engagement, and not for the world would she confess that her hostility was due less to having to drink sherry than to lack of social confidence.

Bony, too, possessed a secret which for nothing the world might render would he tell Alice McGorr. Her dress was wrong. The colour scheme was all colour. The hat was obviously a hat. And there was too much powder on her nose.

Not that his 'cousin's' appearance really disturbed him. Actually he was delighted with her, for no one, not even the most perspicacious, could possibly imagine Alice McGorr in the trim uniform of a policewoman. And further, his own sartorial elegance was emphasised.

"Have you thought up the antidote to plonk?" she asked, her voice edged.

"Oh yes. Robins will call for us at six, and will rush us first to your lodgings. You will at once take two teaspoons of carbonate of soda in a glass of hot water. When your tummy has disgorged the plonk, you must drink a cup of warm water in which six cloves have been boiled. Then lie and rest for half an hour. If you should find the bed behaving like the prow of a ship in a storm, you must take a nobbler of brandy."

"I am serious," Alice said, two edges to her voice.

"I am, too. So much so that I asked Constable Essen to be sure that his wife boiled the cloves."

"Are you going to drink this alleged antidote?"

"No. I have another much less unpleasant."

"And that is?"

Alice watched his slim fingers caressing an object clothed with tissue paper. Having removed the paper, Bony disclosed a small jar having a screw top. From a pocket he produced two teaspoons, presenting her with one.

"I have here a half pound of butter," he told her. "Before arriving at the party, I intend eating half of it. The other portion I am offering to you. The effect of this little meal will be to keep the plonk under a layer of butter and thus prevent the fumes of raw alcohol from reaching the brain and so cause the state called inebriation. I assure you it is most efficacious."

"I love butter," Alice said, slightly impatient.

"Then take your share first."

"Thanks."

"At this exhibition, Alice, we will meet the élite of Mitford. You are my cousin who is greatly interested in criminal investigation as it provides you with knowledge of abnormal psychology, about which one day you hope to write a book. In passing, don't forget the relationship is on my father's side."

"All right. I get that."

"We are being invited because Professor and Mrs Marlo-Jones are deeply interested in me as a particularly rare anthropological specimen. Doubtless they will occupy most of my attention, and it is therefore important that you note and remember scraps of conversation, your reactions to people, and to give your feminine intuition complete freedom."

She watched him remove the last spoonful of butter from the jar, watched the lid being screwed on and the jar placed, with the spoons, on the floor. She saw him glance at his watch, heard him say it was five-ten, and felt the taxi being braked to a stop.

"Now for it," she said, on being gallantly assisted to alight.

She noted his smile, and then was being ushered through a low gateway between lambertianas, to be escorted across lawns studied with small rose bushes. Before her stood a spacious old brick house, having bow windows and venetian blinds. The impression of light and colour gave place to one of chocolate above white linen, the broad face of an aboriginal woman who looked at her with huge liquid black eyes. The face vanished, and in its stead was the picture of people filling a long room, a scene of chaos from which emerged the Viking she had once seen on a cinema screen. Taller than her escort, the Viking stooped to take her hand. And Bony was saying:

"Permit me to present my cousin, Miss McGorr, Professor Marlo-Jones."

"Welcome, Miss McGorr," boomed the Viking. "And I am really delighted you brought the Inspector, because he must be a very busy man. Come along in and meet people. Ah, my dear! Here is Inspector Bonaparte with Miss McGorr."

The woman, dumpy, broad, thick hair greying and brown eyes small and twinkling. The man, huge, vital, old yet ageless. Their interest in Bony was undisguised, paramount, passing her by.

People . . . a thousand. Voices . . . a million. Mr and Mrs Simpson, Miss McGorr. Dr Nott, Miss McGorr. Mrs Bulford, Miss McGorr. Mr Martin, Miss McGorr. Tinkling glasses filled with sherry, glasses massed on a silver salver presented by a chocolate face with large fathomless black eyes. Dr and Mrs Delph, Miss McGorr. Cheers, Miss McGorr. The smell of plonk. The taste of plonk. Plonk sliding down her throat to fight with the butter, and the butter, she hoped, sitting on top. Mrs Coutts, our local author, you know, Miss McGorr. Mr and Mrs Reynolds, Miss McGorr. Cheers. More plonk. Thank heavens that glass is empty. And the same voice saying over and over again, Inspector Bonaparte, as it said over and over, Miss McGorr.

She wanted to scream at the voice to say Bony and Alice for a change, and the voice went on and blessedly away when she was halted by a hand clasped about her arm, and a soft voice urged her to a chair. Her gaze encountered a large woman whose eyes were light-blue and ringed with powdered fat, and whose face was heated and streaked with growing fire.

"Frightfully boring, all these names," the woman said. "Relax, dear, and drink up. The Professor knows a good sherry from a pig's tail." There came a deep-down rumbling snigger. "Are you a detective, too?"

Alice wanted to explain the relationship with Bony, felt it was her duty to him, and managed only to emit a giggle. A tray of filled glasses was presented, and this time the face above the tray was white, and the eyes were grey. The grey eyes commanded her to place the empty glass on the tray and accept a filled one, and somehow she wasn't brave enough to refuse.

Voices. Voices close and distant. Voices harsh and voices slurred, voices malicious. People seated along the walls, groups of standing people, a maniac pounding on a piano. Hands, dozens of hands from which rose crystal stems supporting limpid globes of yellow wine.

Voices: "Wretched day, my dear. Quite off my game, you know." "Yes, he got the contract. He would." "What do I think of her?" "But, darling, I told you he got the contract." "Fancy asking that half-caste person here. A what! Detective-Inspector. Good lord! I must meet him." "Darling, she must be fifty. Couldn't possibly know how." "Oh, didn't you know that? Must be mental, don't you think?" "Writes all day long, I was told. Never mind the baby or the husband. Wants to be a great authoress." Laughter. Voices . . . discord . . . pounding upon the ears.

"Drink up, dear," urged fat face. "Here comes some more."

The lubra stood before her and the fat woman, the black face wide in a fixed smile, the black eyes large and probing and without depth. They seemed to say: "What! You don't like plonk! Silly! They all drink plonk, as much as they can and as fast as they can. It'll be six o'clock soon."

Alice emptied her glass and accepted a filled one. It was peculiar that she was feeling no different than on arrival.

There was no exhilaration, no urge to talk, just a warmth in the tummy when a warm tummy wasn't appreciated on a hot day. The fat woman said: "Cheers, dearie!" Alice sipped, twice, and wanted to fling the glass in the fat one's face.

She could never recall just when it happened, the change which swept away confusion and brought everything to clear perspective. Faces became adjuncts of necks, hands of arms and arms of bodies.

She saw Bony laughing at something said by the Viking, and she thought him the handsomest man present. She saw the local authoress talking earnestly with a young woman who listened with rapt attention, and although she couldn't hear Mrs Coutts, she knew that her subject was writing novels. She watched Mrs Marlo-Jones among the standing groups, the woman apparently deep in thought and oblivious of her guests.

"Funny little woman," mused Alice. "Whatever that lion of a man ever saw in her beats understanding." Mrs Marlo-Jones looked up, but not in time to see Alice watching her. She weaved among the groups, spoke to this person and that, and presently came again to the place where she had been cogitating. That place was just behind Bony, and Alice thought she had returned to continue listening to his conversation with her husband.

It was absurd, of course. For the second time Mrs Marlo-Jones was too late to see Alice watching her, and she stooped swiftly and retrieved something from the floor. The lubra approached again with her tray of glasses, and once more Alice felt impelled to accept yet another sherry.

When the lubra had passed, Mrs Marlo-Jones was over by the mantel upon which were curiously painted bowls; done probably by aborigines. One supported an emu egg, the green surface of which had been carved to reveal the white base of the shell portraying a winding snake. Alice saw Mrs Marlo-Jones drop an object into a bowl, and that object was a button.

The fat woman stood up and mumbled something Alice failed to catch. She made only one false step before reaching the door. Mr Bulford slipped into the vacated chair. He smiled at Alice and said "Cheers," and Alice drank with him, thankful that Bony's antidote was working well.

"How d'you like Mitford, Miss McGorr?" asked the banker, and Alice was saying what a nice place it would be in the winter when it wasn't so hot, when Dr Delph, large, portly and tanned, pulled the chair forward upon her other side and made a threesome. Alice liked his eyes and his clipped grey moustache, and somehow she knew these two men were more than acquaintances.

"I hear you are studying abnormal psychology, Miss McGorr," said the doctor. "Lucky, aren't you? Being able to work with a detective-inspector, watch him work, study his methods, and all that. Tell me, is it true that Inspector Bonaparte has never failed in a case assigned to him?"

"Yes, I believe so," admitted Alice, instantly on her guard. She saw Mrs Marlo-Jones leave the room, and that the lubra watched her leave, and she was certain that neither Dr Delph nor Mr Bulford was aware of her interest in the lubra.

"He's an amazing man," said the doctor. "Had a few words with him just now. He proves how triumphant the mind can be over matter, how personality can conquer insuperable difficulties."

"Certainly a charming man," added Mr Bulford. "I don't think I'd be happy were he trailing me."

"I'd be like the man in the Bible: put a millstone round my neck and drown myself in the river," Alice contributed. A man, tall and gaunt, drifted into Alice's mind, and when glancing up at him she saw Professor Marlo-Jones by the mantelpiece. He was taking the button from the china bowl. The gaunt man was calling to the white maid to bring her tray, and Alice saw the Professor drop the button back into the bowl. She could not see Bony.

"What d'you think of our Mitford parties, Miss McGorr?" asked the gaunt man, and Alice giggled:

"Lovely, Mr Martin. Sherry and crime go well together. I don't know which I like best."

"Must be exciting at times," observed Dr Delph, voice blurred a trifle, eyes bright and complexion to be described now as rosy.

"It's exciting at all times," stated Bony from behind Alice. "I assume you are referring to the mixture of crime and sherry. I have often wondered to what degree crime begets drink and in what degree drink begets crime."

Alice was feeling fire in her tummy, and she hoped her face wasn't blazing red. Now and then she thought how amazing it was that she didn't feel even faintly squiffy, but she was by no means confident. The black maid now was near the mantel-shelf, offering drinks to people whose names she couldn't remember. Mr Bulford said something and she laughed, although not hearing what he said. Only Alice McGorr could watch that lubra without betraying her interest to those around her. The lubra took the button from the bowl and dropped it into the pocket of her white apron.

It was all very hot and noisy when she noticed that people were drifting to the door, and on standing she was gratified that her legs were of use and that the scene remained right side up. She felt slight annoyance when Bony lurched against her slipping an arm through hers and urging her gently door-wards.

They bade their adieus to their hosts in the hall, and when they were walking the path to the gate, again Alice was annoyed that Bony staggered slightly.

"Are you really oiled?" she asked, when they were in the private car owned and driven by Constable Robins.

"Not visually, Alice. How do you feel?"

"Beaut. What's the idea of pretending?"

"Well, I must have drunk at least half a bottle of sherry, and our host would have been disappointed had he thought his wine was wasted. Did you observe anything unusual?"

"No, can't say that I did. Did you?"

"Yes, I learned much of interest, but I was uncomfortable soon after arriving. Er . . . I lost a trouser button."

Alice shrieked and Bony shrank.

The story of the adventures of the button was related, and at the end of it Bony was gripping Alice by the arm.

"You observed something of great import," he said.

CHAPTER 17

A QUESTION OF MAGIC

"CLOSE YOUR eyes, Alice, and try to decide if Mrs Marlo-Jones picked up that button to prevent anyone slipping on it, or if, like a person finding a ten-pound note, she deter-minedly secured it before it could be claimed."

"She was standing just behind you and looking at the floor.

Then she moved away and spoke to people before coming back to the same place. She picked up the button and, sort of carelessly, drifted over to the mantelshelf, where, after a bit of backing and filling, she dropped it in a bowl."

"A piece of the puzzle. Let me picture it. The Professor and I were standing all the time. We were talking nonstop. People joined us but no one stayed, because the Professor was deeply interested in our conversation. When two people talk standing like that in a crowded room, they don't occupy the same place all the time. I remember that button parting company with my trousers . . . at the back . . . and I remember feeling slightly uncomfortable.

"Mrs Marlo-Jones saw the button on the floor, and did not pick it up at the time, but wandered round before coming back to it. The Professor was facing me, and therefore saw his wife pick up something, watched her drop it into the bowl. He didn't know it was a button, and he was driven to find out what his wife had dropped into the bowl.

"Why all that manœuvring over a button? Why should Professor Marlo-Jones be so interested in an object picked up from the floor by his wife? Then the lubra takes up the tale, you watch. Did she see Mrs Marlo-Jones pick up the button, take it to the bowl and drop it there, or did Mrs Marlo-Jones tell her what she had found on the floor and what she had done with it? Silly questions, perhaps, but I'd like the answers."

"I don't get it," Alice confessed. "Why are the answers wanted?"

"Last night someone entered my room, deposited five red-back spiders in my bed and stole all my cigarette-ends from the ashtray. The spiders were meant to put me in hospital for some considerable time, if not into a coffin. The theft of the cigarette-ends was for the same purpose as the theft of the button from the bowl. Button and ends came from me, are a part of me, are necessary objects required for the practice of pointing the bone.

"On one assignment I did have the bone pointed at me, and it was far from pleasant. Why point the bone now? You fell foul of Marcus Clark, or he fell foul of you, and subsequently I approached him in hospital . . . as a friend. Why point the bone at me for what you so thoughtlessly did to him? It doesn't add up. Unless, of course, I am dangerous to those who stole the babies, or to those behind the killing of Mrs Rockcliff, or to those who stole the babies *and* did the murder. I must be dangerous to that lubra and whoever stole my cigarette-ends. Which points to aborigines being mixed up in the baby-thefts and possibly the murder. Good! We have arrived."

"Where?" asked Alice, thankful that they were nearing Essen's home and carbonate of soda.

"The criminals are on the move; they cannot stay still."

"And does the theft of that slab of rock come into it, too?"

"I think it does."

"And this button business is a form of magic?"

"Something of that kind, Alice."

"Something of the kind! It must be either magic or it isn't."

"Magic is dependent on a point of view. When a wild aborigine first hears a radio, he calls it magic. That which is not understood is called magic, an easy word saving us the bother of using our brains to understand how it is done."

"I think I am going to have a headache," Alice declared.

"Well, here we are within a few yards of Mrs Essen and the cloves. And the soda. You have done fine, and I am pleased. Later this evening, if you are well enough, come round to the Station for a further talk on the . . . er . . . plonk party."

"All right, and thanks a lot for the antidote, Bony. It is one hell of a good lurk, I must say. And the sort of headache I was going to have wasn't the sort you thought I was going to have and won't have."

"Quite so, Alice. Now I think I am going to have a headache."

"See you after," she cried, leaving the car, and as Robins made the turn she waved to him.

In the Station office, Sergeant Yoti looked him over, saying:

"What! No lurch?"

"I never lurch."

"No dull, pounding headache?"

"No headache . . . yet. Your tracker and his people came here to Darling River, he says, about five years ago. I'd like you to enquire of the Menindee police if it is known why they left, and what is their record."

"I did so twelve months ago when we took young Wilmot on as tracker. Report then was clean."

"Then you need not bother to seek another."

"You seem a bit hostile."

"I have arrived at the point in this investigation where it's advisable to stir up an ants' nest and watch what happens.

113

But for the moment a cup of strong tea is essential, and I am going to make love to your wife."

"Do. Don't mind me. I'm only the husband."

Yoti smiled. Bony came back from the door to give the crumb for which the Sergeant's eyes implored.

"All my cases are at first like a brick wall presenting an unyielding front. I have to push here and prod somewhere else to find a weakness in the brickwork." Again came Bony's flashing smile. "More often than not it is inadvisable to make a direct attack, but to undermine the foundations, as it might be inadvisable for me to ask your wife point-blank for a cup of tea when she is cooking the dinner."

"I don't know," Yoti admitted. "You may be right. The thing is, this investigation looks like giving. Is that what you are really saying?"

"It is, Sergeant. 'Bye for now."

Bony found Mrs Yoti in the kitchen and, as he predicted, she was cooking the dinner. The kitchen was hot, and Mrs Yoti was hot, and no woman feels at top when she's hot in a hot kitchen.

"Oh, there you are! How was the party?" she asked.

"Rather boring," replied Bony, sitting on a chair at the table littered with pastry-making utensils. "I dislike sherry. Alice calls it plonk. Appropriate, I think. Could you give me a couple of aspirins?"

"Why, of course. Many there?"

"Crowded. The Bulfords, the Delphs, the Notts, the Reynoldses, the novel-writing woman, and others. Two maids, one a lubra, served the drinks as fast as wanted, and most guests wanted fast. The Professor collared me for a session. Most interested in me as a specimen. His wife was, too. I lost a trouser button and gained a headache."

Bony washed down the aspirin with a few sips of water. He stared at the teapot on the mantel over the hot stove, continued to stare that way until certain that Mrs Yoti was aware of the target. He sighed, set down the glass of water, and leaned back.

"You lost a what?" asked Mrs Yoti.

"A trouser button," he answered, standing up. "Well, I mustn't detain you. Thanks for the aspirin." Smiling at her, he glanced again at the teapot, and proceeded to the door.

Mrs Yoti looked at the clock on the mantel, noted the teapot beside the clock.

"Would you like a cup of tea? I could make a pot before my pastry is due out of the oven."

"That is just what I would like," Bony said, returning to the table and sitting down again. "A strong cup of tea would fix this hangover. It's very thoughtful of you. How d'you like being married to a policeman?"

"Wouldn't like not to be married to a policeman," replied Mrs Yoti, pouring boiling water into the teapot. "My father was a policeman, my two brothers are policemen, and now my son is one." The tea was made, the oven was opened and out came the pastry. It looked good, and Mrs Yoti laughingly asked what happened when the button came off his trousers.

"Mrs Marlo-Jones sneaked round the room to pick it up, and then sneaked over to the mantel and dropped it into a bowl. If you found a button at a party would you do that?"

"Not while my guests were present. Afterwards, of course. Good buttons are buttons these days. But that Mrs Marlo-Jones has a kink for buttons."

"Indeed!" Bony sipped the strong tea with intense satisfaction.

"Daughter of a friend goes to High School, and once a week Mrs Marlo-Jones takes the botany class, or something like that. One day she was lecturing the class, and she was wearing a jacket suit. She dived her hand into a side pocket for her handkerchief, and with it she pulled out about two dozen buttons. All kinds, too. The girls shrieked as they scrambled after them all over the floor."

"And now she has added my button to her collection. I didn't like to ask her for it."

"No. You couldn't very well do that," agreed Mrs Yoti. "I'll sew another on for you."

"Thanks. I'm no good at it. Yes, I would like another cup. By the way, is your son a big man, bigger than his father?"

"Six feet four inches, forty-six or something round the chest, weighs sixteen stone. Why, his father's a pigmy to our George."

"I thought he might be, on coming across a pair of his slippers. Size nine foot?"

"Size nine. Takes almost a tin of polish every time he cleans his shoes."

"Is there an old pair about anywhere? I'd like to borrow them."

"Borrow them!" echoed Mrs Yoti. "George's shoes! Whatever for?"

"Merely to make a wrong impression."

Mrs Yoti stared at Bony, and proceeded to nod slowly as though comprehension dawdled like a poodle off the lead. Bony was convinced it was still dawdling when he left for his room and the shower, but the number nines were in his hand and he wondered what it felt like to be an outsize man.

After dinner he found Alice and Essen sitting on his doorstep. Alice said she felt quite all right, and Essen complained that the stewed cloves was wasted effort at home, adding:

"Anyway, I'll try a brew on top of the next Lodge night."

Bony sat with them on the step.

"My mind has been reviewing Mr Cyril Martin. What do you think of him, Essen?"

"Don't care for him. Nothing definite, of course."

"What about his home life?"

"Good enough, I believe. The wife's a semi-invalid. She never goes out anywhere. He does enough of that for both."

"How does he stand financially, d'you know?"

"Couldn't say. Seems to be well heeled. Buys a new car every second year."

Bony musingly looked at Alice, and Alice tried to read his mind.

"How do you feel towards Mr Martin, Alice?"

"I know Martin's type. The older they get the sexier they get. And most of it is in their dirty minds."

"You think he's a nasty man?" disarmingly asked Bony, and Essen chuckled and drew to himself disapproval from Alice, who said:

"I'll tell you what, and I'm serious. The more I see of those people, which includes this Mr Martin, the more I remember what you said about Satan Worshippers and such like. There's something going on that I don't cotton to. Give me the straight-out metho drinkers and city crooks. They're clean beside this plonk-drinking lot."

"Now, now, Alice," Bony reproved. "Let us stick to Mr Cyril Martin."

"All right, we will," Alice swiftly agreed. "There's something at the back of my mind between it and him. I can't dig it out, but I will."

"Let me assist you," Bony pleaded, and went on: "Does he remind you of the man who wears a size eight shoe, and who walks something like a sailor?"

"Why . . ." Alice stared. "Why, that's it."

"He comes closer to the man we imagine killed Mrs Rockcliff than anyone we have met in Mitford," Bony said, dreamily. "But, Alice, I must earnestly warn you not to rush in where even Bony fears to tread. I understand, Essen, that Martin has two children, a boy and a girl."

"Correct. Son would be about twenty-six or seven, and the girl is a couple of years younger. The son used to be in partnership with the old man, but three years ago there was a hell of a bust-up and he cleared off to Melbourne. The sister went with him."

"The reason behind the bust-up?"

"Don't know that one. Could be the father and son are too much alike to get along together."

"Too much like physically or mentally?"

"Both. The son's the dead spit of the old man. I did hear he set up an estate business in Croydon."

"Might dig in behind this Mr Cyril Martin," Alice said hopefully.

"I have already done so, Alice. The day before Mrs Rockcliff leased No 5 Elgin Street, Mr Martin cashed a personal cheque for fifty pounds. That was on October 11th. On the same date every month thereafter he cashed a personal cheque for fifty pounds. That is, to January 11th. He didn't cash a cheque for that amount on February 11th . . . four days after Mrs Rockcliff was murdered. You will both recall that Mrs Rockcliff paid her bills on the 12th of every month."

"That sort of gives me ideas," Alice said, eyes very hard, lines between the brows very deep.

"I took both of you into my confidence, not to provide you with ideas but to ease your minds of the depressing thought that I slumber too much. Could you find me a bike for tonight, Essen?"

"One on hand in the shed out back," Essen replied.

"Too well known. Could you hire one?"

"Easy. Bike shop just down the street."

"Is the tracker still on duty?"

"Went back to the Settlement an hour ago, according to the Sergeant."

"Then hire a reliable bike and leave it here in this room." Essen stood and waited for the reason behind the bicycle hiring. He received a reason. "I'm going out visiting."

There was dismissal in Bony's voice, and Essen grinned at Alice and departed.

"Feeling better?" Bony asked, rolling a cigarette.

"Much, thank you. Ready for work, too."

"The work will come, Alice. I am going to begin tonight. Tomorrow you will begin to work, too. Meanwhile, I'd like you to run along to the Municipal Library and spend an hour or two of relaxation with the magazines in the Reading Room. There is the mystery of the theft of the aboriginal drawing to be cleared up, and then there is the matter of those ceilings being painted duck-egg blue."

"What on earth . . ."

"This afternoon, when discussing the cicatrice patterns of the Worgia Nation with Professor Marlo-Jones, I overheard a man say that the renovations carried out at the Library last November cost much more than the Council had voted. Another man said he thought the work had been well done and was worth the additional cost. The first man then argued that the work need not have taken so long, causing the Library to be closed to the public for an entire week. I would like to know if the Library was closed to the public on November 29th."

"Very well, I'll find out. November 29th! That was the day the Bulford baby was stolen."

"There is the coincidence." Bony smoothly admitted.

Alice walked to the door, her shoulders expressive of irritation. She returned to the desk, glared at Bony, who sat smiling up at her.

"Am I your cobber or am I just a cog in your machine?" she asked. "What's behind the Library ceilings and the Bulford baby? Oh, damn! I'm sorry, Bony."

She had reached the door again when he called her back.

"As you are not a cog in my machine, Alice, you must come under the other heading. We're doing splendidly, so let us concentrate on our respective jobs, that our joint efforts may achieve success."

She nodded, bit her lip, and burst out with:

"All right by me, Bony. But what are you going to do with those enormous shoes and the bike Essen is bringing here?"

"I'm going to stir up an ants' nest, Alice."

CHAPTER 18

PLAYING TRICKS

THE NIGHT was silent and dark. The wind had gone off on walkabout. The famed Southern Cross was as ever the Great Celestial Fraud created by persons cursed with uncontrolled imagination.

It is always sound practice that, if you are unable to command the thoughts of your enemy, you should provide him with material to think anything but the truth; as it is good policy to give your enemy as much worry as possible. Following Bony's visit to the Aboriginal Settlement, the inhabitants would surely be wondering what prompted it, and, when brought to the verge of desperation, those who had planted red-back spiders in his bed, and had stolen cigarette-ends and a button in order to 'sing' these items with their magic, could be expected to make further moves.

Although ten o'clock, the departed day still faintly illumined the western curve of the world. The road was just visible directly ahead of the front wheel of Bony's bike, but, when the end of the made road was reached, the track crossing the flats bordering the river was quite invisible even to him. Constantly he rode off the track, had to alight and find his way back to it, and so left on the dusty soil the imprints of the number nine shoes.

On coming to an old-man red gum growing close to the track, the bike rider was less than a hundred yards from the turn-off to the Settlement. He alighted and leaned the machine against the tree farthest from the track, and sat on a fallen limb to remove the number nines. The shoes he dropped beside the branch and proceeded to employ shaped pieces of wood and cellulose tape, separating his first and second toes from the third, and the third from the fourth and fifth toes.

On proceeding, he left clear imprints of something having three long-clawed toes to each foot.

In the morning sharp eyes would be dilated by tracks surely made by the dreaded Kurdaitcha without his feathered feet. Those prints would be followed back to the tree where the Kurdaitcha put on his great boots and mounted a bike to go back to Mitford. Agile minds would associate the Kurdaitcha with the half-caste police feller, and this police feller had come from far away. To the aborigine, no matter how close he might be to civilisation, the power of magic is assessed in accordance with the distance from which it has come. So if the half-caste police feller is a Kurdaitcha in disguise, then it warrants every aborigine to mind his p's and q's.

Eventually the Kurdaitcha arrived outside Mr Beamer's house, which, with the church and the store, guarded the Settlement.

Bony could see Mr Beamer relaxing on the fly-netted veranda. Within the house someone was playing a piano. Beyond it, the red glow of communal fires illuminated the fronts of the small huts occupied by the aborigines, about which men would be playing the white feller's mouthorgans, and the women gossiping. Only the dogs would be suspicious, but not till the owners slept would they become a disturbing influence.

With a stick Bony scratched in the dust a circle pierced by a shaft of lightning. Outside the store he drew a square, halved it, and in each half placed a triangle. Entering the carpenter's shop, aided by a masked torch, he used chalk to draw a matchstick man on a board leaning against the wall. In the blacksmith's shop he chalked a square on the anvil with a matchstick man fleeing from it. He examined the watch-mender's bench and the inside of a portable cabinet. One drawer was locked, but this he opened with forceps, finding within eleven watches, each neatly tagged with a number. On the top of the cabinet he left a sun making eyes at a prostrate black feller. In a box something like a schoolboy's pencil case he found several pieces of stout celluloid, seven inches long by one and a half inches wide.

Outside the school he drew on the ground six matchstick children, and passed along to the hospital. There were, he knew, three adult patients in this iron and weatherboard building, and that Marcus Clark occupied the partitioned end of a fly-netted veranda. Despite the hour there was a light in this alleged room, and to Bony's astonishment, again despite the hour, Marcus Clark had a visitor, a shrunken old man seated at the foot of the bed. His face was clear in the light cast by an oil lamp on the night table, the lamp being accompanied by a large silver-mounted pipe, a tobacco plug and knife, and a paper-backed novel. It was evident that Mr Bertrand Marcus Clark was above average. He was saying:

"I'm tellin' you I don't clam to all that rot. You can do nothin' to fix this foot of mine, or mend me arm."

The old-'un chuckled, dry and humorous.

"You wait, Clarky, old feller," he said, softly. "You just wait. The kids got what I wanted, and the young Fred will do what I tell him."

Marcus Clark reached for his pipe and proceeded to fill it, and the old man bit a chew from his plug. Although the skin of both was chocolate, they were farther apart than the planets. Chief Wilmot wore the cloak of inscrutable passivity woven by his forebears in procession down the ages, but Clark was naked and neurotic and the sport of a dozen races. He was worried, impatient, victimised by a little knowledge.

"I'm not sayin' young Fred ain't all there," he argued, speaking with the aloofness of the busy parents to the dull child. "But I'm sayin' again what I told Ellen, that mumblin' and moanin' and crying curses into something a man's touched won't give him the gutsache in five minutes. Pickin' a button off the floor what dropped from a man's pants, and snitchin' his cigarette bumpers and the like, and puttin' your curse into them things when yous points the bone at him, is good enough when you've got a month or more to work on him.

"It's time yous blacks woke up and took to modern ways what are faster. Like using them red-back spiders. That was a good idea, and I'll bet it wasn't yours. As I said at the corroboree last week, yous blacks have got to fight with white men's brains and white men's tools. You gotta learn that sitting around on your sterns all day won't ever get you anywhere. Any'ow, yous old blokes is hopeless. Give me the kids. There's hope in the kids."

"That police feller musta found them spiders," offered old Wilmot.

"He's still walkin' about, ain't he?"

Wilmot nodded, strangely cheerful, and Clark snorted

when understanding that all he had said in disparagement of pointing the bone had not registered.

"Young Fred in camp?" asked Clark.

"Came back early. Went up to Big Bend to have a try for that ole cod he reckons is hanging out there. Must be a big feller, that ole cod."

"He ain't muckin' around Sarah too much, is he?"

"No." The Chief chuckled. "Young Fred ain't liking it, though. Says it don't seem fair, them being married only a month, and he can't hang around. I tells him that's the orders, and he went off crook."

"Well, he's got to stay away from that camp," Clark insisted. "It won't last much longer, when we'll be in the clear and them two can romp around much as they like. Oh, hell, damn this busted leg. Time I meet up with them fellers what done it, I'll put 'em in hospital."

"Too right!" agreed the old man. "Damn crook all right. You know when you get outta here?"

"No. Doc Delph he says the more I muck about on the foot the longer I'll be here. Any'ow I'd be here a ruddy long time if you and the others 'sung' it good. And it would get better quicker if you come and see me more. You tell young Fred to come. I can get more outer him."

Bony left when a huge lubra wearing a white apron and a white linen hat suddenly appeared and berated the old man for staying so long, and on the ground in front of the veranda door he drew a particularly venomous drawing of Satan in a fit.

Reaching the tree where he had left the bike, he freed his toes and donned the number nines, and from there pushed the machine all the way to the made road, satisfied that on the following morning his antics would create much ado.

People were pouring from the two cinemas when he arrived in Mitford. Youths astride motor-bikes were ogling girls on the sidewalks, and other young men, with oiled hair gleaming, were escorting women to the milk bars. No one noted the seedy-looking character turn in at the Station, save Alice McGorr and Mrs Yoti, who were about to enter the police residence by the back door.

"Ah, now what have you two been doing this evening?"

"Enjoying our freedom," replied the Sergeant's wife. "We are about to make a pot of coffee and sandwiches for supper before Alice goes home. Would you call my husband and Mr Essen? I think he is in the office, too."

Bony did find Essen with the Sergeant, and on the desk between them a bottle of beer. When Bony clumped across the bare floor, Essen noted his shoes and stared blankly at his baggy trousers and limp black shirt.

"You been to a ball?" he asked succinctly. Bony slipped into a chair.

"I have been employing my artistic talents, Essen. Any news?"

"Nothing," replied Essen, placing a glass before Bony, who drank appreciatively, and from a trouser pocket produced a folded slip of paper.

"Look at this metal dust, and give an opinion," he said, and poured himself another drink.

Whilst the two men crouched forward over the paper, and the white light beat upon the metal dust mixed with other metal scraps, Bony rolled and lit a cigarette. He slipped from his tired feet the shoes belonging to the Sergeant's son, without need to untie the laces, and at last Essen said:

"Too light for gold and it isn't copper."

"Filings, seems to me," said Yoti.

"Filings, all right," agreed Essen, and to Bony: "You know the answer?"

"I have the thought that it's filings from keys made for snap-locks."

"That's it." Essén brought a bunch of keys from a pocket, selected one and laid it upon the filings. "I'll bet my job against a trey bit you're right."

"Your decisiveness pleases me," murmured Bony, and laid upon the desk what looked like . . . just what it was. "Perhaps you could be as decisive with that."

Yoti said quickly: "Plaster of Paris. Look! Part of a key impression on this surface. Yale-type key, too."

"I could not find other pieces to complete the impression," Bony said. "We might then have made a key and tried the lock of Mrs Rockcliff's house, or that on the bank door."

Essen sat back. Yoti eyed Bony, either with suspicion or hopefulness.

"Are you telling?" asked the Sergeant, and Bony presented him with a strip of celluloid. "You found that, same place as the plaster and the filings?"

"In a blacksmith's shop within a hundred miles of this office."

Bony smiled and was saved the bother of answering questions by Alice, who appeared to say that supper was ready, and would they please come, as people wanted to go to bed sometimes. Being domesticated men, they rose and followed her without protest.

Bony first went to the laundry, where he left the number nines and put on his own shoes, before entering the house, where supper was being served in the kitchen. Alice refrained from looking directly at him. No remark was made about the old tweed trousers or the black shirt, because they were Bony's props. Munching a sandwich, Alice was strongly reminded of her deceased father, who, when about to depart on a 'can' operation, invariably dressed as Bony now was . . . in dark clothes and with not a spot of white visible.

Later, when she was crossing the dark yard to enter Essen's car, he to take her to his home before making the rounds of his guard posts, she found Bony beside her.

"You went to the Library?" he asked softly.

"Of course. The librarian said that the whole place was closed to the public on November 26, 27, 28, 29 and 30, while the interior decoration was being done."

"So! You know, Alice, that's good team work."

WET SHOE-PRINTS

CHAPTER 19

EARLY THE following morning Bony returned the bicycle to the shop, and assured himself that no tracks of its tyres remained near the Police Station to be seen by Tracker Wilmot.

It then being too early for breafast, he sauntered down Main Street and took the side road to bring him to the river. Here the river bank was under cut grass maintained by the Parks Department, and the road fronting the residences of the élite ran straight and level and broad to meet the sun. It was going to be another hot day, but there were no signs of wind strong enough to make Mitford unpleasant. The wind came from the north and whispered to Bony the secrets of a million years, tales of tragedy and of love, and of those Beings who created a paradise for the black fellow to enjoy, and then forgot about it and him.

The glorious colours of that paradise faded as the waters dried up and the winds came to scorch and wither and to braise the living with hot and faceted grains of sand. Men were compelled to use their minds to survive, which they did by the rigid application of two practices: the one, birth control, the other, elimination of the unfit.

So there was sustenance for the chosen, and the chosen remained loyal to the Creators of the Paradise, handing down from generation to generation the telling of history by word, by the dance, and the pictures on the walls of caves. And until the coming of the white aliens there was laughter and law in the land.

The first white man to set foot in Australia brought with him the Serpent from the Garden of Eden, when no longer was there in all the land law and laughter . . . only the slow progress of segregation into compounds and Settlements of the ever dwindling remnants of a race.

There was the Aboriginal Settlement supported by Christian Church and controlled by their representative, the purpose of the Churches to make amends, although but a fraction, for the evil done by the Serpent; the ambition of their representative to give back to the aborigine his traditions and his self-respect. Could that ambition be realised by encouraging the old practices only so far as approved by white law and when the white influence had brought the black fellow to a condition of spiritual chaos?

Here and there on the broad and placid plane of the river the currents came to the surface to smile at Bony, slowly crinkling like the dimples on a baby's face, and the simile made him smile although his heart was heavy with foreboding of what he might exhume. Turning, he strolled back the way he had come, arriving at the Police Station to sniff the aroma of frying bacon and good strong coffee.

Yoti came in late, to receive a quiet rebuke from his wife. "Sorry," he said. "Been trouble at the Settlement, and I've been kept by the phone. You know anything about it, Bony?"

"I haven't been near a telephone for days, Sergeant."

"Good at skipping round logs, aren't you?"

"Better than falling over them. What has happened?"

"Padre Beamer rang up to report that a Kurdaitcha visited the Settlement last night. According to the blacks, this monster stands twenty feet high, has two huge eagle's feet, takes a fifty-yard stride, and draws noughts and crosses all over the place. I suppose it was from the blacksmith's shop out there you got those filings and plaster of Paris?"

"It could be. What else did Mr Beamer complain about?"

"Seems that the blacks reckon the Kurdaitcha lives here in Mitford. He rides a bike and cramps his feet into number nine shoes. He wants me to go out there and look at the evil signs drawn on the ground, and chalked on benches and wall-boards and anvils and things, beside those terrible footprints."

"Pleasant day for the trip, Sergeant. I'm sure Mrs Yoti would like to accompany you. She told me only yesterday that she seldom goes anywhere with you."

Yoti snorted something about being too damned busy to go tracking a fool Kurdaitcha.

"Might have to send Robins, and he's been on duty all night with Essen."

"Not possible. I want to borrow Robins's car for the afternoon. Anything on Mr Beamer's mind?"

"Yes, most of the blacks are packing to go on walkabout. Got the wind up. Even Marcus Clark is yelling to be off, roaring for someone to bring him crutches. What in hell did you do it for?"

"Merely to watch what would happen," Bony replied, chuckling. "And, of course, to create a diversion from my examination of the watch-mender's bench."

"Why that? You could have gone out there in daylight."

"One must be subtle when dealing with a subtle people." Bony pased his cup to be filled by Mrs Yoti, who was not pleased by her husband's attitude. "You see, Sergeant, when we investigate a murder we can go straight to the scene, trample all over the place, shout to all and sundry, bring all the inventions of science to bear on the clues. Nothing done or left undone can possibly affect the murdered. I came to Mitford to find what had happened to a number of infants and, until otherwise proved, I must hope to rescue those infants alive. Homicide methods applied to the abduction of those babies, I am confident, automatically destroy all reason to hope."

"And you think those blacks are in this baby-pinching racket?"

Yoti was almost glaring at Bony, and Mrs Yoti, standing by the stove, paused in the act of filling the coffee-pot.

"Yes. Possibly they are in this baby-pinching racket. It is also possible that you are in it, or Mrs Essen, or Dr Nott, or all of you. The vital objective is to find those babies."

"I must agree with you, Inspector Bonaparte," interjected Mrs Yoti, and, stoically, her husband proceeded with his breakfast.

"Mr Beamer can be placated, Sergeant," Bony said a moment later. "Tell him that if a white man drew those figures, the abos would certainly know it and would not fly into a panic. It would seem that one of their medicine men has been up to mischief. Ask him to let us know if Clark goes with them, and later on find out how many abos remain in camp and who they are. And I would like to know if the blacks all went away in one party, or split up into several parties, and which track, or tracks, they took."

"All right! That'll calm Beamer."

"Of course," murmured Bony. "There is no situation so difficult that it cannot be countered with diplomacy."

"Chicanery!"

"The meaning of both words is identical. I presume you are intimately acquainted with the surrounding country?"

"Ought to be."

"D'you know if, say, within twenty miles of Mitford there is an outstanding unusual geological feature, such as rocks balanced on rocks and usually called Devil's Marbles?"

"There are Devil's Marbles not far off the track to Ivanhoe, twelve miles out from the river. You can't miss them in daylight," replied Yoti thoughtfully. "There are several deep caves in the cliff face where the river once took a sharp bend. Take the track to Wentworth. People at Nooroo homestead will tell you where to go from there."

"H'm! Now let us switch from geology to arboriculture. Is there up- or down-river a particularly large or aged redgum?"

"No gum outstanding in those respects."

"Is there a tree or trees which seems to be an oddity out in the red soil country?"

"Yes, there is. About eleven miles from Mitford, the track

to Wayering Station dips down into a shallow depression about two miles across. Almost in the middle of it is a solitary red-gum. It's been burned by grass fire, struck by lightning, and still thrives."

"Sounds promising. Anything else come to mind?"

"No-o. But I'd like to know what's in your mind."

Bony pushed back his chair and rose. Taking both the Sergeant and Mrs Yoti into the range of his gaze, he said softly:

"Dreams."

He went out and they looked at each other silently, and silently Sergeant Yoti rose from the table and, without speaking, left for his office.

It was twenty minutes to ten o'clock when Bony entered the Library and studied the large-scale map of the district and surrounding country. Mentally he plotted the position of the Marbles, the solitary tree, the caves in the original bank of the river, and memorised routes and distances from Mitford. Thus engaged, he became conscious of the curator-librarian at his elbow.

"Good morning, Inspector. I looked into the records about that rock drawing and found that it was presented to the library . . . the original library it must have been . . . by a Mr Silas Roddy in the year 1888."

"It was good of you take the trouble."

"Not at all. Only too happy to be of service. I could find nothing in the records interpreting the meaning of the drawing. It is stated, though, that Mr Roddy brought the drawing back with him when he returned from prospecting pastoral leases in the far north of South Australia. It seems that he brought other aboriginal relics back, too, for the rock drawing is only an item of a list. There are stone and wood churingas, ancient dilly-bags, rain stones and a set of pointing bones."

"Are the rain stones and pointing bones still here?"

"Oh yes. Er . . . Have you any reason to hope the rock drawing will be found and returned to us?"

"Yes. I may hope to return it, or have it returned. Peculiar that no one seems to know what the drawing means. I was talking to Professor Marlo-Jones the other afternoon, and he said he had seen nothing like it elsewhere."

"Only that it might represent an ancestor dropping rain stones."

"Yes, he told me that was his opinion. He said, also, that the drawing would be of little value excepting perhaps to a rabid collector of aboriginal art. It wasn't even a good drawing—nothing like the one in the Adelaide Museum."

"It is of value to Mitford."

"Of course," Bony agreed. "I'm sure you may expect to see it again on the stand in the Reading Room. The books taken out by the late Mrs Rockcliff were returned?"

"Yes, and thank you, Inspector."

Bony departed and thoughtfully strolled up Main Street. The Council men had only now finished flushing the gutters from kerbside hydrants, and the sun was silvering the gutter pools and splashings on the pavement. Two sparrows were taking a bath in one pool, showering themselves with silver and gold, and a woman walked across a wet area of pavement leaving the imprints of her shoes to evaporate on the dry cement. And beside her shoe-marks were the prints of a man's shoes, size eight and worn along the outer edge under the toes.

There were two prints, one perfect, the other almost evaporated. There were other prints, many of them, and passers-by were adding to the number. There were the tracks of a dog. It was the one perfect human print and the one imperfect print which halted Bony.

So the murderer of Mrs Rockcliff was still in Mitford, had been walking ahead of him by perhaps less than a hundred yards.

Bony hurried, almost ran, seeking the next wet patch. The patch at the next hydrant extended merely a foot in from the kerbing, and gave nothing of the murderer's footprints. He passed Martin & Martin's Estate Offices, Madame Clare's Frock Shop, the Olympic Bank, but the next two hydrants had done nothing to assist him, and when he returned down Main Street, the sun had dried the cement.

Standing in black shadow, he looked at a display of books and saw only the jumbled colours of the jackets. He mopped his face with his handkerchief, seeing only the mental picture of that wet shoe-mark which tallied in every detail with those left on the linoleum at No 5 Elgin Street. A man taller than himself, who took a longer stride, who walked on his toes as though inebriated or just off a ship. Now it would be too early to be drunk, and the seafarer long since would have gained his land legs. A man who walked forward on the balls of his feet like one ever anxious to arrive.

He entered the Estate Offices of Martin & Martin. The clerk at the counter of the outer office was listening to a woman complaining of the front fence of her home. It was about to collapse on to the sidewalk, and it appeared that the landlord had promised to have it seen to months previously. She was a woman determined to have her say and the supercilious clerk wilted.

The door to the inner office was closed. From beyond it drifted the murmur of voices, proving that Mr Cyril Martin was there. He was taller than Bony, and he walked like a man ever anxious to arrive. He could have come in, five minutes back; he could have trodden on that wet patch of pavement.

Then the door opened, and a man said:

"Well, that's how it is and how it's going to be."

He came out, brown eyes angry, wearing his hat. He closed the door with unnecessary vigour and kicked the floor mat as he crossed to the outer doorway. He was taller than Bony. Bony followed him to the street, watched him walk down the street. Mr Cyril Martin could not deny this man was his son. Save for the lines of age on the father's face, they could have been twins.

His reason for calling must wait upon events. Bony sauntered to the Olympic Bank, and without delay met Mr Bulford, who stood behind his desk to greet him nervously and invite him to be seated.

"Phew! Hot morning," Bony said, and again wiped his face with silk.

"Must expect it at this time of year, Inspector."

The manager was alert, a trifle too alert. His voice betrayed tension, and his hands allied the voice. Bony replaced the handkerchief in his breast pocket, and from a side pocket brought out tobacco pouch and papers. With these in his hands, he looked at Mr Bulford, and then looked down at his fingers working at the cigarette. Mr Bulford was silent. He took a cigarette from the silver box and lit it.

"Your child was abducted on November 29th, Mr Bulford, was it not?"

"Yes, that was the date, Inspector."

"From November 26th to 30th the Municipal Library was closed to the public as renovations were being carried out."

In the parlour, silence. From without the faint clinking of money and the muted sound of voices. Bony drew at his cigarette, slowly exhaled, looked through the smoke at the man seated behind the desk. Mr Bulford stubbed his half-consumed cigarette, and dropped his hands below the edge of the desk.

"I forgot that the Library was closed that day."

Bony waited. Mr Bulford waited. Neither spoke until Bony leaned forward and pressed the end of his cigarette into the ash-tray.

"One, Mr Bulford. You were working here when the child was stolen. Two, Mr Bulford. You left shortly after your wife and met Mrs Rockcliff in the Library. Three . . . Could you let me have number three statement of what you did between four-thirty and five-thirty on the afternoon of November 29th?"

"Yes, I could, Inspector," Mr Bulford said softly. The window light illuminated the beads of moisture on his forehead. "My first statement is the correct one."

Slowly Bony shook his head.

"I am afraid that won't do, Mr Bulford."

"No, I suppose not."

"You might like to give me the truth."

"Perhaps you know the truth, Inspector."

"No." Again silence, that inner silence made the more poignantly complete by the sounds without. "Only the other day I was mentally comparing the American Third Degree methods of interrogation, and those said to be practised by the Hungarian authorities, with our Australian methods of conducting an investigation. While our Australian methods tend to prolong the investigation, I concluded that they provide an irresistible challenge. So that when I am asked to investigate a crime, Mr Bulford, detection becomes an icy slide with truth inevitably at the bottom. Why delay? Would you dally in the act of taking castor oil?"

Bony stood to smooth down his impeccable tussore silk jacket. He looked down at Mr Bulford, brows raised just a fraction. The manager brought his hands into view and gazed at them as though seeking help. Bony waited. Presently Mr Bulford looked up and slowly shook his head.

Bony's shoulders expressed the shrug of resignation, before he turned and walked out.

CHAPTER 20

A TRIP FOR ALICE

WITH BONY beside her driving the racy sports car, Alice McGorr silently vowed that if this was one of the methods by which Detective-Inspector Napoleon Bonaparte tracked down criminals, then the ways she knew were no more. The car was red, low-slung, long-bonneted, a two-seater. The canvas hood was down and the sun was hot and the wind whipped round the shield like puffs of hot air from an oven and yet astonishingly invigorating. She was reminded of Sweet Seventeen out with the boy friend, and she wanted to let her hair stream in the wind behind her.

Once away from the green belt, and up and over the lip of the river flats, the world became even brighter and remarkably clean and stereoscopically clear. Alice did actually look upward for the passing cloud, to see the sky unblemished in blue-washed perfection. With unexpected abruptness she was introduced to a strange world.

The road was merely a track languidly avoiding acacia clumps and box tree groves, running straight over the flats covered with blue bush, and for ever being teased by the dancing horizon.

Contented sheep lay in the shade cast by old-man saltbush, and rabbits dived into their holes among the foot-high herbage. Far away she saw toy-sized horses beneath box trees, and mottled cattle grazed on a brown grass field. Kangaroos stilled, to gaze curiously at her, and three emus daintily trod a minuet on a bar of red sand.

The hot sun was forgiven. The flies were left far behind or clung to the rear of the machine like small boys having a 'whip behind'. And this Alice McGorr, reared in a semi-slum and associated with crime and vice in a close-packed city, felt she was being swiftly carried to some place beyond the mirage of life, a home-place from which she had been absent for centuries.

Several crows raced the car, low-down and cawing derisively like urchins ya-hooing Sweet Seventeen and her escort. Alice wanted to laugh at them, felt like ya-hooing in return, resisted the thought because she was so utterly content. It was unbelievable that she was Policewoman Alice McGorr, and absolutely impossible that her escort was an inspector of the Criminal Investigation Branch of the Queensland Police Department. Jet-black cockatoos with scarlet under-wings shrieked at this unreal reality, and a flock of rose-breasted grey galahs supported them.

Into the lullaby of the engine and the singing of rubber on sand drifted the voice of her companion, and during the fraction of time before she glanced at him she was conscious of mental effort to break the spell.

"Did you ascertain the date of the new moon?" Bony asked.

She moved her gaze from the slender dark hands about the wheel to rest upon his face in profile, and it seemed that time halted while she looked at the firm chin, the straight nose, the high forehead and the straight black hair which even the wind failed to disturb.

"It's due today," she answered.

"Today! Someone once said of the moon: 'The maiden moon in her mantle of blue.' And I think it was Shakespeare who wrote: 'The moon, like a silver bow new bent in heaven.' Do the thoughts build anything for you?"

"Not clearly," she replied, hesitantly. "I'm not educated like you."

"A mythical problem, Alice. The quotations came to mind to support a theory. Like a silver bow new bent in heaven . . . a maiden moon in her mantle of blue . . . a maiden and a bow . . . Cupid's bow."

After a half minute of silence, Alice said:

"I don't get it."

"I did think the dates those babies were stolen might have been chosen to coincide with a phase of the moon."

"Moon madness or moonshine," Alice said, teasingly.

"I sought the possible significance," Bony said reprovingly. "Just why the new moon is of importance, if at all, to the abductors I have yet to learn. The new moon comes today. We shall see it just after sunset."

On a white splodge of mullock hiding the surface of a dam appeared four emus that stupidly must race the car and dart across the track, heads low, tail feathers sweeping up and down, clawed feet at the extremity of long shanks throwing up miniature dust clouds.

Shortly after the ground colours had painted out these birds which never flew but could run at forty miles an hour, Bony stopped the car to scan the world ahead with binoculars.

"Something like two miles out are what is commonly called Devil's Marbles," he said. "Far to the north-west a dust cloud denotes sheep travelling to a watering place. There are no smokes, nothing to indicate the presence of aborigines, so Padre Beamer was right when he said his blacks went east up-river on their walkabout."

Soon the Devil's Marbles appeared on the image of the landscape like a figure on developing film. Then it seemed that under pressure of vast volcanic forces they jumped over the edge of the world. Alice wondered why Bony drove past these great brown boulders, a Stonehenge here as strange as that on the downs of England.

Bony braked the car to a halt, again stood and examined the scenery.

"We must walk," he said. "Half a mile, that's all. You may remain in the car, if you wish. I could drive to those Marbles, but the wheel tracks would be noted when the new moon wears her mantle of blue."

"I'm being left out far too much," Alice protested, and almost hastily alighted. Then she wondered why he didn't walk direct to the heaped boulders, why he angled this way and that to walk on a chain of cement-hard claypans, and once when she looked back at the car it was easy to believe they were space travellers exploring another planet.

Of brown granite huge smooth rocks supported others upon their shoulders, some with seeming eternal security, others with knife-edge balance which, Alice thought, possibly she could upset. She was asked to stay put, and Bony walked round the little mountain, noting one place where a camp fire had burned.

The journey back to the car seemed to take longer, and still Alice failed to understand why Bony deviated from the direct line to follow the hard claypans. She was glad to arrive, to welcome the cooling breeze from the moving car as Bony drove on for a further mile before turning back toward Mitford.

Half an hour later the car was stopped, and Alice couldn't remember having seen previously the windmill and iron tanks. She strove to recall the gate which Bony alighted to open, drove through and closed. She was sure they hadn't gone through a gateway before, or passed a windmill, and just where they were she hadn't the remotest knowledge.

"I suppose you wouldn't like to tell me why we're touring about out here?" she asked, when Bony stopped before another closed gate and she was feeling the apprehension of the lost.

"Your patience, Alice, hasn't gone unnoticed," he told her when they were once more on the move. "Our business here is to prospect a theoretical lode which could show paying results; prospecting which must be done before the effects of stirring up the Settlement are further made manifest. It is all a matter of distances, angles, and compass points and what not."

"Now everything is made clear to me," Alice jibed. "Do you know where we are?"

"Yes. Ahead of us is a well called Murphy's Triumph. Far to your left is the Murray and Mitford. If we continued in the present direction for a month we would arrive at Perth, in Western Australia."

"What would we do if the car broke down?"

"Walk fifteen miles to Mitford . . . walk south."

"I'm glad we brought Mrs Yoti's flask of tea and something to eat," Alice said, adding: "I hope the car doesn't break down."

She only just saved herself from giggling, and then was furious at the thought which had captured her mind.

"We'll have our tea in the shade of a tree to which I want to present you," Bony said, and Alice was thankful he hadn't guessed what was in her mind. "We should be there in twenty minutes. As the tree was something more than a sapling when Dampier first saw the coast of Australia, it is now the Aged King of Trees. Therefore, you must be presented to it."

The world continued to roll towards them, parading its endlessly different faces, and then there seemed to be an end of the world and nothing but sky beyond, and the end came swiftly, to mock them by revealing yet another face . . . a vast flat depression covered with a russet carpet.

The car dipped downward to tread the carpet, in the centre

of which was one small shrub. The carpet was woven with dried herbage upon a base of broken clay chips, and the shrub was a blot, a flaw. The blot grew under fairy magic, became a tree, and the tree grew and grew like Jack's beanstalk to tower over the carpet, over the world. When abreast of the tree and some four hundred yards from it, Bony stopped the car, and Alice wanted to say to the tree:

"How silly to grow there all by yourself. You must be lonely, and you don't look at all friendly."

They drank Mrs Yoti's tea and ate her salad sandwiches before beginning the walk to the tree. Alice was thinking she should have rested in the car when this image of eternity tore from her mind all lassitude. The girth of the trunk awed her. The grey and brown mottled bark was smooth and yet wrinkled like the skin of a pumpkin, and from high the old bark hung in long streamers to rustle and sing softly in the wind. Four great boughs sprang from the bole to support lesser branches draped with bark shed by the eucalypt instead of its leaves.

At the base of the trunk was a cavern, black walls of charcoal telling of savage attacks by grass fires, and the cavern was floored with wind-blown sand, rose pink and faintly rippled. Alice was invited to enter the trunk-cavern with Bony, and found ample room for a dozen people to shelter from the rain.

"A proper monarch," she said, and Bony nodded agreement and stepped out after her. With him she circled the tree, but she did not follow when he climbed it to disappear among the branches. The wind rustled the bark streamers, and abruptly she felt herself dwindling into the emptiness of space materialised.

She didn't see Bony descend on the far side of the trunk, didn't hear him until he called to her, and she found him smoothing the sand within the cavern, first with his hands and then by flicking his handkerchief. For the second time she verged on giggling, and again she was furious, this time made so by the thought that he was smoothing the sand so that Essen would never know they had been in there.

When nearing the southern hem of the depression, she looked back, seeing the tree as an aged giant not to be defied, a living monument erected when the world was young, and as they passed up the slope to gain the rose-red plain, she was sorry for it in its immense and terrible solitude.

The sun was dipping into an opaque haze above the horizon

and three minutes later, when she looked again, its gold was tarnished. Sand dunes were crimson on the floor of grey saltbush, shadows beneath old-man saltbush were now purpling, and the shadows of the passing trees were purple splashes, too. The wind dried easily, gladly, and the sky beyond Bony was as bluely grey as oily smoke.

"Wind tomorrow," predicted Bony.

Alice smiled, restful and content. A 'roo raced the car, small and brown with a white apron, a tiny patch of brown on the apron, and when the brown patch moved she saw the head of the baby outside the mother's pouch. The 'roo swung away, and wherever its bounding feet touched the earth there arose scarlet puff-balls.

"Like a silver bow new bent in heaven," quoted Bony, and Alice looked again at the sun, saw a slim crescent above it and said happily:

"The maiden moon in her mantle of . . . of rubies."

The sun went down as they dipped into the green belt about Mitford, and abruptly the world darkened and all the glory of the uplands was only a picture in imperfect memory. Alice roused herself, sitting upright, bracing herself to return to the mundane world and keenly regretful that this day was ending.

"It's been wonderful," she told Bony. "I never dreamed the real Australia could be so lovely." A flock of galahs wheeled above them, softly conversing, and the last rays of the sun were filtered to paint them with rainbow colours.

The dust of a car in front hung like smoke on a frosty evening, and thus they returned to Mitford. It was darkening fast as Bony swung into Main Street. It was time to switch on the lights when he turned to enter the Police Station yard.

Essen came from the Station office by the back door, reached Bony's side as the engine was cut. He said, as though giving evidence:

"At about four-twenty-five this afternoon, sir, Mr Bulford committed suicide in the manager's office at the Olympic Bank."

CHAPTER 21

FRANTIC ANTS

Bony sat at the Sergeant's desk, hands resting on blue papers, tapping fingers betraying his mood. With him were Alice McGorr and Essen.

"Everyone satisfied it was suicide?" he asked, when they were wondering why the silence.

"The bank was closed for the day, and the teller and the accounts officer were working late. Within three seconds of the shot they were in Bulford's office. He was sprawled over his desk, the office revolver between his right hand and his head. He had cleared his desk of all papers as though knowing they would be ruined by his blood. The rear door of the bank chamber was ajar; the side door was locked." Essen paused, to add with emphasis: "Suicide all right."

The long dark-skinned fingers continued their slow tapping on the blue documents, and presently Alice said impatiently:

"Did you expect it, Bony?"

She was examined by blue eyes unusually blue, steady, cold, inscrutable. Memory of him that afternoon created regret for having spoken and she was glad that the fingers ceased their tapping to become busy with a cigarette.

"Yes, I did think suicide might be the road Mr Bulford would choose," he admitted. "There was another road open to him which could have led him to the foot of the rainbow. We discussed that road. You see, Alice, Mr Bulford was unfortunately weak, but he had three shining attributes: honesty, loyalty and veneration. I am risking contradiction by events, yet believe my assessment is correct. Essen, where is Yoti?"

"Still at the bank when I left twenty minutes ago."

"Contact him. Ask him to ascertain from the bank staff if either of the Cyril Martins interviewed Bulford today."

"Either! But the young feller . . ."

"Is in Mitford."

Essen stared, frowned, withdrew to the telephone on the wall of the outer office. Bony lit his cigarette, and Alice forgave his inattention to her. She heard Essen speaking, wanted to ask questions and instead obtained a cigarette from her handbag. When Essen returned, he was still frowning.

"The Sergeant says that young Cyril Martin interviewed Bulford shortly after two this afternoon."

"H'm! I could be wrong in my assessment," reflected Bony. "I don't think so. I want to know when young Cyril Martin came to Mitford, and especially if he was in Mitford about the time Mrs Rockcliff was murdered. He must not be aware of the enquiry, and that is of extreme importance."

"I'll get going right away."

"Wait. Have dinner first. Both of you go along now. And do please keep in mind that our baby investigation continues to take priority. Return after dinner. I've work for you both."

He accompanied them to the outer office, and on looking back from the main doorway Alice saw him at the telephone.

Bony heard Essen's car leave the yard before hearing the voice of Mr Beamer.

"Ah, Mr Beamer! Inspector Bonaparte! Have your people returned from walkabout?"

"Oh no, not yet, Inspector. They won't come back for several days at least."

"Sudden, wasn't it? The Sergeant said something about them being afraid of a Kurdaitcha, or something equally silly."

"Yes. I don't believe it, of course. As Sergeant Yoti suggested later, it must have been one of themselves out for a joke. Making all those drawings on the ground and what not."

"Seems obvious, Padre. The Chief didn't go on walkabout?"

"No. Neither did his son, Fred, and half a dozen others. The hospital lubras wanted to clear out, but Chief Wilmot ordered them to remain as there are several patients as well as Marcus Clark. Now my wife has to keep them pacified, too."

"When did they go on walkabout last time?" Bony asked.

"Oh, let me think. Not long ago. About a month."

"And the time before that, d'you remember?"

Mr Beamer chuckled.

"I do. We were all set ready to be visited by the Premier, and they all cleared out the day before, that is, all except about a dozen. The Premier had to inspect an almost deserted Settlement."

"You must find life amusing as well as crowded, Mr Beamer.

Anyway, Mrs Beamer and you will be able to take it easy for a while."

"I wish we could, Inspector," ruefully replied the Superintendent. "There's no chance of that; we're always behind with our work. Er . . . it's dreadful news about Mr Bulford."

"Yes, it is. I've only just heard about it."

"He must have been frightfully grieved about the baby. We liked him so much, my wife and I. We bank at the Olympic, you see, and came to know him really well."

"I rather liked him, too," Bony said. "He must have broken under the strain. Well . . . Thanks a lot, Mr Beamer. I'll run out again to see you some time."

"Yes, do."

Bony rang off, and paused before the duty constable, who stood.

"When did you come on?"

"Four, sir."

"D'you keep a record of inward calls?"

"Yes, sir."

Bony checked the sheet pinned to a board and bearing that day's date. The Olympic Bank had called at 4.29 pm. Yoti at 4.41. Dr Nott at 4.44. The next call was made by Dr Nott at 5.14."

"Do you know why Dr Nott rang twice?" Bony asked the constable, who was able to provide an item not without interest.

"Yes, sir. The first time Dr Nott rang to say he couldn't possibly leave a case at the hospital, and to call Dr Delph. I rang Dr Delph's house and someone there told me the doctor was out. So I rang the hospital and asked them to tell Dr Nott that we couldn't contact Dr Delph. I was getting anxious, knowing the Sergeant was at the bank and what for, when Dr Nott rang again saying he would be leaving the hospital within five minutes."

Bony renewed examination of the day sheet, found nothing more to keep him. He had but stepped from the side door when the telephone shrilled and he paused, waiting, expecting news from Yoti. The constable spoke:

"Police Station. I couldn't say, marm. Who is speaking? Oh! yes, something like that, I think. I don't know. Sergeant Yoti is attending to the matter, and he's not here at the moment. Yes, all right!"

Bony went back, raised his brows in question, and the constable reported:

"Mrs Marlo-Jones, sir. Wanted to know if it was true about Mr Bulford. As the Press has already been informed, I didn't blank her out."

"Quite right, Constable. By the way, did anyone else ring asking what had happened to the bank manager?"

"A Mrs Coutts did, and so did Mr Oats from the Library. I told them the same as Mrs Marlo-Jones, and nothing more. Can't keep anything like that dark too long in a place like Mitford."

"No, it would get around," agreed Bony.

Mrs Yoti and Bony had almost finished dinner when Yoti appeared. He looked at Bony as though displeased, and Bony discussed the river flats. Afterwards, when they were smoking and Mrs Yoti was clearing away, the Sergeant asked:

"What do you know?"

"That Bulford committed suicide with the bank's revolver."

"You saw him this morning, they tell me."

"Yes, I did call on him."

"Oh!" Yoti glared. "You won't talk, eh?"

"No. I want to listen."

"Well, he shot himself through the mouth." Sergeant Yoti sighed. "A bloody policeman isn't supposed to have any feelings, but when I looked at him sprawled over his desk I thought what a terrible waste of life. I've played bowls with him, and I've met him at Lodge, and I won't believe he did himself in over pinching the bank's money. There can't be anything like that."

"Has it been suggested?"

"No. The teller took charge, and the bank inspector's due to arrive from Albury. Do you know why he committed suicide?"

"I've a half-cocked kind of idea," countered Bony, and the phrasing did not escape the Sergeant, who said:

"Funny how life treats some people. You know, me and the wife never had any trouble, always got along well. Looking back, we sort of changed for the best as the years went by, but there's a lot of people who begin to change for the worse immediately they're tied. You met Mrs Bulford, of course?"

"Yes. Alice McGorr says she is the type of woman who get themselves 'Crippenised'."

Yoti grinned, the grin became a genuine chuckle of laughter.

141

"Good one, that," he said. "That lass is about right regarding the wife. Bulford was meek as milk, but liable to blow up. Poor old Bulford! If only he'd had guts enough to knock her down once a week."

"You appear to dislike Mrs Bulford."

"Nothing new about that. Now she's blaming you for hounding her husband over the disappearance of their baby, for getting him alone and defenceless in his office. The long worry over the baby, plus you, drove him to suicide. What about giving a little? It's my turn to listen."

"Very well, I'll give you what I know," assented Bony. "In his first statement to me, which was identical with that given to the previous investigator, Bulford said he remained working in his office after his wife left until half past five. Subsequently he stated he had not remained at work after his wife left, but had gone to the Library to talk to Mrs Rockcliff. This morning, I informed him that on the day his baby was abducted the Library was closed to the public while renovations were being carried out. I asked him for the truth, and he declined to give it. When I left him, he knew I would discover the truth; in fact, it could be that he was convinced I knew all the truth concerning the abduction of his child."

"So that's it," Yoti slowly exclaimed. "And do you know the truth?"

"I may be right in my guess. Now, how did the trouble with the doctors turn out?"

"It seems that the teller of the bank rang for Dr Delph after he rang me and, being understandably upset, he merely asked for Delph to be sent to the bank at once. When Delph didn't turn up, I rang Dr Nott, and the house said he was at the hospital. I told Mrs Nott why we wanted her husband, in a hurry, and she said she'd get him. Then Nott rang the man on duty, saying he was on a serious case which he couldn't leave, and the duty man rang Delph and was told Delph was out. Meanwhile, Nott finished up at the hospital but did not want to leave his patient if he could help it, and he rang Delph. The cook at Delph's house told him the doctor couldn't answer the call because Mrs Delph had been taken ill.

"Mrs Delph suddenly ill! H'm! She seemed to be well enough at Alice's plonk party."

"Drinks like a fish," growled Yoti. "Haw! Ought to be

'Crippenised'. Good one, that. How did you know about the doctors?"

"Your telephone record. I'd make it a must at every Police Station. Think you could enlist your Postmaster friend to aid us again?"

"Why not? What's the use of friends if you can't use 'em?"

"I'd like a list of all the calls made by Mrs Bulford after four this afternoon, all the calls made by the Delphs after four this afternoon, and all the calls made by and to the Aboriginal Settlement. Up to, say, midnight tonight. Think he would do that?"

"Do it for me, anyway. Now, why the interest in young Martin?"

"I'm keeping that angle to myself." Yoti watched the eyes harden, and the chin firm. "You must travel with me, Yoti, and I have to tread with the spring, and silence of a stalking cat. As I have already said, the babies must take priority over the murder of Mrs Rockcliff. I've put Essen on to the Martin angle, and Martin mustn't know our thoughts. The same attitude applies to the stolen drawing, itself of much less importance. I know why it was stolen, and until the investigation into the abductions is concluded I am not interested in who stole it or where it is. When did the Premier come to Mitford?"

"Eh? Oh, the Premier ..."

"January 3rd, Inspector," interjected Mrs Yoti. "And if you wouldn't mind, I'd like to remove the tablecloth."

"Mind? Of course not. As your husband is so argumentative, make him do the washing-up." Bony smiled, and withdrew before the glare in the Sergeant's eyes.

He found Alice and Essen in his room, the former wearing a dark-brown dress and a small black beret with a large red bobble perched to one side. The ensemble disagreed somewhere or other. Was it the brown and red or the bobble on the black? ... Bony gave up.

"All ready for the job of earning our wages," he remarked cheerfully. "You haven't got a line on young Martin already, Essen?"

"Only that he came in his own car, which is garaged at a Service Station. A pal of mine is manager of the garage, and he's going to nose around this evening without mentioning me."

"Good! Now for another job. I want a boat, light and shallow draught. I want it at eleven tonight. Can do?"

"Yes. Know just the thing."

"There's an old jetty a hundred yards up-river from the bridge. Have the boat there at eleven."

"On the dot," agreed Essen.

"How far up the Settlement Creek does the river back water?"

"Don't know that one. Could find out from the town butcher who runs stock on the far side of it."

"Obtain the information . . . with your usual caution."

Essen left, and Bony regarded Alice, and Alice knew she had not previously met this particular Bony.

"Mr Bulford committed suicide, Alice. And Mrs Delph becomes suddenly ill. As soon as it's dark, pay the cook a visit and find out just what the illness is, and if possible the cause. Let me know by phone. Then skip along to the Olympic Bank and keep an eye on Mrs Bulford. Clear?"

"Quite. You stirred up the ants' nest, didn't you?"

"You're guessing, Alice."

"P'haps."

"Well, stop it. See you tomorrow. I must talk to Yoti."

He left her mutinous but high on the peak of action. He passed Essen at the telephone and sank into the chair beside Yoti. Yoti put down the pen with which he was writing a report on the Bulford suicide, and Essen came to state that the water in Settlement Creek lay as far back as the lantana swamp. Bony asked him to draw a rough map, and the sketch showed the lantana swamp due north of Mr Beamer's house at the entrance to the Settlement.

"I was hoping that was so," Bony said, distinctly gratified. "In the morning, Essen, I want you, accompanied by two constables, to proceed to the Aboriginal Settlement, leaving here exactly at nine o'clock. On reaching the Settlement, I want you to tell Beamer that you have information concerning Marcus Clark's trespass in Mitford which necessitates interrogating every aborigine remaining at the Settlement. I want every aborigine called to the hospital ward where Clark is a patient and there kept for at least an hour. Cross-question them on the imaginary information, and permit not one to leave Clark's ward during that hour. There will be, so Beamer told me, not more than a dozen to be rounded up, and I want them out of the way for an hour only. Clear?"

"Yep. That'll be done," answered Essen. "With two men, I'll leave town at exactly nine. Meanwhile . . ."

"Your patrols on duty?"

"Yes."

"Good! Now I have to make my own preparations. I'll see you again, Sergeant, before I leave."

Bony vanished beyond the doorway, and Essen looked at his superior with the ghost of a smile widening still further his wide mouth.

"Busy little man . . . sometimes, isn't he?" he remarked to the wogs flying about the light.

"Reminds me of a Chinese I knew and sometimes played draughts with," Yoti said seriously. "Ah Chung let me win a man off him, then perhaps two more, and then another, and I'd think I had him well sewn up. And he would sort of hesitate and say: 'I gibbit chance'. He'd move a man to make me move, and then he'd clean the board. And do it every time."

"Yair! This half-caste seems something like your Chow," Essen drawled. "Plays his leads, then stirs up a mob of abos, and we get what? Nearly all the abos clear out, and a bank manager shoots himself. And now he's going off on a boat trip, and tomorrow I'm to bale up the remaining abos on fake information. I'd better go after that boat."

Yoti nodded, and returned to his endless writing.

At eight o'clock the duty constable reported, was told to lock up and go home. At eight-twenty Alice McGorr rang up and spoke to Sergeant Yoti. At nine-fifteen the Postmaster came in with two bottles of beer and to talk for fifteen minutes. At nine-forty Bony reappeared.

He was dressed in black. There wasn't a speck of white about him. He wore a pair of old black canvas shoes, and about his neck were slung a roughly made pair of sheepskin over-shoes with the wool on the outside.

"Fancy dress ball this time?" mocked Yoti.

"Something of the kind. Anything further?"

"Yes. Your Alice McGorr rang to say that Mrs Delph has had a nervous breakdown."

"Indeed!" purred Bony. "She gave me the impression she was heading for it."

"From information received," continued Yoti grimly, "it

is alleged that Dr Delph communicated with a Dr Nonning in Melbourne, saying his wife was seriously ill, and asking him to come to Mitford at once, to assist him with his practice."

"Promising, Sergeant," Bony almost lisped. "Nonning is Mrs Delph's brother, the well-known psychiatrist."

"Any good to you?"

"It gives. Dr Nonning is also a collector of aboriginal relics. I wonder if he would be interested in that missing drawing?"

CHAPTER 22

THE SECRET CAMP

SAVE FOR the talking ripple at the bow, the boat and its crew made no sound. The 'maiden moon' had vanished and her starry lovers were lustreless.

The flow of the stream was negligible, and the only discomfort was created by mosquitoes. Facing to the bow, Bony pushed at the oars for three hours before he saw on the skyline of the north bank the tree marking the turn-off to the Settlement. Ten minutes later he was resting under the bridge carrying the main track over Settlement Creek.

By the stars it was then two o'clock . . . when all good aborigines should be fast asleep, sheltered and safe from the dreaded Kurdaitcha.

Under the bridge it was completely dark and, in this creek, no currents. The boat rested motionless, and Bony made a cigarette, lit it when hands and head were enfolded by a bag, and thereafter kept it cupped by his hands. Here the surfacing fish were almost lethargic, when those in the river had exhibited élan in their chase after smaller fry. The bull-frogs 'clonk-clonked' like bells minus tonal strength, and the invisible night birds committed their murders with unemotional efficiency.

There was no need for haste, and Bony, having finished his cigarette, greased the hole in the square stern of the craft to take a rowlock, and greased the rowlock before laying an oar in it. From now on he would propel the boat by the oar astern, and steer without error.

The bridge passed, and the trees almost met over the narrow waterway. The sculling oar and its rowlock made no sound, and it seemed to be the trees passing the boat, not the boat in motion. The lovesick stars were no lamps upon the dark waterway, and the trees slept unattended by wind. There was plenty of time to reach the far end of the waterway and hide the boat before dawn, when Bony hoped to be high in an ancient gum within fifty yards of the blacksmith's shop and about that distance from Mr Beamer's house.

Presently the trees halted in their procession to make way for clumps of lantana growing along the edge of the now shallow water. A few minutes after having entered this lantana section, Bony smelled smoke. Camp-fire smoke at three in the morning! Smoke when all camp fires would be out or damped down for the night! The air movement was from the Settlement to Bony, but such was the strength of the aroma its origin could not be a fire banked with ash ready to be broken open for breakfast cooking in the Settlement.

Bony ceased sculling, and the boat continued to 'drift' through the still water, and then abruptly the aroma was cut off and the rancid smell of mud returned. Gently the stern oar brought the boat round, and slowly it was propelled back over its course until again it was centred in the ribbon of invisible smoke, so sweetly aromatic.

Doubtless it was the weight of a cold twig which broke through the white ash covering the burning heart of the fire, because in the wall of black velvet suddenly appeared a flaming ruby to become an angry eye staring at the man in the boat. And for five long minutes Bony stared back at the angry red eye. It was then that the embers beneath the eye subsided when for a brief three seconds there lived a tiny flickering blue flame.

It wasn't an old tree stump smouldering away for days. It was a camp fire, and just beyond it was a rough humpy constructed with tree branches. That much the tiny flames revealed before retiring to permit the red eye to continue its angry watch.

Bony sculled silently down the creek till coming opposite a large lantana clump partly growing in the water. Here he went ashore, pulling the boat into the cane-mass, and then as silently boring through the mass to dry land. On stepping forth from the lantana he was wearing the sheep-skin over-shoes which would leave no imprints on these hard river flats.

147

He stalked that camp fire without making sound enough to disturb a finch, seeing its red eye where he expected to see it, and finally squatted behind a clump of low cane-grass situated within a few yards of it.

Save less than a dozen, all the aborigines had gone on walkabout. Those who had remained would be sleeping in huts, not here beside this stagnant backwater. There was no normal reason for this lonely humpy, indicated by the fire as being inhabited, excepting perhaps that an aborigine had brought here his newly-wedded bride. In view of the prowling Kurdaitcha not even the most obedient bride could be expected to honeymoon in such solitude.

The false dawn came, followed by darkness more intense, and a little cold wind to make Bony shiver. A fox barked as though at the squatting man, and seconds later barked again from far away. It was when that second bark had been blanketed by night, and Bony saw the first shaft of soft light high in the sky, that the baby cried.

There reached him the low murmur of gentle soothing; the baby quietened. The dawn shafts were spearing the night when the child cried again, this time demandingly. A woman said sleepily:

"Was'matter, little feller?"

The voice was the voice of an aborigine. The baby yelled, old enough to know how to claim attention, and, a moment after, the red eye vanished. The baby continued to cry, and soon there appeared a faint glow which grew swiftly bright to reveal the aboriginal woman tending her fire.

The blazing fire proved the humpy to be a tent almost made invisible by green tree branches. Bony could not see the mouth of the tent. The woman stood and the firelight showed her to be tall and graceful. She was wearing male attire, a suit of flannelette pyjamas, and her black hair was banded with a blue ribbon. Bony remembered her. She had been with old Wilmot when he visited the Settlement with Alice. She left the fire for the humpy, soothed the infant who wouldn't be soothed, and came out carrying a feeding-bottle, a tin of powdered milk, and an old billycan. The billy she filled at the creek and placed over the fire.

The infant, understanding that screaming failed to bring instant doting attention, stopped as abruptly as it had begun. Like all the mothers of her race, this woman loved babies and was versed in the exquisite art of being cruel to be kind. The baby was hungry and so food must be prepared for it, but to worry about the screaming would be the height of folly because the cry lacked that poignant note of pain. Calmly this woman watched the water heating, and only when it was boiling did she go to the tent and bring out a jug in which to mix the milk.

She brought cold water from the creek to cool the milk before pouring from the jug to the bottle, her movements unhurried, her face expressive of abiding content. Taking the bottle to the tent, she spoke to the baby and the baby started a yell which was stopped by the bottle teat. Thereafter the soft voice lullabyed.

Bony could remain no longer, for now the water of the creek was visible and the kookaburras were greeting the New Day with their ironical laughter. The boat was safe enough from chance discovery, and silently he walked up the creek and so to the red gum near the blacksmith's shop.

The tree was bent by the years and scarred by innumerable climbing boys. They had made a path upward by the only way, and Bony climbed this path to reach a rough platform at the junction of two branches with the trunk, the work also of the Settlement children.

Like the woman at the fire, his movements were deliberate as he made himself comfortable on the roughly-woven sticks. He smoked two cigarettes, and now and then he smiled at little mental images and refused to permit ugly thoughts to disturb his mind.

Having pocketed the two cigarette-ends, he told his mind to sleep till nine o'clock. His mind slept. His mind awoke at nine o'clock when the sun was high and the ants already were up the tree gathering its sweet exudations.

A bull-ant objected to his presence, and he flicked it into space with a snapping forefinger. The maurauding red ants took no notice of him, and he politely ignored them. He climbed, and at the higher elevation commanded a clear range of the Settlement.

Three magpies were warbling on the office roof, and the smoke from the Superintendent's chimney was almost the colour of washing blue. Then a lubra in a white dress and white shoes emerged from the hospital to take something to the incinerator, and Dr Beamer appeared from his veranda to cross to the office. After him trotted a grossly fat fox terrier, who quickly gave up the idea of escort duty for the pleasure of rolling his left ear on the ground to remove stick-fast fleas.

At twenty past nine Bony saw the dust rising behind the car bringing Essen and his constables, and five minutes later the noise of the car propelled Mr Beamer from his office and his wife to the door of the house veranda. A conference was held, and ended by Mrs Beamer and one constable walking to the hospital and Mr Beamer with Essen and the other constable making for the lines of huts.

All quite normal. The Superintendent would know who of his people had not gone on walkabout, and what huts they occupied. Several figures rose from beside a communal fire, and others appeared from the huts, totalling nine. Finally, all gathered into a small party and walked from the huts to the hospital, Bony recognising old Chief Wilmot, his son Fred, the watch-mender, and he who ran the store. There was an ancient crone and two young women.

Questions. Did the Beamers know of that woman and baby living in the tent shrouded by green boughs? Did old Chief Wilmot know? Almost certainly, for nothing and no one would escape his notice. Bony gazed over the lesser tree-tops to the area of dark-green lantana, and failed to see the faintest wisp of smoke from that camp fire.

The policeman and Mrs Beamer entered the hospital, and Essen and Mr Beamer with the aborigines filed in, leaving one constable on guard at the door. Bony waited five minutes for the woman with the baby to appear, watched for the slightest betraying movement and saw nothing. Then he went to ground, the entire Settlement his for examination . . . for one hour.

The constable at the hospital door saw him cross behind the blacksmith's shop to the lines of huts, noted the extra-ordinary footwear, and with great interest watched him as long as possible.

The ground was dry, flaky, hard beneath the flakes. Only from point to point was the ground powdered by feet; about the Superintendent's house, where all traffic stopped, about the school and the hospital, was the ground churned to dust. Paths made by naked feet skirted the lines of huts, because off the paths waited the three-cornered jacks having needle-pointed spurs.

Bony's first objective was the communal fire, still alive, and the huts closest to it. They were single-roomed shacks, containing a table and hard-bottom chairs, and mattresses of straw lying on the floor.

Utility blankets lay on one of two mattresses in the first hut he visited. A military greatcoat and a couple of cotton singlets served for a pillow. Hanging from nails driven into the walls was a military felt hat with the brim unclipped to the crown, an expensive stockwhip, a pair of goose-neck spurs in which the rowels had been replaced with sixpences to produce the louder ringing, and a gaudy silk scarf denoting feminine ownership.

The scarf was the only feminine item in this hut. There was a litter of comics, a pair of tan shoes, a bridle and a .22 rifle in a corner.

Bony pondered on the two mattresses, so close together; only one in use. Taking great care not to displace the blankets, he looked under each mattress and found nothing. Whereupon he translated what he saw. The things hanging upon the wall, especially the hat and the spurs, said this was Tracker Wilmot's hut. The unused mattress beside the used one, told of an absent wife. Recollection of Marcus Clark's reference to a lubra named Sarah, the month-old bride, now added that to this, which totalled a graceful young lubra in the secret camp among the lantana.

In the next hut he found evidence of occupation by Tracker Fred's father. Here again were two mattresses, both being used, and placed as far apart as possible. The place was clean enough, due to Mr Beamer's regular inspections, but the litter was an offence. Under one mattress Bony found a set of pointing bones and a skin bag containing many precious churinga stones and a set of rain stones as large as the hand and as green as polished jade.

The fact that these sacred articles were hidden under the Chief's mattress and not in a sacred store-house, such as under a rock or in a tree, indicated that Chief Wilmot was unsure of the degree of his rejuvenated authority over his people, and that he was aware many of them were so 'ruined' by white civilisation that they would steal these tribal relics and sell them for a few plugs of tobacco.

The hut occupied by the watch-mender and the store bookkeeper gave nothing, as did those other huts into which he flitted.

As he anticipated, he found a path running direct from the huts to the secret camp in the lantanas, and so crossing an open space of two hundred yards. Convinced that the lubra with the baby would lie quiet within the tent, he followed the path and so came to another junctioning with it. This path came from the direction of the office. On this path he found imprints of the shoes worn by the woman who had crept under Mrs Rockcliff's bed.

The wearer had visited the secret camp, and she had returned by the same path. He followed the returning prints, followed them till they passed by the office and continued to the Superintendent's house. The woman who had been under Mrs Rockcliff's bed had emerged from and entered Mr Beamer's house by the back door.

CHAPTER 23

REPORTS

WITH AN oar thrust astern, Bony propelled the boat with a minimum of exertion, satisfied with the assistance of the current and aware that for a further fifteen minutes the Settlement aborigines would be boxed inside the hospital. To defeat the glare, his eyes were reduced to mere slits, and now and then the upper lip lifted as it had done when he had cut the prints of that woman who had crept into No 5 Elgin Street.

The woman had worn the same shoes when in the Aboriginal Settlement the day before this glaring golden day. She had departed via the back door of the Superintendent's house to visit the secret camp, and had returned to the house and entered it by the back door. For Bony that was proof incontestable.

There were sound reasons for not following those tracks into the Superintendent's house to find the shoes, a minor reason being that either Beamer or his wife might become bored with being in the hospital with Essen and the others and return to the house. Essen could keep the aborigines for an hour, but had no power over the Beamers, who naturally would protest at Bony's trespass without a search warrant.

The major reason for ordering Satan again to his rear was given by the study of Mrs Beamer's shoe-prints made when she walked with the constable to the hospital. Her shoe size tallied. She was wearing wedge-type shoes. The prints, however, proved to Bony that she was accustomed to wearing low heels, while the woman who entered the house in Elgin Street was accustomed to wearing high-heeled shoes. While not positive, for human memory cannot be a thousand-per-cent infallible, Bony was satisfied that it wasn't Mrs Beamer who had visited the secret camp.

He permitted the boat to drift and smoked another cigarette. The one pair of shoes worn by the one woman linked Mrs Rockcliff's murder and her abducted child with this Aboriginal Settlement, and this link strengthened the supposition that the baby in the secret camp was a white child.

There was nothing to support opposing argument. There could be no other intelligent explanation for that small tent masked by tree boughs, a mere hundred yards from twenty-eight weatherproof and comfortable huts. And no lubra could have her baby secretly, and in secret keep it.

It could be accepted as certain that Chief Wilmot and his men knew all about that lubra and the baby. There were two further certainties. The reason for the baby being kept in that secret camp was a community secret, and a community secret is something which cannot be levered from the aborigines by any method of interrogation accepted by western civilisation.

He moored the boat at the old jetty, and by a devious route arrived at the rear af the Police Station and entered the yard via the back fence. Unobserved, and with the sheep-skin over-shoes under an arm, he entered his office-bedroom to find Essen and Alice McGorr playing poker.

Essen said, faintly smiling:

"You look as if you've been sleeping with the dog."

Alice said:

"Have you had any breakfast?"

"Not yet, Alice." Bony swept his black hair back from his forehead, sat at his desk and began the inevitable cigarette. "Would you try . . ."

"I'll fetch coffee and something to eat from the kitchen," she told him, her face severe. "Enough to go on with so's not to spoil your lunch. And don't go telling Essen anything till I get back."

"Not a thing, Alice. I'll tell him nothing at all." After she had gone, he said to Essen: "Now you tell me everything."

"I followed your instructions, all but," Essen began. "Arrived on time and left on time. Had no difficulty with the Beamers: in fact, they helped. Beamer came with me and a constable to the huts and we rounded up all the blacks left on the scene. You told me to keep 'em off the grass for an hour and I added ten minutes extra because shortly after I began on 'em I felt something under the surface I couldn't understand.

"You know how it is with abos. You can lead 'em but never drive. I put Marcus Clark into a blue sweat, and against the full-bloods he's a weakling. Couldn't shift him an inch from his first yarn of having met a cobber down-river and getting drunk with him. I cooked up a couple of yarns hinting we knew he was buying booze and having beanos with other blacks outside the Settlement at night, and that altogether he was a nasty bit of work to have around. No go.

"Old Wilmot just sat still and kept his face shut. Fred, his son, looked anywhere but at me. The others wiggled their toes and looked frightened. And the Beamers looked at me as if I was murdering the innocents. That's all, on the surface, but under the surface was something. It was like charging a man with theft when he expects to be charged with homicide. They weren't concerned with what I was asking them, but by what I might have in mind to ask them later on."

"That was your reaction to the attitude of Chief Wilmot and his son and Clark? Not to the attitude of any of the others?"

"Not to any of the other men, but it was to the lubras, even to the two acting nurses."

"Did you probe into the walkabout?" Bony asked.

"Mentioned it in the beginning. The mob went up-river to Big Cod Bend all right."

"How far from the Settlement?"

"A good nine miles. How did you get along?"

Bony smiled.

"Remember the order to tell you nothing until the breakfast is served?"

"Yes, I remember," Essen chuckled. "What a girl! Ten

154

thousand women in one, and to date I've only seen about six of them: mother, man-handler, sleuth, home-manager, infant-welfare expert, and dictator."

"The order doesn't prevent you informing me on the movements of Mr Cyril Martin, Junior."

"That's so. Young Martin's been in town two days, arriving late the day before yesterday. The last time he was here he stayed with a pal who owns a vineyard about two miles down-river. That was from January 26th or 27th to February 10th. He was in Mitford on February 1st and 10th, because on those days he booked petrol at the Service Station."

"Where is he staying now?"

"With his parents," Essen replied. "Must have patched it up with the old man."

"The patching could have fallen apart, Essen. I heard them in heated argument at the father's office." Bony paused, to add:

"Even that must wait."

They were discussing Tracker Wilmot's spurs when Alice returned with a tray, which she set before Bony and at once poured his coffee. She returned Bony's smile before sitting beside Essen on the far side of the desk and examining her chief with critical eyes.

"What have you to report, Alice?" he asked, sipping coffee and holding a sandwich in the other hand.

"I went to the Delph house and called on my bosom friend the cook. They seem to treat her pretty well, and as she had cleaned up for the day she'd gone to her room. Her room is at the back of the house, where there's a small cottage for the domestic staff, but she's the only domestic. There's a house telephone in her room.

"Anyway, we settled for a half bottle of gin and a few bottles of dry, and I got the news of the day. Everything went as usual until half past three in the afternoon, when the doctor came in and Mrs Delph rang for afternoon tea. The cook took it to the lounge, where there was a hot argument going on between the doctor and his wife over the usual; the usual, according to the cook, being the monthly plonk bill.

"The cook had cleared away the tea things and was preparing the vegetables for dinner when the telephone in the hall rang and Mrs Delph answered it. Mrs Delph called loudly to her husband, who came from somewhere. She said something the cook couldn't hear, and then let out a screech like a reefered galah. The doctor shouted, and then spoke a bit softer into the phone. A moment after that he shouted for the cook.

"When the cook reached the hall, the doctor was bending over Mrs Delph, who was lying on her back on the floor and yelling over and over the one word 'No'. The doctor told the cook to try to pacify her, and he rushed away to his surgery and came back with a hypodermic and gave his wife a shot. It put her out in under the minute, and they carried her to her bedroom and the cook undressed her and put her to bed. Afterwards, Dr Delph told the cook they had received a bad shock, that someone at the bank had rung to say Mr Bulford had killed himself.

"Later, when the cook was setting the table for dinner, she heard the doctor phoning a telegram to the Post Office. It was to Dr Nonning, Mrs Delph's brother down in Melbourne, telling him she had had a nervous breakdown and asking him to come up at once and help. After that nothing happened. When she had cleaned up, she asked Dr Delph if she could do anything for Mrs Delph, and he said he would nurse her and she could go off for the night.

"I left most of the gin with Cookie and found a phone-booth and reported to Sergeant Yoti as you ordered. From there I went to the Olympic Bank. There were three cars outside. There were lights in the rooms over the bank, and the light outside the private door was on. So I got into the vacant place next-door and took a stand against the fence opposite the private door and waited to see who came out.

"I had been there less than twenty minutes when Dr Delph drove up and came along the lane to ring the door-bell. It was Professor Marlo-Jones who let him in, not Mrs Bulford, and as neither said a word, I thought they'd done a spot of telephoning and Dr Delph had come to give Mrs Bulford a shot, too.

"Anyway, I spent two hours fighting the mosquitoes, when the door opened and the visitors came out. With them was Mrs Bulford, so she couldn't have had a shot, and by the look of her she didn't need one.

"There was Professor Marlo-Jones and his wife, Dr Delph, that Mrs Coutts and her husband, the Town Engineer, and another man and woman I didn't know by name. They were at the plonk party. After they'd gone I waited around, and when all the upstairs lights were out I reckoned Mrs Bulford had gone to bed, and I went off to get a couple of cups of coffee and a meat pie before going back to the Delph's place.

"In the hall there was a light on, and lights were on in one of the front rooms and one at the side. I had seen a seat just inside the front gate and I sat there and again squashed my blood from mosquitoes. Nothing happened all night, and the lights remained on. It was near dawn when the car came, and then I happened to be out in the street walking up and down to keep the circulation going. This car was a big one, and it drove straight through the gateway as though the driver knew the place well.

"Even before the car stopped at the front entrance, Dr Delph came out. He said to the driver:

" 'Hullo, Jim. Made good time.'

" 'Yes, I let her go and the road's empty at night,' said the driver. 'Could only bring one nurse at such short notice. How's the patient?'

" 'Keep her quiet, Jim,' said Dr Delph, and Jim opened the door of the car and helped two women out. One of them was introduced as Miss Watson, but the other was known to Delph, who called her Dicky. The women went inside, Dicky apparently knowing her way round, and as the men were unloading the luggage Jim said: 'Brought Dicky along to run the house for a bit. Miss Watson's a good nurse, and discreet. She can be trusted.'

" 'If you say so,' Delph said. 'Good of Dicky to come. What about those other people? The sooner this last business is cleared up the better.'

" 'That's what I thought,' said Jim. 'I told them to come at eleven tonight, and gave the husband the usual instructions.'

"And that was all they said for me to hear," concluded Alice.

"Usual instructions?" pressed Bony.

"Yes," replied Alice. "As it was getting too light for me to stay any longer, I went home for a couple of hours' shut-eye. Driver Jim is Dr James Nonning."

"And Dicky?" Bony asked, faintly mocking.

"Must be Nonning's wife."

"How come you to think that?"

"Both the doctors were polite to Miss Watson the nurse.

157

They didn't bother about Dicky, so she must have been Nonning's wife."

"Sound deduction, Alice, and ninety-per-cent correct. But remember there are a few husbands like me. Now off you go, both of you. Go back to bed and rest, because we'll all be on the job tonight."

"I'll be ready. I'm sure I could sleep for eight hours and Mr Essen must be really unconscious." Alice rose and Essen looked at her suspiciously. At the door Alice paused to enquire, expectantly:

"Did you do any good last night?"

"Oh, yes," airily replied Bony. "I found another Moses in the bulrushes."

"What . . . You found . . ." Alice's face lost its official woodenness, became swiftly eager. "Not a . . . a . . ."

"The admissions you drag from me, Alice! Nothing more. Now be off and let me change. Report at eight tonight."

CHAPTER 24

WHITE TRAIL OR BLACK?

SHAVED, SHOWERED and dressed, Bony sat at his desk and read his inward mail delivered by plane that morning. The first opened was in his wife's handwriting, and most of what she wrote dealt with the hypothetical case of a woman who bore a child long after she had given up the idea. There was nothing of the jargon of psychology, but profound knowledge of feminine complexes expressed in simple and therefore powerful phrases. Bony's old friend, the Chief of the Victoria CIB, enclosed a note when forwarding a Research Report concerning people named Nonning and Martin; and there was an official communication from Superintendent Canno which, in civil service confines, is called a 'Please explain'.

The explanation required concerned the entire lack of progress reports.

When Sergeant Yoti looked in from the open door, Bony was sitting upright in the chair, his hands relaxed upon the opened mail, and his eyes closed. At first he thought Bony to be overcome by fatigue occasioned by being at work all night, and then changed the thought for another on studying Bony's attitude.

He went in and Bony opened his eyes.

"Good day, Sergeant?"

"H'm! Thought you were asleep. Doing a spot of thinking?"

"Yes, I was teasing a problem." Yoti sat down and began loading his pipe. "What does one do when situated precisely midway between two impulses, equally compelling?"

"Poor old Bulford knew the answer to that one," replied Yoti. "And he's being buried tomorrow."

"Inquest over?"

"An hour ago."

"Who was there beside the officials?"

"Mrs Bulford, the teller and the ledger-keeper and the bank inspector. The Press, of course, nine city reporters as well as the locals."

"None of the Bulford friends?"

"No. Excepting Dr Nott, Mrs Marlo-Jones and Mrs Coutts."

"Clear verdict, I suppose?"

"Yes. Unsound mind. Probably caused by loss of the baby. The bank inspector found everything in scrupulous order."

"Poor fellow."

Pensively, Bony stared at the opened mail, and Yoti smoked abstractedly, until under pressure of silence he said:

"I did come to call you to lunch."

"Then we must obey. But first, did your tracker report for duty this morning?"

"Haven't seen him about, but then I've been at Court most of the morning."

"Make sure whether he came or not, and I'll entertain your wife."

At lunch, Yoti said that Fred Wilmot was not on the job, and then referred to Bony's problem. Mrs Yoti glanced at her husband, and he frowned warningly, for Bony was again pensive, an unusual mood at table, and they talked of other matters of no consequence until Bony said:

"Because I cannot be at two places at once I am feeling distinctly thwarted. Faced with the twin trails of White and Black, and free to choose, I would choose the White. However, being sentimental, and because I cannot call on anyone of equality with me in bushcraft and knowledge of the aborigines, I have to choose the Black."

"Enlightening, isn't he?" Yoti put to his wife.

"Could you let me have a bottle of strong coffee without milk or sugar, and sandwiches for two meals, Mrs Yoti?"

"Of course. And cake?"

"No cake. Too hot for sugar. But do you happen to have an empty sugar sack I could use as a tucker bag?"

"Yes, I think so."

"I'll call at the kitchen door for the coffee and sandwiches in the bag at ten to three. Thank you, Mrs Yoti. Now, Sergeant. Could you take me for a ride of some four miles, starting at three this afternoon?"

Yoti was exceedingly busy but could not resist plunging a finger into this pie.

"You will find me waiting in your car at three o'clock. Both of you I thank for co-operation. Now I must write instructions."

Bony having left them, the woman looked at her husband. The Sergeant said:

"Worrying like hell."

"But not about himself," argued Mrs Yoti.

"How d'you know that?"

"Because I do."

"Damnation! Ask a woman why and all she says is 'because'. Lemme get back to my office."

Yoti relented, affectionately kissed his wife's ear and departed. At work, constantly he watched the clock on the wall, and when it was three he stumped out to the public office and told the duty constable he would be away perhaps for an hour, or maybe a week.

The yard and the driveway between Station and residence pulsated with heat. There was no one about. Crossing to the garage, he opened the doors and went in. He saw no one in the car. He climbed in behind the wheel, started the engine, was backing the car out to the yard, when a voice said:

"Take the Ivanhoe track."

Yoti waggled his rear mirror, and still could see no one. Leaning back over the seat, he then saw Bony crouched on the floor.

"Hiding from the goblins?" he asked.

"I wish to leave town unnoticed. Tell me when we're clear."

Yoti drove down the almost deserted Main Street, turned right to the boulevard, travelled to its ornamental extremity and finally angled north between the drowsing orchards and vineyards. Where the track rose to the red soil plains which had so entranced Alice, Bony was given the 'all clear' and he clambered over to sit beside the Sergeant.

"I'm leaving in the dash-box these three envelopes," he said, with something of urgency in his pleasing voice. "Those addressed to Alice McGorr and Essen contain specific instructions. The third envelope is addressed to you and marked not to be opened until six o'clock tomorrow evening, and then only if I should not claim it before that time. Clear?"

"Perfectly."

"If I should meet the misfortune between now and six tomorrow, my investigation of the Rockcliff murder would be lost to the Department, and so I have outlined the work done and this should be ample for you to proceed against the woman's murderer."

"Are you telling me that the name of the murderer is in that envelope?" Yoti asked.

"Yes, although the evidence is not yet conclusive. I must again emphasise that the arrest of the murderer is of less importance than the solution of these baby abductions."

"I shan't forget that. The killer and the kids are the Black and White trails you spoke of, I take it?"

"No. The White indicates one place and the Black another, and obviously I cannot attend both places at the one time. Therefore, because the safety of a baby must take priority, I have no choice."

"You located one of those babies?" Yoti shouted.

"I have reason to hope so."

"Haw! And there's me and old Canno thinking you been up the same street as all those other CID nitwits. What have I got to do tonight? Sit and chew me fingernails?"

"Yes. You may have your turn tomorrow . . . after six o'clock. I'll leave you in the middle of this clump of she-oaks ahead. Don't stop. Slow down enough for me to jump out, then drive on for another mile before turning back. Anyone seeing you turn will concentrate on the car, not on these she-oaks . . . and me."

Bony slipped on the sheepskin overshoes and tied them to his ankles. Taking up the sugar bag containing his meagre rations, he opened the door, and as the car rolled between the she-oaks, he jumped to the ground. Yoti drove on for another mile, where he turned on a hard claypan. By then Bony was under an old-man saltbush half a mile from the she-oaks, and before the car dwindled to a black dot-head of a long shaft of rising dust, he was high in a tree and employing powerful binoculars.

At the end of five minutes, he was sure that, other than Yoti in his car, nothing moved on that landscape. Animals, both wild and domesticated, would be hugging the shade and waiting for the sun to go down before leaving to graze or make for the man-made water supplies. Man's actions could be different. Other circumstances could drive a man into the searing sunlight as he was then being driven.

But nothing betrayed movement, animal or human, and Bony went to ground and arranged his tucker bag across his shoulders like a rucksack, slung his glasses like a punter, patted the automatic in its holster under his arm-pit. He was approximately two miles north of the Settlement.

There was plenty of cover ... patches of saltbush, clumps of trees, dry watercourses. Canny white scouts can put up a good show ... against other white scouts. When opposed to aborigines, however, there is no show. The Australian bush north of the Murray looks to be splendid scouting country to anyone not conversant with its trickery. You think you are walking uphill when the ground is table-flat. You see a shallow creek, and the water does run uphill. You'd bet on it, and lose. You think a sand-dune is ten miles away and it isn't even one mile distant. You know that a tree clump is only a couple of hundred yards to the left and you would walk an hour before gaining its shade. And should you think you can escape the aborigines hunting for you, just think again. The mirage you can see spreads over the horizon like vast inland seas; the mirage you cannot see makes a giant gum of a blue-bush, and a patch of red pig-weed a hundred-foot-high sand-dune. You'd never see the wild aborigines deep in the mirage because they know how to make a mirage cover them.

From trees, from dune summits, from behind old-man salt-bush, Bony looked for dust spurts, for smoke spirals, and he maintained watch on the eagles and the crows, and his ears reported the moods of cockatoos and galahs.

Finally, heated to the point of exhaustion, wet with perspiration, and slightly groggy on legs unaccustomed to such prolonged exertion, he lay behind a lantana bush and peered between its thin cord-like stems to see water, and beyond the water the green branches masking the small tent. The lubra was preparing food for the baby.

Being thus assured that the baby was still at this secret camp, Bony retreated to a tree growing on high ground, and he hadn't to go far up into that tree before gaining a position from which he commanded all approaches to the camp.

On his perch high above the ground, he sipped the tepid coffee and ate sparingly of Mrs Yoti's sandwiches. A rabbit couldn't enter that camp without being noted, and as the Ruler of this World reluctantly moved down the western arc of the sky, his nerves were tautened by the waiting upon events, and his mind became increasingly anxious by the shadow of doubt cast upon that old reliable—Intuition.

A rabbit ventured from its burrow to run swiftly to the creek and drink, and this seemed to be a call to the birds. The blue wrens and the lovebirds poured into the sky, and the eagles dropped lower to earth. The galahs and cockatoos appeared in flocks to take their evening drink. And from behind the nearest tree to the camp stepped Tracker Fred Wilmot.

He must have called, for the lubra came from the tent and joined him at the lazy fire. Bony could see their white teeth when they laughed and joked, and when Fred poked the lubra in the ribs and she playfully slapped his face. That they were lovers was plain enough; that they were newly weds was proven by the ready acceptance of the woman's orders.

Fred filled a billycan from the creek and placed it on the fire. He accompanied the lubra to the tent, where she handed to him a tin bath and a blanket and supervised the spreading of the blanket and the placing of the bath. He was then ordered to bring water from the creek for the bath, and add warm water from the billycan over the fire.

The lubra carried a bundle and knelt on the blanket, and the man stood near, watching the woman unfolding the bundle. She looked up at him and laughed, and then from the wrappings she lifted the naked child.

A burnished shaft of sunlight fell upon the group. The chocolate skin of the man and the woman gleamed in that golden shaft, and, between them, the white skin of the tiny infant.

163

CHAPTER 25

THE SOWER

Through the binoculars Bony observed the lubra bathing and dressing the infant in garments taken from the suit-case and wrapping about it a large white shawl. The man sat on his heels watching the operation and sometimes laughing at the lubra, and, when all was done, the bath was returned to the tent and they sat with the baby between them.

Bony could see the flash of their teeth when they teased and laughed, and his own eyes shone like sapphires. He was feeling elation stronger than satisfaction engendered by prog-nostications proved to be correct, for now the curtain was about to rise on a drama first created in the womb of Time, and the child was prepared and waiting to play its part.

The shadows had further lengthened by twenty minutes when from the trees masking the creek to Bony's left appeared a buckboard drawn by two horses and driven by white-haired Chief Wilmot. The elderly aborigine appeared to be in no haste, and of this the horses seemed to be aware, as the turn-out leisurely continued along Bony's side of the creek until stopped opposite the secret camp.

Tracker Fred Wilmot took up the suitcase and the blanket and led the way across the shallow water, the lubra following with the child. He held the baby whilst she climbed to the body of the vehicle and settled herself with her back to the high driving seat. She reclaimed the baby, and the suitcase and the blanket were stowed on what looked like firewood.

All these preparations for a journey were accomplished without the excitement normal to aborigines. There was no shouting, no flurry, proving that the purpose of the journey was not associated with an ordinary walkabout. Further, wily old Wilmot had left the Settlement via the river road bridge, then followed the course of the creek where the creek trees were between himself and the Reverend Mr Beamer. Hence no shouting at the horses, and no shouting when near the secret camp.

Fred Wilmot having joined his father on the driving seat,

the Chief urged the horses into action with his whip, and they were heading towards Bony's tree. That tree was a shield for Bony as he raced away across open country to gain cover in a clump of needlewoods, there to wait for the buckboard to appear and confirm the driver's course. Thus from cover to cover he kept ahead of the travellers, who, he was convinced, had one of but two destinations in mind, and he was gratified that the speed of this 'Flight Into Egypt' was only slightly higher than that of the original exodus.

Going ahead of the travellers gave him all the advantages. The general direction being north-westerly, the men on the driving seat of the buckboard were facing the westering sun, where the sharp-eyed lubra sitting with her back to the driving seat would encounter no such hindrance to her watch for possible pursuit.

When a mile from the creek, the driver became less cautious, shouting when laying his whip to the horses, and doing both from habit rather than to increase progress, and this the animals understood, for their spasmodic trotting quickly relapsed to an indolent walk. Thus Bony on foot was not extended, his only concern on leaving each successive cover was being sure no one waited ahead of him.

Eventually he crossed the track to Ivanhoe not far from the she-oaks where Yoti had dropped him, proceeding then to the cover of an old-man saltbush. If the aborigines on reaching that track drove towards Ivanhoe, their destination would be those Devil's Marbles recently visited by Alice McGorr and himself. Should they continue across the track, then their journey's end would be the Ancient Tree dead centre of the wide depression.

The Wilmots were not interested in the Ivanhoe Track.

Now assured, Bony sped westward, in an hour coming to the rim of what in the long ago had been a large lake, roughly circular and two miles across. For a minute he scanned the entire rim, and for another made certain that no one was camped under or in the vicinity of the Tree. Between it and the rim there wasn't cover enough for a cow to hide her calf. When the Wilmots reached the rim, Bony was concealed in the Tree and so watched the vehicle advancing across the depression, the dust from wheels and hooves rising to float above it like a veil of spun gold.

The sun was setting when Chief Wilmot shouted at the

horses to stop, when they would have stopped anyway at the merest pressure on the reins. They parked a hundred yards south of the Tree, the men jumping to the ground, stretching bodies and kicking dust with their boots as though they had been on their way for twenty-four hours.

Action normal. No unusual excitement. No hint of urgency. Obviously plenty of time in hand.

The lubra handed the baby down to her husband of one month. She passed to Chief Wilmot a large tucker box, a four-gallon tin of water, the suitcase, the blanket, and finally tossed off the load of firewood. On gaining ground, she demanded the baby and young Wilmot laughingly refused, turning his back to her and telling her to make a fire. She pleaded but failed, and in good humour gathered brushwood and started the camp fire.

Meanwhile, Chief Wilmot drove on for a further fifty yards, where he unharnessed the horses and freed them in hobbles to find sustenance on the herbal rubbish.

There were thus several abnormalities, for Bony all establishing the importance of the great tree in which he lay hidden. It was unusual for the camp fire to be lit so far from the tree which offered companionable shelter. It was unusual to park the vehicle so far from the fire. And the manner in which the baby was fussed over by both the lubra and her husband would have been abnormal even had the baby been their own.

The heated Earth took the Sun. The wind dropped to a faintly cooling southerly, and the smoke of the fire was barely visible. Silence came to the aborigines, and over them and Bony flowed music made by the bells suspended from the necks of the horses.

Young Wilmot crossed to the buckboard and returned with a filled sugar bag, the contents obviously not sugar. And Chief Wilmot removed his shirt and boots, revealing the cicatrices on chest and back, cut with flint and kept open to heal with mud, done to him at his initiation.

The years had neither bent his back nor drained his strength, and the shirt was a tragic disguise, the uniform of a tragic civilisation. Head up, shoulders squared, he came to the Tree, his eyes unmasked, clear beneath the beetling brows lined white. Bony beheld the veneration for the Tree on the calm face as Chief Wilmot paused to regard a living monument to which he was linked in defiance of Time and Death.

166

To the Tree Chief Wilmot revealed himself as never in his life had he done to a white man, and rarely to one of his own race.

Unlike his son, and his son's generation, Chief Wilmot had known the days when the aborigine possessed the remnant of tribal independence. He could recall when, as a small naked boy, he had watched his father and elders fight with spears and waddies the warriors of invading tribes, forced by drought from their rightful country. He could remember his father being speared to death in one such battle.

His father had died like a man; he had lived on to be robbed of his birthright by the white man, and shackled by the white man's laws and taboos. His own son and his son's generation felt not the shackles, cared little for the lost birthright, and even less for the tales of history handed down by generation to generation for five thousand years.

This lonely representative of a race remarkable for its morality, its justice, its freedom from greed was now gazing upon the repository of the faith and the beliefs of the generations who had sunk into the graveyards of Time. It was not just another tree, an oddity because of its age. It was The Tree smitten by a Devil that had jumped from a cloud, burned by another Devil who had come running across the world to gouge a cave in its belly, and yet preserved by Altjerra to go on living for ever and ever. Altjerra himself had once slept at the foot of the Tree. For centuries The Tree had been the Sacred Storehouse of the people living in this country. It was here that famed Orinana had come to meet her lover of a forbidden totem, here that her brothers had caught her and slain both her and her lover.

As Bony expected, Chief Wilmot espied the tracks left by Alice and himself, and instantly became alert and shouted in his own tongue, so long in disuse that his son failed to understand and shouted in reply:

"What's up?"

The old man's urgency, however, brought Tracker Wilmot at the run, and together they examined the tracks, agreeing on when they were made, that a white man and a white woman had come from the road to the tree and had returned. They were wrong, of course, in one detail. Bony had walked like a white man, angling his feet at twenty-five minutes to five, and he had been careful to leave no evidence of having climbed the tree.

"Came here yesterday?" Chief Wilmot said.

"Yair," agreed the son, who now had springs in his feet. "White people all right. Could be old man Jenks from Wayering Station. He brought a white woman here to see the tree. I better look-see, though. Be dark soon."

The Police Tracker faultlessly followed the tracks to the distant road where Bony had stopped the borrowed car. Watching, Bony could see by his actions that he was satisfied.

The Chief returned to the camp fire and stood with his back to the blaze as Man has always done. Dusk was sweeping in from the east, impatient because the day wasn't dying fast enough, and the furnace glare of the sun's couch stained red the returning young man, the lubra nursing the baby, the aloof man at the fire. And upon the warmth of the colourful sky reclined the slender maiden moon.

Chief Wilmot spoke to the lubra and she put the infant down into a nest she made of the blanket and strode gracefully to the buckboard. Taking a large hessian sack she gathered dead roly-poly, light as air, which quickly filled the sack and puffed it to its fullest. Having returned the filled sack to the buckboard, she was given the task of gathering brushwood on a site selected twenty feet beyond the tree cavern. Her husband set wood upon the kindling, and the old man brought a bottle and liberally splashed the heap with kerosene.

The kerosene intrigued Bony, for the brushwood was tinder-dry. Still carrying the bottle, the old man took a stand ten feet from the tree cavern and marked the place with a boot-heel.

"You lie there," he said to the lubra.

"All right," she assented, adding: "But not on the three-cornered-jacks."

"I'll fix it good," her husband volunteered, and with a branch-tip swept the place clean of the skin-piercing burrs.

They returned to the camp fire without igniting the one just prepared, and there they squatted to eat. Laughter had sped away from them, the fire-flames moulded to a tall candle vying with the purple dusk.

Bony ate and drank prudently, and afterwards managed to get a cigarette going by thrusting his head and shoulders into the hole excavated by the lightning bolt. He marked the change in himself brought about by the events since he had jumped from Yoti's car, analysed it and was not ashamed that the subtle spirit of this vast land could sway him through his maternal ancestry.

The maiden moon rested herself languorously on the tree-spiked horizon. The spikes cruelly took and devoured her, and cold rage took possession of the sky. The Southern Cross was low to the south-east and not worth looking at, but the Three Sisters, perfectly spaced and aligned, each the exact counterpart of the others, were faithfully following the path of the Sun and able to tell Bony it was eleven o'clock. It was then that the lubra built a little fire near the buckboard and there squatted, rocking the child.

She kept her back to the main fire, for it is not lawful for a woman to witness what followed.

Tracker Wilmot slipped off his clothes and donned the pubic tassel fashioned from the dove-grey skin of the Queensland duck. From his neck he suspended with string of human hair the dilly-bag of the initiated man, made of kangaroo hide and containing his personal treasures. With white ochre the old man painted wide lines longitudinally round his body, and horizontally up his legs and down his arms. The effect was to give likeness to the week-old emu chick, and the final touch was the band of woven human hair about his head which bunched his sleek black hair to a solid plume.

The old man stepped away to view his 'creation' with some satisfaction . . . and stepped from his trousers.

Standing on the tucker box, he was taller than his son, and the firelight glistened on his skin and banished the tiny hollows pitted by the years. He found ecstasy in the caress of the light wind, and raising his arms he exulted: "Orri ock gorro!" meaning: "I am a man!", and Bony in the Ancient Tree was tempted to strip and himself experience that primitive pride in his body.

Chief Wilmot was like the snake that had sloughed its old and tattered skin. He was now smooth and hard and straight, hair and beard and brows white and fiercely virile with an aura of authority bequeathed him by five hundred generations of forebears.

For the first time Bony saw deference in the son's attitude. He handed to his father and Chief the pubic tassel of emu skin, and the dilly-bag of kangaroo hide containing the precious churingas, into which so much magic from afar had been rubbed. With white ochre he striped the Chief's legs from waist to ankles. That done, both arms were completely painted in white, and the Chief sat on the box. The son opened the sugar bag, and taking from it a pinch of kapok dipped it into a solution of tree gum and stuck it on his father's chest.

As this ceremonial task proceeded, white bands became a pattern, and the pattern grew on chest and back and shoulders till Bony recognised the Mantle of the Medicine Man. White ochre marked the cheeks and mouth and nostrils, and on the forehead kapok again formed the letter U, representing The Devil's Hand. Again, the final touch was the headband mounting the white hair to foam. And tiny claw-like hands clutched at Bony's heart at sight of this Being of Magic Who Knows All, Who Can Kill with Pointed Bones, and Who Can Heal by removing the Stones of Pain.

Not once had the lubra dared turn and look, continuing to squat over her fire not for warmth but spiritual comfort, and as still as her sleeping babe. The Medicine Man slowly pivoted, that the gum adhering to the kapok might the sooner dry. Presently young Wilmot announced that the drying was complete, and he draped a blanket about his father to hide from unauthorised eyes that dreaded Mantle. He himself donned his military greatcoat, and then called the lubra, who, being freed from her invisible bonds, returned to the main camp fire.

The fire was permitted to dwindle, to become one large bright ruby on the black velvet world. The Three Sisters marked off two hours. A newly-risen star was so bright it could be mistaken for a lamp in a stockman's hut. There appeared another star, low to earth, far to the south, and this star seemed to dance and then slide down into a pit and there tremble like a lost glow-worm.

Brushwood was thrown upon the camp fire, and minutes later Bony heard the singing of the car engine coming from Mitford, and knew that the driver was being aided only by a parking light. His headlights would have flooded the sky to be seen a dozen or more miles away. The car was driven off the track and stopped near the buckboard.

Car doors were slammed shut, and two figures emerged from the dark background to advance into the firelight. One was tall, the other was short. The waiting aborigines gave greeting to Professor and Mrs Marlo-Jones.

The Professor spoke with grave mien, and Chief Wilmot replied. Mrs Marlo-Jones talked with the lubra, who uncovered the infant's face and laughed her pleasure at the compliment given by the white woman. Together they removed the infant's white shawl and placed about it one of black.

Minutes passed, for Bony slowly. Then two 'stars' appeared and behaved as had the first. Each driven by a single parking light, two cars arrived to park near the Professor's car, and by that time the Professor and his wife and the aborigines were hidden by the night, and the camp fire was dwindling again to a bright ruby.

For Bony the World spun in reverse back and back into the Days of the Alchuringa, and his pulses leaped and his mind reached with mythical arms to encompass All Knowledge.

The ruby gave birth to a spark of light which whirled and circled as Tracker Wilmot handled the fire-stick, ringing himself with bands of light. He sped out upon the plain to come in behind the Tree, to round the Tree and race by the prepared fire into which he flung the fire-stick. Flame leaped high, its light pursuing him into the darkness. And a brolga far away vented its fearsome cry.

Something was coming from the direction of the road, something without shape in likeness to any thing created. It stood ten or eleven feet high, and it walked stiltedly like a bird unused to walking upon land. The red glow from the camp fire made it appear to shrink back upon itself, and then the light of the leaping fire near the Ancient Tree found it and clung.

It had the head and the graceful feathered neck of the emu, and the long and ruffled tail of that bird. It had the body and legs of a man, and on one shoulder rested a great sack. The man-bird advanced, becoming clearer in the firelight to those about the cars, and to Bony thrilling high above.

The bird-man wore the Mantle of the Medicine Man, and he circled the Ancient Tree. Coming again to the cavern in the great trunk, he withdrew from the sack what might have been white bird's down, and the fluffy things fluttered to the ground, where Whispering Wind urged them to hide in the cavern.

For a little while the man-bird lingered, gazing upwards at

the treetop, and Bony could hear him speaking in gentle tones. Then he passed into the Wing of Night, and the foot-lighted stage was empty save for the majestic backdrop.

But not for long. A tall and graceful figure rose from near the ruby and walked hesitantly toward the lighted stage. The footlight accepted her, illumined her nude body, revealed a young and ripe lubra.

Her hair was plumed in glossy black, fine and straight and living. Against her breast she hugged the baby in his shawl the colour of her skin, and all the while keeping the infant from being seen by the audience.

Before the Tree she stood as though humbled in prayer, and then gracefully she sank to the ground, arranged herself that the child should still be hidden, and composed herself to sleep. Time passed. The brolga flew over the treetop, and Bony shrank beneath its haunting scream.

Two figures advanced from the dark wing concealing the cars. One was a tall and lean man wearing a beret, and this man had his arm about the waist of a woman wearing a duster coat whose head was enveloped in a gauzy scarf. She might have been conscious of her surroundings, but she was unable to walk without the man's support. Her hands, finely shaped, were bare and white of skin.

They came to the 'sleeping' lubra. They moved round her and came to the tree cavern, and there the man eased the woman into the cradle of his arms and carried her into the Tree of Trees.

Young Wilmot came silently to bring a blanket to clothe his wife, and she took the baby to the man within the Tree. With her husband she stood away, and a moment later the white man appeared and returned to the camp.

The lubra sped away to the buckboard, and Tracker Wilmot scooped sand with his hands to douse the 'footlight' as the play was ended. Brushwood was tossed upon the camp fire and gave light to those standing about it—Professor Marlo-Jones and his wife, the tall man who had carried the woman into the Tree, a short, stout man, and yet another whom Alice could have identified as Dr Delph.

The firelight illumined their faces. The Professor was in jovial mood, his wife vivacious. The tall man shook hands with the stout man as though heartily congratulating him. Dr Delph looked tired and alone.

172

Presently they left the fire for the cars. Two cars were driven away, the drivers again aided only by parking lights. The short man reappeared at the camp fire, and lit a cigar. Then Tracker Wilmot appeared and was given a cigar. A moment later, again in coat and trousers, Chief Wilmot joined them and openly demanded a cigar. And finally the lubra came into the firelight, dressed and excited.

They were there an hour later, obviously waiting for the dawn, and Bony silently climbed down the tree, knowing himself free from observation by those blinded by the fire, and himself energised by memory of a woman's hands.

Within the tree cavern it was totally dark, and he knelt and found the woman lying on her side, the infant resting in the cradle of her arm. Bony found her hand, traced it lightly with his fingertips. His fingers, now impatient, found the woman's face. The scarf had been removed. She was Alice McGorr.

CHAPTER 26

ALICE McGORR'S STORY

BONY SAT at the feet of Alice McGorr. Within the frame of the arched entrance Night portrayed the distant camp fire and about it the stilled figures seemed to be waiting for the Dawn to free them. Within the heart of the Ancient Tree it was so dark that Bony could see nothing of the recumbent form of the woman and the child nestling against her. The child continued to sleep, but Alice, Bony suspected, was drugged.

Within himself, the tension which had been steadily mounting for several days was now being submerged in the warm glow of satisfaction that yet another assignment was about to be completed, that once again the ever-present menace of failure had been subdued by triumph.

Although unable to see the eastern sky, he knew when the Dawn stole softly over the earth. Young Wilmot added fuel to the fire, and the lubra brought water. Chief Wilmot stalked away to the buckboard, where he obtained the bridles and departed for the horses. The stout and prosperous-looking white man sat on a blanket for a cushion and waited expectantly for the billy to boil.

The Day fought Night and the picture for Bony was etched on rose-tinted steel until the sun flashed above the rim of the world and all the metallic hardness vanished. It was then that Alice opened her eyes, to close them swiftly for a little while longer. When again she opened her eyes, she gazed wonderingly at Bony, and then at the black roof of the cave. She was trying to answer Bony's encouraging smile when the infant stirred, and the miasma vanished as she turned quickly to look down upon the babe.

That was a moment never to be erased from Bony's memory.

Her caress woke the child. It kicked against the enfolding clothes and yawned, and Alice continued to gaze upon it in unbelieving amazement. Then the baby yelled for breakfast.

The group about the fire came to startled attention, beyond them Chief Wilmot roping the horses to the wheels of the buckboard in readiness to be harnessed. The white man hurried to the tree, the lubra behind him, and, stooping, peered into the cave . . . and into the muzzle of Bony's automatic.

"Good morning!" Bony said, interrogation under the cheerful greeting. The white man jerked away, and Bony followed to confront him outside the tree. The lubra shouted, and the Wilmots came running. The white man demanded:

"Who the hell are you?"

"Forgive me," murmured Bony at his suavest. "I am Detective-Inspector Napoleon Bonaparte. And you?"

"I . . . What in . . . Where's my wife? What's all this mean?"

The stout man was well dressed, accustomed to being answered obsequiously, the city tycoon off balance in the vital Australia. Behind him, young Wilmot nudged his father and grasped the lubra by the arm. They retreated hastily.

"Step back a dozen paces," ordered Bony. "This automatic is too temperamental even for my liking. That's better. You are under arrest. Your accomplices, I observe, are deserting you."

The white man turned to see his supporters swiftly harnessing the horses to the buckboard. Compared with them a fire-engine crew were sleepy dolts. Again turning to Bony, he saw Alice standing with him and the child in her arms.

"Where's my wife?" he shouted. "Where's my wife?"

"In hospital where she belongs, you baby-snatching swine," replied Alice, her voice raised to straddle the yells of the infant. "I suppose you've got baby's food in the car over there. Get it."

The man waved his arms in the hopeless gesture of defeat, and proceeded to obey the order. At the car, he found Bony just behind him.

"The ignition keys first, please," commanded Bony. In possession of the keys, he stepped away while the other man burrowed in the boot for a hamper, and the blacks climbed aboard their chariot. They began to shout at each other and the horses, and young Wilmot stood to wield the whip with greater vigour. The speed of their departure made Bony chuckle. The old man was pointing to the south, and Bony saw slipping down the distant rim of the plain the glitter of a speeding car.

Flushed with anger, the stranger carried the hamper to the camp fire, Bony hard on his heels. He dumped the hamper beside the tucker box, and was told to stand on the far side of the fire and remain there.

Alice McGorr placed the baby in Bony's arms, and proceeded to mix milk. The child yelled its impatience, and the stranger said:

"Who did you say you are?"

"I am the Bridge built by a white man and a black woman to span the gulf dividing two races," replied Bony, grandiloquently. "To all my friends I am Bony; to you I am Detective-Inspector Napoleon Bonaparte."

Thus, when Essen and a constable arrived, trailing a tall cloud of rose-pink dust, they were confronted by a domestic tableau, the paramount figure being 'The Bridge' supporting an indignant baby.

*   *   *   *   *

"Wish I owned a machine like this," Bony said when making Alice comfortable in the front seat of the tycoon's car. He peeped at the baby lying on her lap. "Head better?"

"Much, thanks," she replied and giggled. "Wish you did own a car like this. Wish you didn't have a wife."

Somewhat startled, Bony closed the door and firmly passed to the driver's side, to slip behind the wheel and start the engine. Far away on the depression rose the dust from Essen's car in which the constable sat with the white man who said his name was Marsh, and who had mislaid his wife.

"Envy is a corroding sin, Alice," Bony ventured, when they reached the track to Mitford. "I knew a man who owned a Rolls-Royce, and he wished he were young again and driving a T-model Ford with boon companions and rich red wine. Now tell me how you came to be here."

"Well, as you ordered, I went to the Delphs' house last night. I was a few yards off the front gate when I met the cook, dressed for an outing, and I walked back with her to Main Street while she told me she had been given the night off with a ticket for the pictures, and a box of chocolates as a present from Dr Nonning for looking after Mrs Delph. She told me that Mrs Nonning was running the house and nursing Mrs Delph, and that she was still very ill. Dr Delph had been out on his rounds, driving himself as the chauffeur-gardener had been sacked."

"That chauffeur-gardener didn't sleep at the house?"

"No. He's married, and lives at his own place. Anyway, after leaving the cook, I hurried back to the house. It was then quite dark. Dr Delph's car was parked on the opposite side of the boulevard, and Dr Nonning's car was parked outside the front door. On the lawn side of the car was a flowering tree growing there just for me, and I could watch the front door and the hall through the car's two windows. The hall light was on, but not the outside light.

"Nothing happened until half past nine, when Dr Nonning came out and took from the boot of his car a long flattish case. He put it on the hall table. At twenty to eleven Nonning and Delph came out, and Delph backed Nonning's car to the street and drove away. Nonning went in again and opened the case on the hall table. He was fiddling with something there when Dicky, his wife, appeared and said something I couldn't hear. I heard him say not to worry as it was going to be the last, and she'd better stay with Flo.

"At a quarter past eleven Delph came back in Nonning's car, and right on his tail was another car. Delph drove past the entrance to allow the second car to stop at the front door.

"Beside the driver of this car was a woman, and she was on my side. . . . The driver switched off his lights and got out, and was met by Nonning, who said: 'Good trip?' The driver said it had been okay, and Nonning then said: 'You gave your wife the tablets?' The driver said he had stopped at ten o'clock to give them. Nonning then came round to my side of the car and opened the door. The hall light was good enough for me to see the woman. She was wearing a light duster coat over a brown dress, and she had a filmy silk scarf about her head.

176

She didn't speak, and from the way she was sitting and never moving I thought she must be doped.

"Anyway, Nonning said: 'Well, Mrs Marsh, and how are you?' The woman just mumbled. That was all it was, a mumble like she was very sleepy. I saw Nonning take her pulse. Then he turned back to Dr Delph: 'She's all right. I'll give her a shot later on.' Delph nodded, and they went back round the car to the driver and Nonning said: 'The wife's all right, Mr Marsh. Care for a bite and a drink?' Marsh said he would, and that the long drive from town had knocked him. Then Nonning said: 'You can relax from now on. Go in Delph's car, and I'll drive yours.'

"They all went inside, leaving the woman sitting upright and me under the garden tree. I went over to her, and I said: 'Are you all right, Mrs Marsh?' and she only mumbled again as though not wanting to wake up. I opened the door and found she'd been propped with cushions on each side, and try as I did I couldn't see her face clearly enough to recognise her if I had to. And, to clinch everything, she was just my size and height, and I was wearing a brown dress, too.

"You telling me in your letter that you thought this Nonning business had to do with the baby, and that I had to tail these visitors, backed up the feeling I got that this Mrs Marsh was to be given the baby you'd found. I thought I'd hide in the back of the car, you know, down behind the front seat, and then I thought it was just likely they might change their plans and Dr Delph and the Marsh couple go off in Marsh's car. That led to deciding to take the woman's place.

"I heaved her out on to the lawn and under the tree, and I was taking off her coat when suddenly Essen was behind me and asking what went. I told him to lend a hand, and explained what I was doing while he helped me with the coat and scarf, and fixed the cushions. He wanted to dump the woman in the shrubbery, but I didn't like that because she was so wonky, and so he carried her out to where he had his car parked, and took her to the hospital. I told him if he was quick enough he could get back in time to tail the cars.

"It seemed a long time I waited before the men came out again. Marsh and Delph went down the drive to Delph's car in the street. Nonning came to my side of Marsh's car, opened the door and said: 'Can you hear me, Mrs Marsh?' Like she'd done, I mumbled. He said: 'Now we're off to see Altjerra the

Giver. As I've so often told you, Altjerra the Giver can make dreams come true, so you are going to sleep in a tree and wake up with your own baby in your arms. And you will be happy then, very happy.'

"With that, he closed the door and got behind the wheel and backed the car out. The other car was waiting and we followed it. We left made roads and followed an ordinary track, and after a little of that we came to a junction. We still followed Delph's car, and soon after that the lights of the first car went out, excepting the tail light, and Dr Nonning switched off our headlights and drove slowly only by a parking light. How he managed, I don't know.

"A long time after, I saw the glow of a fire ahead, and when we got opposite this fire Dr Nonning drove off the track to it, and another fire lit up and showed the big tree, and I remembered you and I had been there before.

"When we stopped beside Dr Delph's car and another one, Dr Nonning got something from the back, pushed up my sleeve and gave me a shot. He didn't say anything until he'd put the needle back in the whatever it was on the rear seat, and then began to say soothingly over and over: 'Mrs Marsh! Mrs Marsh! You are going to see Altjerra the Giver. You are going to see his spirit babies run to that big tree . . . and wait. Wait, Mrs Marsh, for women like you. Other women have come here, hoping, made happy ever after. Now you have come hoping . . . Mrs Marsh. You are going to fall asleep inside that tree, and when you wake you will have your very own baby in your arms. You will remember all you see, Mrs Marsh, but you will not remember my voice or what I've said. Remember, always remember that the truth is what you see before you fall asleep.'

"And so on over and over again, and the dope working in me so that I felt like I was floating along on air, and wanting with all my mind to stay awake. I still knew I was Alice McGorr and not this Mrs Marsh. I wanted to shout questions at the Voice going on and on about Altjerra the Giver. But I couldn't move, and really I didn't want to. I wanted you there to find out what it was all about, and somehow I knew that this auto-suggestion job, or whatever Nonning was doing to me, wouldn't work because I hadn't been given those tablets Marsh had doped his wife with before they arrived at Mitford.

"Nonning told me to forget his voice, but I didn't and

haven't. I just waited and a fire grew bright to light up the tree, and then I saw the half-bird man thing carrying the huge sack and going to the tree and dropping things. I saw them run and hide inside the tree, little things no bigger than butterflies. I watched the aboriginal woman go there and lie down, and I wanted to tell Nonning she mustn't do that, that this was my night to sleep in the tree, and all the while knowing I was Alice McGorr, your offsider. . . . I was lifted and carried from the car. I was walking to the tree but I couldn't feel the ground under me. Inside the tree it was dark, soft, warm, sleepy darkness, and somewhere I heard Nonning saying: 'Sleep, Mrs Marsh, sleep.' "

Alice fell silent, and Bony made no attempt to disturb the stream of memories. They were passing through the green belt to the town when she said:

"I expected to find, I don't know what, but it was heaven, Bony. Please tell me what it all means."

CHAPTER 27

ACCOUNT RENDERED

NOT SINCE the Fruit Pickers' Riot had the Mitford Police Station been so busy.

Showered, dressed and breakfasted, Bony sat at the Sergeant's desk with Policewoman Alice McGorr on his right and a shorthand writer over in the corner. Yoti wandered in and out like the office boy fearful of the sack, and First Constable Essen acted as Master of Ceremonies.

Mr Robert Marsh, night-club proprietor and sportsman, was brought in and invited to be seated. He was now less agitated, having received a favourable medical report on his wife and, moreover, had had the opportunity to review his position. Bony said:

"Now, Mr Marsh, be advised and tell me all about it . . . from the beginning to the moment you expected to find a stolen baby with your wife in the heart of an ancient tree. From information already in my possession, I incline to the belief that you have been actuated less by criminal intent than by your wife's state of mind. What d'you think about that?"

Mr Marsh agreed with the analysis, and he had already decided to get out from under. His story was clear and to the point, and when the stenographer had typed the statement and it was read to him, he signed almost eagerly.

Marsh having been returned to the lock-up, Dr Nonning was presented by Essen and invited to be seated. Nonning was much more difficult. He continued to be stubborn even after the gist of the statement signed by Marsh was given. It was the reminder that a murder had been committed when the child intended for Mrs Marsh was stolen which loosened his tongue.

The Master of Ceremonies returned him to the lock-up and produced Dr Delph. Dr Delph was given a résumé of the statements made by Marsh and Nonning, and he was more amenable to reason. By the time his statement had been typed and signed, Bony was thinking of morning tea.

Again in the yard between the Station and the residence, Bony asked the Sergeant for the envelope he had placed in the dash-box the previous afternoon. Yoti produced it from a pocket of his tunic, and having examined it Bony gave it back, saying:

"Yesterday afternoon I said that this envelope contained the name of the murderer of Mrs Rockcliff, although the evidence against him was inconclusive. Now being able to locate the remaining four babies, I can finalise the murder of Mrs Rockcliff by pointing him out to you for arrest. Essen!"

"Sir!"

"Take two constables and proceed by car to invite Mr Cyril Martin and Mr Cyril Martin, Junior, to call on me. With these two men, stop the car outside this yard entrance. Have them escorted to the side door of the Station, the two men to walk together, a constable either side of them. You will not enter the yard until I signal. Clear?"

"Yes, sir."

Essen called Robins and two constables, and they drove from the yard and up Main Street.

"Now, Yoti, a rake and a broom, please. Quickly." The Sergeant brought the implements. "As I rake, smooth with the broom. Order your men to keep out those reporters."

The surface of the yard was of sand compressed by boots

and car tyres, and Bony proceeded to rake the ground in a wide swathe from the gateway to the rear door of the Station. As he raked, the Sergeant smoothed with the broom, producing a fine tilth. Both men were heated when the work was done, but Yoti was given no time to idle.

"Plaster of Paris, water and the trowel, please. Hurry."

So the stage was set for the actors to strut. Bony stood just within the gateway, Yoti and Alice admired the flowers in the tiny garden in front of the residence, the Sergeant having with him a tin of 'superphosphate' and a trowel.

Essen drove up. The constables alighted, then two civilians. The elder Martin nodded to Bony; the younger stared moodily. They were marshalled together and, with a constable either side of them, walked into the yard.

Moving across the prepared surface, the party left four distinct sets of shoe-prints, the two civilians of the same height, the same build, the same manner of walking, the same Christian name. And one of them was the murderer of Mrs Rockcliff.

Bony followed the four lines of prints, slightly crouching. Then swiftly he drew an arrow indicating a print made by the right-hand Martin, and Yoti immediately filled the print with sloppy plaster. Another arrow indicated a second chosen print made by the right-hand Martin, and then Bony signalled to Essen to join him, at the same moment calling:

"Constables! Just a moment!"

The party halted, each man in his tracks. To the right-hand Martin, Bony said:

"I charge you with the murder of Mrs Pearl Rockcliff on the night of February 7th. Take him, Essen."

"Come on, Mr Martin, Senior," Essen said, with immense satisfaction.

*   *   *   *   *

For an hour before lunch the Sergeant's office was the scene of much activity following the arrival of a large car manned by police who brought in Chief Wilmot, his son and the lubra, the old watch-mender, and Mr Beamer who came to see fair play. Instead of sullen silence, they surrendered to Bony's quiet assurance that after confession they would be returned to the Settlement. Mr Beamer, anxious for them, witnessed the statements they made, and at the State's expense they were returned to the Settlement.

At two o'clock Professor and Mrs Marlo-Jones were presented to Bony in the Sergeant's office. They were a strange pair: the man regal and dynamic, the woman nondescript and yet vital. There was fire in her small brown eyes, and the wide mouth was truculent.

"Now," she exclaimed, "now we may be able to make sense of all this extraordinary police behaviour. Please explain, Inspector . . . if you are an Inspector."

"Don't be so vitriolic, dear," boomed the Professor. "Inspector Bonaparte is but doing his duty, and you will remember that I advised against taking the rock drawing."

"I know," agreed the woman. "Still . . ."

"We intend to restore the drawing, Inspector," asserted the Professor. "Merely a stupid prank, that's all." He chuckled. "We are quite ready to accept punishment for borrowing our neighbour's goods, you see."

"But why, Professor?" Bony mildly asked. "You told me when I was your guest that you couldn't decipher the meaning intended by the aboriginal artist. Or did you steal it because you didn't want me to see it, because you knew that if I saw it I might know the legend portrayed by the artist?"

"Oh no, it wasn't that," said Mrs Marlo-Jones.

"And then I would know the inspiration behind your plan to steal babies?"

"Oh!" exclaimed Mrs Marlo-Jones.

"Ah!" breathed Professor Marlo-Jones.

"I am glad you accept the idea," murmured Bony. "I suggest that you tell me all about it, from the beginning and including the murder of Mrs Rockcliff that night that you, Mrs Marlo-Jones, entered her house and stole her baby."

"Me?" snorted Mrs Marlo-Jones. "I didn't murder the woman."

"You were under the bed."

"Under the bed! Henry, you're a traitor. You told this man what I told you."

"I did not, dear," boomed the Professor. "How did you find out that my wife was under the bed, Inspector?"

"As a famous fictional detective used to say: 'Elementary, my dear Professor.' When your wife crept under Mrs Rockcliff's bed she was wearing gloves, the identical gloves she is now wearing. One of the glove fingers has been mended. You see the darn, both of you? On the floor about and under the bed the imprint of that mended glove was left on the linoleum. It was also left on the Library window, proving that Mrs Marlo-Jones was engaged in the theft of the rock drawing. You see how difficult it is to make real crime pay."

"I didn't murder the woman," Mrs Marlo-Jones loudly insisted.

"Tell me, who did?"

"Yes, dear, do tell," urged the Professor. "I'd hate to see you hanged for it."

Mrs Marlo-Jones shrugged despairingly, as a queen deserted by all her courtiers.

"I was under the bed, as you said, Inspector. I had to get under it because I didn't know anyone was inside the house until I heard him knock something over. He came into the bedroom, in the dark, and then I heard the front door being opened. I knew it was Mrs Rockcliff by her shoes on the floor covering in the hall, and I couldn't understand why she'd come back so early. She came into the bedroom and switched on the light, and then I heard the blow and saw her body fall to the floor. And then I saw the man stoop over her, and I knew him. I saw his face distinctly."

"You knew where Mrs Rockcliff had gone that evening?"

"Oh yes, Inspector. She used to meet the man twice a week. But this time he couldn't have been at the house where they met, and she came home and he was waiting to kill her."

"Why didn't you report all that . . . to me?"

"Tell you about it? How could I? There was the other thing . . . the babies."

"And knowing this man was a murderer, yet you did nothing about it?" pressed Bony.

"Yes. You see . . ." She looked helplessly at her husband, and he took over.

"Mr Martin knew all about Nonning's experiments, for he and the Delphs have been friends for years," explained the Professor. "However, he took no active part in our little schemes, and it was from the Delphs that he learned the details of our plan covering the Rockcliff child, for we didn't take him into our confidence that much. If, after the murder, our attitude to him had altered, he would have guessed we knew who did it. And to cover up that crime he might have killed us, too. I had better narrate the story, don't you think?"

Bony inclined his head in assent, and the Professor asked if he might smoke. His cigarette lit, he settled himself comfortably, cleared his throat from long habit in the lecture room, and only once glanced at the stenographer.

"The germ of the, ah, plot, was born last August when we were spending the evening with Dr and Mrs Delph. Staying with the Delphs were Mrs Delph's brother, Dr Nonning and his wife.

"The conversation that evening turned on a visit paid by Dr Nonning to our local Museum. He saw the drawing, and asked Mr Oats, the curator, what the picture portrayed, but Mr Oats, only recently having taken over, just happened not to know it. So I related the legend, and Nonning was greatly impressed. Subsequently he was inspired to formulate a plan to help certain of his patients.

"Among his patients were several women of a peculiarly neurotic type. I cannot employ Nonning's phraseology and, in fact, have little sympathy with these new sciences, but it appears that in women there is a sickness of the mind caused by inability to bear children and aggravated by a hunger for them and by an obsession that they are the object of universal contempt. And Nonning evolved the notion that if such a woman could be made to believe she received a child as the legend describes she would recover her mental, spiritual and physical health.

"You will agree that receiving a child in this, shall we say, spiritual way would give these women psychological balance, deep and complete; far greater than selecting a child from an orphanage as one would choose an appealing object.

"Nonning came again to Mitford in September, when Mrs Delph's child was born, and he told us that his sister didn't want the child and that he had a patient who would greatly benefit if a child was introduced to her in accordance with the legend. We then decided to stage the legend, with the assistance of several of the aborigines at the Settlement, and also planned the abduction, as Mrs Delph would not dream of the public ever knowing she didn't want her baby. We arranged with the aborigines to . . ."

"Pardon, Professor, but I know all about that arrangement

for the aborigines to take over and care for the baby, and to act the part of the Beings in the legend," Bony interrupted.

"Oh, you do, do you, Inspector?"

"Yes, I saw you both at the show last night. I was in the gods, up in the tree. Tell me, how did you work the abduction?"

"It was quite easy. We bought a pram identically the same as the one bought by the Delphs and, with the co-operation of Mrs Delph, we duplicated the child's clothes and the fly-net. The girl was sent to the frock shop with the pram. We knew she would have to leave it outside when calling for the parcel. Our lubra maid wheeled the second pram beside the other one, paused there for a moment or two, and then walked away with the pram holding the baby. She continued to wheel the pram to the lower end of the boulevard, where an aborigine waited with his truck. A lubra on the truck took over the child, and the pram was ultimately taken to the middle of the river and sunk with heavy stones. There was no hitch."

"And then you gained possession of the Bulford baby with the co-operation of Mr Bulford," Bony interposed. "One of you took position behind the fence separating the bank from the disused premises, and another rang the bell and took the child from Mr Bulford, who was waiting to pass it."

"You are a very clever man," remarked Mrs Marlo-Jones. "I'm sure Mr Bulford didn't tell you."

"That is so," admitted Bony, to add, being unable to resist: "Mr Bulford committed suicide because he realised I am a very clever man. Mrs Bulford didn't co-operate, I take it?"

"No, that woman wouldn't co-operate in anything or with anyone. She couldn't be trusted," replied Mrs Marlo-Jones. "But she was glad the baby disappeared; the fool thought everyone was laughing at her, and the way she treated her poor husband was shameful. We were all glad, too. The babies were taken from homes where they were a nuisance, unwanted, and were given to women who were figuratively dying for want of one."

"And after the Bulford baby was given to Nonning's selected patient, more babies were wanted and you turned to stealing them?" Bony pressed.

"Yes, we turned to real theft," continued the Professor, quite cheerfully. "We knew the Eckses, husband and wife, and knew the latter often went to the River Hotel. The child didn't receive proper attention from such a drink-swilling mother, and Dr Nonning was most anxious for another infant for a really desperate patient. It was all very easy. So, too, was the theft of Mrs Coutts's child. Mrs Coutts was a worse offender against a helpless baby than Mrs Ecks. All she thinks about is dreaming of becoming a great author."

"And that Mrs Rockcliff was the worst of the lot," added Mrs Marlo-Jones. "Cyril Martin didn't know we knew all about her and him. And how she visited him at a cottage he had down the river a bit, leaving the baby alone in the house for hours. That was why we took her baby. We've done nothing morally wrong, Inspector. All we did was to transfer unwanted children to people who wanted them and would give them wise attention and affection. Besides, these four women who were given our babies recovered from their illness and are now happy and well. Dr Nonning is delighted with his successes, as well he should be. And the other sick woman will recover, too."

"What of the mothers who lost their babies: Mrs Coutts, Mrs Ecks, and Mrs Rockcliff, had she lived?"

"Pooh! Inspector!" exclaimed the indignant Mrs Marlo-Jones. "To those women a baby was like an attack of sandy blight . . . an irritant. That was why we selected their babies for Dr Nonning's patients."

"What was the reason you selected male children? Was it because the aborigines declined to, ah, officiate over a female child?"

"Precisely. Female children are quite unimportant."

"Tell me, what did you do to prevent Mrs Coutt's baby from crying when you stole it from its cot?"

"Nothing. We knew that Mrs Coutts's baby seldom cried. But it did. It cried after I had put him in the suitcase and was out in the street. It was very awkward, but fortunately there was a thunderstorm and people were hurrying for shelter."

"Go back to Mrs Ecks's baby."

"I took a bottle. He was ready for it and gave no trouble."

"Cow's milk?"

"Oh yes." Mrs Marlo-Jones smiled. "We agreed it wouldn't do for us to purchase a preparatory food which might have been traced back to us."

Bony pondered, and they watched him like children who, having finished their lessons, hope to be released from school.

To them, stealing five babies for the purpose which they freely avowed was much less reprehensible than stealing the rock drawing from the Municipal Library, and even this relic was merely 'borrowed' and was to be replaced. The problem they presented was unique.

"I am going to permit you to return to your home," he told them. "You will, of course, not attempt to leave Mitford until a higher authority decides what is to be done. You have no children?"

"No," replied the Professor, in manner revealing so much.

"H'm! Mrs Marlo-Jones . . . when under the bed, which Cyril Martin did you see stooping over the body?"

"Why, the father, of course. He's been carrying on with Mrs Rockcliff since before Christmas. Could have been before then. That was when we found out about him and her."

Bony glanced at Yoti and Essen, and their slow nods affirmatively answered his unspoken question: 'I tracked the right one, didn't I?'

CHAPTER 28

'WHAT'S THE LEGEND?'

"So THAT completes a very strange case," Bony said when the Professor and his wife, having signed their statements, were released. "Mrs Marlo-Jones is unclassifiable to the lay-man. As for the Professor, he is out of this world. He did not learn to adventure until six months ago, and I think his most absorbing anthropological study has been his own wife.

"Now having interviewed Dr Nonning, we can understand how those two were so easily dominated by him. Nonning belongs to the class of ruthless scientist who spares neither himself nor others in the furtherance of his work. Delph is Nonning's antithesis, satisfied with himself and life in general, happy to ramble around on his cases, wanting only peace at home and relaxation. In vulgar parlance, his wife wore the trousers, and because she wanted their baby to be passed to another woman, he agreed . . . for peace' sake . . . fatal error . . . the first step taken down the grade. And how like Dr Delph was John Bulford."

Pensively Bony rolled a cigarette and Yoti felt urged to make the effort himself, so badly was it done by the long dark fingers. The Sergeant was tired. Essen felt his mind so crowded that it would be hard work to arrange all the oddments. Alice looked at Bony with eyes soft with unmaidenly adoration, and she was about to ask a question when he continued speaking.

"Mrs Delph didn't want the world to know about her baby, and Dr Delph found comfort in the idea behind the legend and agreed to the abduction and Nonning's experiment. Now observe. The abduction was to be carried out, and the legend staged, by two people the least capable, one would think, of ever becoming successful criminals. The very simplicity of their plan to take the baby off Main Street assured its success. Then the mother's pretence of grief was good enough to deceive men who talked to her about it: good enough to deceive men, but not good enough to deceive a woman . . . you, Alice.

"The plan to abduct the Bulford baby was also a gem of simplicity, having, of course, the co-operation of the father. The moral weakness of the father spoiled that case for the abductors. His first statement covering his actions during the period in which the child was taken wasn't strong enough to withstand my attack, and his second attempt fell down because he forgot that the Library was closed that day for renovations. What really upset Bulford was the murder of Mrs Rockcliff. He thought, without doubt, that she was murdered by the very people to whom he had passed his own child, despite the denial made to him by Mrs Marlo-Jones. And when he committed suicide Mrs Delph realised that the crisis for her was near.

"The successful abduction of the Eckses' baby required the degree of luck which no experienced criminal would have accepted in his calculations. That same degree of luck entered the abduction of the Couttses' baby, and both these cases provide proof that to achieve success in crime the best course to adopt is to commit the crime in broad daylight, and with as many people as possible in the vicinity. That and the ability to behave normally under abnormal conditions.

"Each child in turn was whisked to the Aboriginal Settlement, where it was cared for in the secret camp under the very noses of the Beamers. When the time came to enact the legend, the aborigines were sent away on walkabout by wily old Chief Wilmot, not because his people were to be kept in ignorance, but because when they were on walkabout Mr Beamer and his wife were able to catch up on the clerical work and so would remain long at their desks.

"We can clearly see Professor Marlo-Jones taking his long walks late at night when it is cool and meditation is a tonic. We see him by merest chance watching the Estate Agent entering a house down the river, a house which the Professor knows is not his home. The light is switched on in the front rooms, and a little later a mysterious woman arrives and is admitted. The Professor stands by and observes them leave separately at two in the morning.

"Thus the spice of adventure which drew both the Professor and his wife to investigate, to use the wife's words just now, these goings-on. They see Mrs Rockcliff passing their house to and from Main Street. They know when Mrs Rockcliff enters the hospital, and when she leaves with her baby. They know its sex. They have known for a long time Mr Cyril Martin's domestic background.

"It appears that Martin met Mrs Rockcliff in Adelaide, where she went under the name of Jean Quayle. Further, it appears that Jean Quayle wasn't easy to snare, and she brought Martin to the point of proposing marriage. When she found she was going to bear his child, she pressed for advancement of the marriage date, and Martin slipped the cable. Or thought he did. He had mentioned his business, but not his place of business, and the Register of Estate Agents told her where he lived.

"Thus she arrived at Mitford and put the screws on a hard bargain. He was to pay her fifty pounds a month in cash and every month was to pay into an Adelaide bank a further fifty pounds. He was to find her a house and pay for the furnishings. Because this was so favourable to her, she took steps to erase her former identity, and to keep secret her association with him.

"Martin, however, found paying out a hundred a month most irksome. He knew the night when Mrs Marlo-Jones would steal Mrs Rockcliff's baby. He knew all the details from Mrs Delph without Mrs Delph realising the significance of the information. He knew that Mrs Marlo-Jones would gain entry to the house by means of a strip of celluloid to force the front-door spring lock.

"He knew even the time Mrs Marlo-Jones was to take the baby, or thought he did, because Mrs Marlo-Jones was delayed an hour. When he entered the house via the scullery window, he expected the child to have been taken. Being the agent for the owner he was familiar with the interior of the house, knew from Mrs Rockcliff where the baby was left, and so went direct to the front bedroom. He was no sooner there than he heard Mrs Rockcliff come in and, so he tells us, had no time to be sure the cot was empty. Thus he rid himself of an incubus by making it appear that the abductors of the baby had murdered the woman who found them stealing her child.

"The deed done, he left at once, not knowing that the child was still in its cot and Mrs Marlo-Jones under the bed. Believing that he had successfully saddled the baby-thieves with murder, he was able to stay still after the deed.

"The Marlo-Joneses were unable to stay still. Horrified by the murder, they had to know what was being done about it. They put Clark to shadowing Alice, and Wilmot thought he kept me under observation. Stealing the rock drawing was the height of foolishness. They hoped I would not associate the theft with the abductions; they thought I would not find out what the drawing meant. They feared that if I saw the drawing I would quickly associate the legend with their activities.

"When Mr Oats supplied me with a sketch of the drawing made from memory, I was relieved of my worst fears of the fate of those infants. The placing of red-back spiders in my bed, I am glad to say, was the act of Marcus Clark and his pals, and not of the Marlo-Joneses. They didn't fear me nearly as much as did the aborigines, who took independent action.

"That about covers the twin investigations. My chief concern was the fate of the babies, as I have so often asserted, and we must all rejoice to know where they are and that they are being well cared for. Their respective parents will be told where they are to be found."

"Now, please, tell us the legend," Alice pleaded.

"The legend!" Bony smiled at her provocatively. "It happened a long, long time ago in the Days of the Alchuringa, when the world was young and waiting for the aborigines to come and take possession of it. In those far-away days the world was peopled by all kinds of monsters, and one day there came wading through the seas a strange being who was half-bird half-man. Its name is Altjerra, the Creator of All Things.

"On coming to dry land, Altjerra was very tired because he carried on his shoulder a huge sack filled with spirit babies with which to people the world. He sought for a resting place in the shade and found such a place at the foot of a great baobab tree. When he awoke he was very hungry, and he saw in the tree a poor old kookaburra, which he caught and ate. Whereupon the tree began to cry, saying: 'You've killed my only friend, and now I am so lonely without him.'

"That made Altjerra very sad for the baobab tree, so he opened his great sack and took out many spirit babies, which ran to the tree and hid in its trunk. Leaving the now happy old tree, Altjerra travelled on across Australia, and wherever he came to an ancient tree, or a heap of Devil's Marbles, or a hill having a strange shape, he dropped spirit babies from his sack, and the spirit babies ran to hide away in those unusual sanctuaries.

"After a long time hiding in the baobab tree, the spirit babies got tired of being so imprisoned. Of themselves they could not leave the sanctuary and roam the wide world, and no matter how much the baobab whispered patience with its leaves, the spirit children became sad and still more sad.

"Then one day there came another Being, this time an aboriginal lubra. She was both tired and sorrowful, tired because her husband had chased her away from camp, and sorrowful because the cause of it all was her failure to give him a son. So she laid herself down in the shadow of the baobab tree and cried herself to sleep. And then a spirit baby more venturesome than the others crept out from the tree and hid himself in the lubra's body and eventually was born a human child. So ever afterward when a lubra wanted a baby, she would leave the tribe and lie down and sleep beside an object said to shelter spirit children, and her wish would always come true."

The ensuing silence was broken by Alice, who said:

"That is a beautiful story, Bony."

Yoti snorted, saying sarcastically:

"Still, which did come first, the egg or the chicken?"

Bony stood, and sighed:

"Must you be so practical, Sergeant?"

Essen chuckled, but Alice was silent. Yoti said:

"Well, that ties all the knots. I thought I knew most about crime and criminals, but I'm only a starter. Come on, Essen. Give us a hand with the damned reports on this lot."

They departed, and Bony crossed to his suitcase and began to pack. Alice remained silent, and presently he asked:

"Any questions, Alice?"

"Yes. I want to keep the baby. That little fella came out from the tree just for me to love him. You'll let me keep him, Bony?"

He returned to the desk and she stood to meet him.

"A wise woman would not submit your problem to Solomon," he told her, softly smiling. "I'm not Solomon. I'm only your good friend, Bony. We are catching the plane for Melbourne, leaving in an hour. So be ready. Remember, Melbourne isn't in New South Wales. Remember, too, that possession is nine-tenths of the law."